*In remembrance of Private Thomas Clarke,
19th King's Liverpool Regiment, who died near Trone's Wood
on the Somme, 30th July 1916. Also his beautiful niece,
Muriel, my mother. Rest in peace.*

THE GOOSE ROAD

ROWENA HOUSE

WALKER
BOOKS

Based on *The Marshalling of Angélique's Geese*, a short story by the same author,
first published by Andersen Press in 2014

First published 2018 by Walker Books Ltd
87 Vauxhall Walk, London SE11 5HJ

2 4 6 8 10 9 7 5 3 1

Text © 2018 Rowena House
Cover illustration © 2018 Leo Nickolls

The right of Rowena House to be identified as author of this
work has been asserted by her in accordance with the
Copyright, Designs and Patents Act 1988

This book has been typeset in Bembo

Printed and bound by CPI Group (UK) Ltd, Croydon CR0 4YY

British Library Cataloguing in Publication Data:
a catalogue record for this book is available from the British Library

ISBN 978-1-4063-7167-3

www.walker.co.uk

One

I'm turning hay in the top meadow when I hear the squeak of rusty wheels and look up to see Monsieur Nicolas, the postman, pedalling up the lane. I stiffen, suddenly afraid that I know the reason why he's here.

Please, God, let it not be Pascal.

Soft summer sounds surround me now that I'm still. Grasshoppers. Distant birds. The eternal hum of bees. The creaking of the bicycle is like some infernal machine, let loose in the Garden of Eden.

Please, God, not my brother, Pascal.

I think about that other August day two years ago, when the jangling of church bells shattered the peace of the valley. Pascal and I dropped our pitchforks and ran to the village square just in time to hear the mayor announce, "Men of France! To arms!"

Father left straightaway, but Pascal stayed long enough to

show me how to gather the harvest, how to scythe and how to plough. I was twelve years old and so excited. Now my hands are calloused and my back aches like an old woman's.

Monsieur Nicolas clatters slowly past the orchard, waking the geese. They flap and hiss as they waddle towards the fence. Mother appears at the kitchen door, wiping her hands on her apron. Her back is very straight.

Monsieur Nicolas clambers awkwardly off the saddle and pushes his bicycle up the hill towards our gate. I hold my breath. My legs shake. My vision blurs with tears.

Please, God. Not Pascal.

Monsieur Nicolas stops again. He rests his bike against our fence. The geese clamour and shriek as he opens the gate to our yard. Stifling a cry, I pick up my skirts and run.

It's Father, *Mort pour la France* on some distant battlefield. The letter telling us is crushed in Mother's hand. I bow my head and make the sign of the cross, then ask, "Who's the letter from? May I read it?"

She turns hollow eyes on me. "It's from your brother, my angel."

"*Pascal!* Is he safe? Is he well? Oh, Maman, does he say when he's coming home?"

Relief bubbles inside me. I'm torn between laughter and tears. But when I reach out for the letter, Mother's knuckles whiten as she tightens her grip on it.

"Your father is *dead*, Angélique. Have you no feelings at all?"

I hang my head, the pain in her voice cutting through me. For her sake, I try to remember something nice about him. One small thing. But I can't. All I recall are his fists and his belt and his leather razor strop. Pascal got the worst of it, but sometimes late at night I'd hear Mother whimpering too.

"Well?" she asks, sounding weary now rather than angry.

My gaze remains fixed on the earthen floor and the dust-flecked shaft of sunlight falling across it while the ticking of the kitchen clock grows louder between us.

Am I wicked, I wonder, a heartless, unforgivable child because I'm not sad he's dead?

I try to squeeze out a tear, but inside my head I can hear the *thwack, thwack, thwack* of his drunken anger, and Pascal's sobs as he rushed up to his room, and Mother's muffled voice through his closed door, hushing him, telling him not to fuss.

"I am sorry," I say at last.

"Are you?"

I give a tiny shrug. "For you, yes."

She sighs, then turns her back on me and takes her apron off.

"See to the animals," she says, "then come in to change. We'll go to Mass this evening."

My mourning dress is stiff and tight, a laced-up hand-me-down. Mother is almost invisible behind her long black veil. As we walk down the lane to the village through the warm, rosy dusk, I half expect a bat to blunder into her or a fox to stop and sniff the air as we pass.

Outside the church, the village widows flock around Mother like crows. There are Madame Villiard and Madame Arnauld, and poor young Madame Besançon, whose husband was just nineteen when both his legs were blown off at Verdun.

Old Madame Malpas draws me aside, wringing her bony hands and crying, "What's to become of you, Angélique? You'll very likely starve! La Mordue will go to rack and ruin without Monsieur Lacroix!"

"Pascal will be home soon," I say. "Maman and I can manage till then."

"Manage, child? When your corn's still in the ground in August?"

"The farm men have been promised leave."

"And you expect the generals to keep their promises?"

She sniffs loudly, then stumps off, calling to Mother, "Madame Lacroix! What terrible news! Tell me, did he suffer?"

My best friend, Béatrice Lamy, hurries over to me.

"That woman!" she says, rolling her eyes. Then she kisses me on both cheeks and hugs me tightly. "This is unbearable, Angie. I can't begin to imagine how you feel."

Guilt prickles me because, just then, I'd been thinking how much I hate wearing black and having to pretend to be sad. I wish I'd told her the truth before, but Mother always said the beatings would get worse if

Father suspected we talked about him behind his back.

And now it's too late. I can't speak ill of the dead, condemn a brave soldier *Mort pour la France*. What would Madame Malpas say?

"I'm fine, Bee," I say. "Really, I am."

She cups my cheek in her hand. "You're so brave, Angie. I'd be in pieces if I'd lost Papa. How did you hear the news?"

I lean forward, hiding a smile, and whisper, "Pascal wrote."

"Pascal!"

"Shhh, Bee. Not so loud." I glance around, but the village women are too busy comforting Mother to take any notice of us. "Come on. Let's talk inside."

The cold stone church is empty. We sit in the front pew, the one allotted to the newly bereaved. Béatrice takes both my hands.

"Is Pascal safe?" she asks. "Is he hurt?"

"I don't know. Mother wouldn't let me see his letter."

"Why not?"

"Oh, you know. She's upset."

"Of course. Silly question. I'm sorry."

Her eyes brim again with sympathy.

Quickly I say, "Do you want to hear the good news?"

"Good news?" Her eyes widen.

I smile conspiratorially. "The farm belongs to Pascal now — the house, the land. Everything! It's *his*."

"Oh."

"Bee! Don't you see what this means?"

She shakes her head.

"He can get married whenever he wants!"

"Oh!" Her eyes widen further. "But … Papa won't let me. I'm too young."

"Pascal will wait, I know he will. And when you're both ready you'll live with us, and we'll be sisters, a real family. Won't that be wonderful?"

Her eyes shine, then she blushes. "I do love him so much."

We start to hug, but just then the door opens and the village widows seep inside like shadows, a horde of veiled and silent wraiths.

"I should go," Béatrice says.

"No. Please stay."

"But your mother—"

"She won't mind."

"Are you sure?"

"Absolutely."

I slip my arm through hers while we wait, each looking up at the brightly painted statue of Saint Joan of Arc, high on her pedestal. She's wearing a full suit of armour, and spearing the devil through his blackened heart.

"I hate that statue," Béatrice whispers.

"I don't know," I reply. "I rather like it."

Two

Next morning I'm up with the larks, whistling a tune as I strip the sheet from Pascal's bed.

Dust erupts from his mattress and his pillow smells fusty and stale. I throw open his shutters and the dewy dawn floods in.

Downstairs two wooden pails stand in the middle of the kitchen floor. I look around in surprise. They're the pails Mother takes to market.

"Maman? You're not going to Monville today, are you? Wouldn't you rather rest?"

"I can weep for your father on my feet as well as in a chair," she says, emerging from the pantry, her arms laden with pats of butter wrapped in fresh green leaves.

I smile at her, not wanting to argue again. "Shall I come with you? We could go shopping afterwards. You know, buy something nice."

"Buy something nice?"

Her voice seems to crack. She shuts her eyes tightly. I drop the sheet and run to her, taking her hands in mine. Her skin feels like worn-out leather. Sobs shake her body.

"I'm *so* sorry," I say, pressing her hand to my face. "I didn't mean to upset you. And I'm sorry about yesterday too. I know I should be sad."

She shakes her head. "We can't mend the past, Angélique, only forgive it."

I nod solemnly – even though I know in my heart I'll never, ever forgive Father. Kissing her hand, I say, "We'll be all right. Pascal will be home any day now."

She opens her eyes and sighs. "Fetch me the *palanche*, would you? I'm late."

The palanche. How I hate that thing. It stands in a corner of the yard, a yoke of solid wood with a hook at each end for her pails. She says it balances the load, but I think it makes her look like an ox in harness or a shackled slave.

She shudders when I bring it into the kitchen and shuts her eyes again as I lift it over her shoulders.

The butter pail is heavy. I have to brace to pick it up. She sucks air through her teeth as the weight of it bears down.

At least the pail of eggs is lighter. Mother has made a nest for them out of clean, golden straw. But as I pick it up, something catches my eye. I peer inside, then put the pail down again and part the straw with my fingers.

I look up at Mother, amazed.

"Goose eggs?"

I look down again, just to make sure, but there's no doubt about it – they're twice the size of the hens' eggs.

"Maman? Why have you taken Pascal's goose eggs?"

A shadow crosses her face. She glances at the door. I stand up and reach for her arm, more puzzled than cross. She knows Pascal told me to hatch them. We've talked about it often enough.

"Not now, Angélique. I haven't got time."

She brushes my hand away. I just stand there staring as she adds, "Put the bucket on the hook, would you, or do I have to do it myself?"

"But … Maman, we're not meant to sell them, you know that."

She rubs a hand across her face, then takes a deep breath and bends at the knee, stretching out for the pail. My foot is in her way. I decide not to move it.

"Angélique!"

I stand my ground. This is for Pascal. He *loves* those geese. He told me to hatch every egg. With an aching heart, I watch her shuffle sideways. The unbalanced palanche makes her clumsy. I ought to help her, I know, but this is too important to let pass.

She looks up at the ceiling, her eyes wet. I'm sure she doesn't want to take them, really. So why is she?

"Maman, what's going on? Please tell me."

She squats down, breathing heavily, and pulls the pail of eggs towards her, then hooks it awkwardly onto the end of the palanche. Slowly she stands, the strain clear from the set of her jaw.

"So what are we going to tell Pascal?" I ask. "That the geese aren't laying? He'll never believe it."

"Open the door, Angélique, then the gate."

"It's not like the hens aren't laying well. I'll go out right now, if you like, and find loads of eggs! The hens always hide them."

"The door," she repeats, "and the gate."

"But Pascal *said*—"

"I know what he said! But he's not here, is he? And I've got enough mouths to feed!"

I step back, my heart racing. She hardly ever loses her temper, but now her face is twisted and there's spit on her lips from shouting.

"But, Maman—"

"Stop it! This instant! And get out of my way!"

At last I step aside, my eyes burning with tears. Her words felt like punches. Turning around, I fling open the door and run into the yard.

Out of the shade of the house the sun blazes down.

In angry silence, I watch her manoeuvre the palanche through the gate and into the lane.

Grim-faced, she turns uphill, towards the woods and the long, long road to Monville. I know how hard her day will be, but still I can't forgive her.

A slight breeze rattles the overripe seeds in the corn

field on the far side of the lane. She glances towards the sound.

"If you want to help Pascal, start the harvest – and don't give me any nonsense about wash day, not when there's work to be done."

Without waiting for an answer, she trudges off, weighed down, a thin black figure under a cloudless sky. The scraping noise of her clogs on the hard-baked earth is quickly swallowed by the seething, rasping insects and the heat.

I turn my back on her and walk down to the orchard, where the geese are grazing on the last few blades of parched grass.

They're tall, handsome birds with greyish-brown backs and dusky orange beaks. Toulouse geese. Pascal's pride and joy. We call the biggest gander Napoleon Bonaparte.

He raises his head when he sees me and waddles over to the fence, expecting me to feed him. Poor thing. They're all so hungry in this drought.

I hurry over to the corn field and gather a handful of grain for them. The seed heads clatter and sigh, and grey patches of mould catch my eye.

If only I knew Pascal was on his way home I'd happily start the harvest for him – and finish it, too. I'd scythe the whole field and thresh the grain, and mill it as well, if that would bring him back any sooner.

But Friday is *my* day, the only time I see my friends now we've all left school. We do our washing together at the old stone *lavoir* in the village, then swim in the river afterwards.

As I return with the grain, Napoleon snaps at me greedily through the fence. I jump away from his beak, which could take my eye out with one peck – or so Pascal once said.

Back in the house, I pick up Pascal's bed sheet from the floor and put it into our big wicker washing basket. Then I look round for his letter.

I search the pockets of Mother's apron first, then the dresser, the bread drawer, the sooty shelf in the brick chimney breast.

I lift up rugs and examine nooks and crannies, then try the pantry.

It's cool and cramped, white-tiled with a pitted stone counter. I look behind Mother's butter churn, under her bottles of pickles, in the crate of potatoes. I even check the wire cheese cage which hangs from a rafter, out of the reach of the mice.

Finally, with a sense of trepidation, I climb the stairs to Mother's bedroom.

Father's coat still hangs from a nail in the wall. I squeeze past it, avoiding its touch. On her bedside table, she's draped her black veil around the photograph of Father in his uniform. The picture of Pascal as a soldier stands beside it.

And there it is, between the two photographs. His letter. Snatching it up, I run to my room to read it.

Three

33e batterie du 35e RAC
d'artillerie de campagne
IIe Corps d'Armee

Vieil Dampierre, Marne
August 8th, 1916

Ma chère Maman,

There is no kind way to say this so I will just tell
you straight. You will soon get a letter from Father's
regiment telling you he is dead. *Mort pour la France* on the
banks of the Meuse. It was a direct hit, which is a great
mercy. He did not suffer, as many poor devils do.

Forgive me if I cannot mourn him. Not because
of what he did (the past is forgotten here) but because
of this War, which makes us all soulmates of Death.

His close companions, for on the Battlefields of Verdun, we eat, sleep and live with corpses. The air stinks of them. The land is grey and brown, and we cannot tell flesh from filth.

Thank God my *batterie* is out of it at last, and the guns grow quieter.

The roads hereabout are full, night and day, with ammunition trucks and ration carts, and infantry-men slogging up to the trenches. Poor beggars.

Tonight, though, home is a hayloft where our rations will be delivered by a man standing up, not crawling on his belly through mud, and desperately hoping smoke and darkness will hide him from the snipers' bullets.

Poilu, my little terrier, is inside now, dispatch-ing rats for me and my mates so we don't wake up with them eating our faces, as if we too were dead.

Tell Angélique she will like Poilu. He is an ugly three-legged fellow, left behind when they aban-doned the village of Esne.

We have orders as far as the camp at Mailly. Rumour has it we will be sent north after that to this madness on the Somme, which was meant to take pressure off us at Verdun, yet here we are! Off to help the Tommies! This war is full of such jokes.

There was talk of harvest leave a while back, but we have heard nothing more about it.

May God be with you, *ma chère Maman*, for I fear He forsakes the sinful soldier, who prays for nothing more than the sight of green grass or a tree in leaf, not burnt and broken by the ceaseless artillery shelling. Here we worship blue sky, and dance in the sunlight at the joy of leaving the Hell of Verdun behind!

Be happy for us, Maman. Be safe. Know that home is Paradise with you and Angélique there.

Forever your loving son,

Pascal

I read the letter again and again, searching his words for the laughing, teasing, funny big brother who went away to war.

I wouldn't believe he wrote it, except that his spidery handwriting hasn't changed since school. *Good French citizens write with their right hand, not with their left.* I can almost hear our teacher, Monsieur Cousin, saying it as he tied Pascal's left hand to a chair.

I read the letter one more time. How can he be a soulmate of Death and worship blue sky? That sounds mad to me. And all this talk about corpses...

My eyes flick down to his offhand comment, *There was talk of harvest leave a while back, but we have heard nothing more about it.* It's like he's left me dangling over an abyss, not knowing whether I'll see him or not.

Shutting my eyes, I try to picture little Poilu in the

hayloft and Pascal dancing in the sunlight surrounded by green grass and trees, but the rats and the shells and the snipers somehow seem more real.

With a deep sigh, I fold his letter in two, put it back in the envelope and return the envelope to Mother's room.

Outside, the heat is brittle, the empty sky almost white. The hens flutter past me as I open the door of the little stone barn, which nestles against the side of the house.

Inside, the moist, dung-heap warmth of the pigsty wraps itself around me. King George, our pig, presses his snout through the bars of his gate. I kneel down to scratch his ears. He grunts with contentment – until the cow shifts in her stall, reminding me I'm meant to be milking her. I fetch the stool and sit beside her, resting my cheek against her velvety hide.

As my fingers find her udders, I try to lose myself in the rhythm of work. But I can't. I try to picture Béatrice and Pascal living here together. But today I can't do that either.

Instead, a deepening sense of unease settles on me, a fear that I can't trust Mother to keep the farm safe for Pascal any more. But then I can't let the geese starve either, or leave the corn in the ground. And I certainly can't go swimming.

Taking a steadying breath, I think about the long days ahead. The heat. The weight of the scythe and the sheaves. Then I make myself a promise.

When Pascal comes home from the Front – whenever

that might be – he'll find the farm exactly the way he left it, with the harvest safely stored in the barn and his animals contented and fed. I'll sharpen his tools and put them in their proper places. I'll clean his room, polish his boots, and wash his bowl and knife ready for the table.

I think of it like a magical spell. If I can stop time, if nothing ever changes, then maybe he won't change either and life can start over, just like before.

No! It'll be better this time because Father won't be here.

Four

Pascal's scythe hangs from hooks on the threshing barn wall, the long curved blade rusted and blunt. I oil a whetstone and sweep it along the edge of the metal until it's razor sharp.

But the shaft is too long for my arms and when I try a practice swing, I dig the blade into the ground. Pain jars my arms and across my shoulder blades.

In the corn field I try again, but this time I hit a stone and the jarring is worse. I have to stand very tall, which makes the angle of the blade all wrong, and all I manage to do at first is bash the corn, not cut it.

A fox watches me working from the shade of the hedgerow at the top of the field. Lucky him, I think. I'd love to laze about all day and then go and steal my supper.

I avoid the stands of mouldy corn, and by mid-morning the field resembles the face of a scrofulous tramp, badly shaven, with tufts of grey sticking out.

When my shadow reaches its shortest, I lie down in the shade of the solitary oak tree that grows in the middle of the field, and look up at the sky through its leaves.

Here we dance in sunlight and worship blue sky…

I can't bear to imagine Pascal's nightmare world of brown and grey.

The fox sits up. I expect him to stretch and yawn, and trot off to chance his luck with our hens in the yard, but suddenly he's gone, a golden streak in the hedgerow.

Then the geese honk. There's someone in the lane. My heart skips a beat. Could it be…?

I tell myself to stop being daft. It's probably Béatrice, come to find out why I didn't meet her at the *lavoir*. Stiffly I stand and hobble to the gate, squinting against the sun.

It *is* a soldier! In a pale blue uniform, a rifle slung over his shoulder, he's kicking up dust with his down-at-heel boots as he walks slowly up the lane.

I stare at him, hardly able to breathe…but no. As he gets closer I see he can't possibly be Pascal. This man is grizzled and heavy, with a salt-and-pepper beard. His eyes glitter from under the peak of his cap like two bright slits.

"Gettin' an eyeful, are ya?" he shouts.

Blushing, I look away, hoping he'll pass on by. But he stops by the gate and gazes over the corn, scratching at his belly through the straining buttons of his tunic.

"Well?" His eyes fix on me. "Ain't you never seen a soldier before?"

"My brother," I reply as stoutly as I can. "But he wore red trousers and dark blue."

"An early recruit, hey? Where's he at now?"

"He just left Verdun."

"Haven't we all, mademoiselle."

He says it with a sneer, as if calling me a liar, and I straighten my back and square my shoulders. But the soldier smirks, then saunters across the lane and leans on the orchard fence.

I open the gate and follow him, asking his back, "What do you want?"

"None of yer business."

"It's my farm! It is my business!"

"*Your* farm?"

As I glare at him, Napoleon – bless him – waddles towards him silently.

I plant my feet apart and put my hands on hips, holding the man's gaze as Napoleon draws back his head and opens his sharp, fierce beak...

"*PUTAIN!*" The soldier leaps backward. "Look what he's done to me britches!"

"Naughty bird," I say as blood oozes through the rent in his trousers.

He looks me up and down, furious at first, but then his expression changes, and he chuckles and casts his eye over Napoleon and the rest of the geese as they gather along the fence, hissing at him and beating their magnificent wings.

"Fine birds," he mutters.

"They're not for sale."

"Who says I'm buyin'?"

His smile is more of a leer.

I glower at him, but he takes a step closer, grinning wolfishly. I swallow hard, my blood quickening as he casts his eyes over me too, like I'm a horse at a fair. Rapidly, I look about.

The soldier is standing between me and the yard. My scythe is still under the oak tree, although what I think I could do with a blade against an armed man I really can't imagine.

My legs take me backwards as fear sets in, but he swaggers after me, matching me step for step. His fat, pink tongue moistens his lips, and his eyes follow me hungrily.

"Stay back," I say.

"An' who'll make me? You?"

But then he falters. His gaze slides over my shoulder, and a twitch of consternation wipes the leer from his face. I whip round. A figure is limping frantically up the hill. Tall and thin, his left leg drags behind him.

"René!" The baker's boy. I've never been so glad to see him.

"You all right?" he shouts back.

I am now.

I turn on the soldier and growl, "Off with you! Go on! There's nothing for you here."

He summons a snarl as well. "I saw what I came for, *girlie*."

Then he spins on his heels and makes off uphill towards the woods, and I run down to René.

Five

"You saw him off," I cry as I run. "How clever you are!"

"What'd he want?" René calls back, still limping madly up the lane.

"I don't know! Oh, wait there. I'm coming."

He stops to catch his breath, his dark fringe plastered to his forehead and his white shirt stuck to his chest.

"Thank you," I say as I reach him, panting from the heat and feeling foolishly weepy now the soldier's gone. "I'm so glad you came. But why…?"

René glares up the hill. "They were talking about *him* in the village." He jerks his chin at the soldier's retreating back. "And you weren't about…" He shrugs.

"So you came to find me? Oh, René! That's sweet."

"Sweet?"

"Yes! It was nice."

"Sweet and nice? Great."

"Stop it. You know what I mean."

He shoots me a quick, shy smile, then stares at the ground, blushing and grinding the heel of his outsized boot into the dirt. Looking away from his withered leg, I ask, "What were they saying about that soldier in the village, then?"

"I don't know. Didn't stop to listen." He shrugs again.

"And you're telling me that's not sweet?"

I bump his arm with my shoulder.

We stroll along the hedgerows, picking blackberries. They stain our lips and fingertips.

He finds me ripe hazelnuts too, and a little round wren's nest hidden in a tangle of honeysuckle. Then, suddenly, he squats down and reaches deep into the hedge, pulling out two hen's eggs. "Yours, I think." He gives them to me with a grin.

"But I looked there before!"

"Outsmarted by chickens, huh?"

"Shut up, René."

We hunt along the lane for more secret nests until we've found them all, then we stop by the corn field gate and look at the half-scythed corn.

"Not waiting for Pascal, then?" he says.

"Harvest leave's cancelled."

"Again?"

I nod.

He looks at me from under his fringe. "You know I'd help if I could."

"I know." I lean against him and he smiles.

After a minute, he says, "I should go."

"But you only just got here! What if that soldier comes back?"

"Why would he?"

"I don't know. Maybe he's a deserter, come to steal food. He might be waiting till you've gone. You know, watching us from the woods."

René looks up the hill, his face thoughtful. He chews on his lip for a moment, scanning the shadows under the trees, then says, "They might've found out who he is in the village by now. At least, old Ma Malpas will pretend she has."

"I'll race you! Come on!"

"Like that?" He nods at my filthy work clothes.

"Oops."

Giggling, I run to the house and change into mourning black.

The sun burns through the fabric of my dress as we gallop down the lane, jockeying to be first at the old stone horse trough. It's fed by a trickling spring that never runs dry.

René leans against the mossy bank while I splash water on my face and neck, but when I bend lower to drink, the stays in my bodice dig into my flesh.

"Stupid dress," I mutter, and try to pull it away from my sweltering skin, but the stays' grip is like an iron claw. *Mon Dieu!* I hate this thing."

René looks at me sideways.

"What?" I say.

He pulls a face, then scoops up a handful of water to drink.

We idle through the water meadow, watching swallows swoop above the tall grasses and butterflies dancing among the late summer flowers. Then, on the edge of the village, we stop by the Brett brothers' farm. It looks more derelict than ever, the yard choked with brambles, the barn roofs sagging and full of holes. Rusted plough shards stick through the nettles and the air smells of scorched cow pats.

Sighing, I say, "Do you think they'll come back from the war?"

"The Bretts? I guess." He glances at me when I sigh again, and adds quietly, "You didn't like him much, did you?"

"Who?"

His eyes flick to the dress.

"Oh. Him. Can we not talk about it?"

"Fine by me, but you might want to try looking sad, you know, if we're going to see Ma Malpas."

I glower at him. But not for long. What's the point?

I say, "He wasn't a nice man, you know."

"Never said he was."

I look back along the empty lane, then towards the silent village, and take a deep breath. "Promise you'll keep this a secret?"

"Course."

"He was a monster. The devil himself. I *hated* him."

René looks at me sadly. "He's not coming back, Angélique."

"I know! It's just…he makes me angry. He ruined our lives."

"And you want everyone to know that?"

"Of course not! Mother would hate it!"

"So look sad for her."

"I am trying."

René cocks his head.

"All right," I say. "I'll try harder. Don't nag."

The first of the village houses are squat and square, with four stone windows each, and pots of red geraniums. The cobbled streets echo with the screaming of swifts, but there's no one about at the lunch hour.

On a corner, I peer into the window of Monsieur Lamy's pharmacy to see if Béatrice is there, but the blind is pulled down behind the front door and the coloured glass bottles glow dimly.

René nudges me. "You've got hair stuck on your face."

I wipe the strands off my forehead and tuck them back under my cap, using the window as a mirror. Sweat pours off me even in the narrow shade of the building and the collar of the dress nearly chokes me.

"There. How do I look?" I ask.

"Red as a nice, sweet tomato."

"You're a terrible person, René Faubert."

He bumps my arm with his shoulder.

Turning into an alleyway, the hubbub of the market square reaches us. I compose my face and plan what I'll say if I am asked about Father.

Of course, very sad... Mother is coping... Pascal's letter was a great comfort...

But then a thought strikes me and I stop abruptly.

What if the villagers think I'm gadding about with René and not mourning properly? Have I got an answer for that? I duck into a doorway to give myself time to think.

René frowns. "What?"

"Um. I'm just wondering..."

It seems mean and ungrateful to ask him to leave me after he's been so kind, but I can't find another solution.

"Maybe, you know, I should be...alone?"

He looks puzzled for a second, then his shoulders sag. "Yeah. Course. You go." He sticks his hands in his pockets and looks down.

"I'm sorry, René. Really, I am. See you next week?"

"I guess."

"Bye, then."

"Bye."

He thrusts his hands deeper into his pockets and starts scuffing the ground.

I watch him for a moment, then, feeling wretched, hurry away, head down, into the sudden sunlight of the market square, where I cannon into Claudette Danton,

Béatrice's cousin, coming the other way.

"Watch out!" she cries as she drops her washing basket. "Oh, it's you. Where've you been? Bee's been worried sick." She pecks me on both cheeks. Then, looking over my shoulder, her eyes light up.

"Oo-oo! What have you two lovebirds been up to? Had a row?"

René scowls at her from the doorway.

"Stop it! We're not lovebirds," I say. "We're here about this soldier. He came to the farm."

Claudette's eyes widen. They dart from me to René, then she grabs my wrist and tows me into the square, shouting at the top of her voice: "Everyone! Listen! He's been at Angie's place too!"

Heads swivel from every direction. Young boys crane to see me. Old men look up from their tables outside the café. The women at the *lavoir* turn as one.

I glance back into the alley, but René is already limping away.

Six

I shake off Claudette's hand and stride into the square, surprised to see so many people — and not just villagers. There are boys from outlying hamlets, old farmers and their wives. The crowd of women at the *lavoir* parts and Béatrice elbows her way towards me.

"Angie, what happened?" she calls. "Are you hurt?"

"She's fine," Claudette calls back. "René ran to her rescue!"

"Shut up, Claudie!" I glare at her, but she just giggles.

Béatrice smacks her wrist. "Behave," she says. "This is serious." Then she takes my arm and ushers me towards the *lavoir*.

The women listen to my story in silence, but as soon as I've finished Madame Malpas folds her arms and loudly declares, "Well, doesn't that just prove it? It's what I've been saying all along! Ever since my sister wrote,

I knew this would happen here too."

"Knew what would happen?" I ask her, my imagination on fire, but she purses her lips and looks around as if waiting for everyone's attention.

"Here we go," Claudette says with a titter, but the women seem to have heard it all before. They turn to each other and gossip in groups, speculating about the soldier and where he'll appear next. I ask Madame Malpas again, "What did you know would happen?"

She glances around one last time, then wrings her hands.

"You won't remember my sister Adèle," she begins. "She's the one who married that awful blacksmith and moved to Canigou—"

"All that way? How terrible for you," Claudette breaks in, her eyes bright with mischief. "Why *would* she do that?"

Béatrice digs her in the ribs.

"Tell Angie about the *soldiers*," Claudette says, fending Béatrice off. "Tell her what they did in your sister's village."

The voices around the *lavoir* hush and heads turn again to listen.

Madame Malpas sniffs noisily, then leans towards me and lowers her voice. "It was awful! Horrible! My sister was terrified for her life."

"Why?" My mouth feels dry.

"They had guns, of course! They were *fully* armed!

They came in the middle of the night, with lorries, dozens of them, so they didn't leave any behind."

"Didn't leave any what behind?"

"Cattle, of course! It was the Requisition!"

"But... I-I don't understand. What's that got to do with this soldier? He was just one man."

Madame Malpas shakes her head as if I'm being deliberately stupid.

"He's a scout," she says slowly. "A scout for the Requisition. They're coming back."

I hear myself gasp. I feel my hand fly to my mouth. It's like an anvil just fell from the sky. The Requisition? It can't be! Béatrice takes my hand. Even Claudette has finally stopped grinning.

"But... But... They already came!" I cry. "They took our horse and cart!"

Madame Malpas folds her arms again, nodding knowingly. "Which is why they'll be after cattle this time, mark my words. In Adèle's village they took every last cow — and hanged a farmer too."

"Why? What did he do?"

I cling to Béatrice as Madame Malpas brings her face close to mine.

"He wouldn't let them take his cow," she says. "He only had one, you see. He told them. He said, 'Without that animal, my family will starve.'

"But the officer lost his temper. He said the men at the Front needed meat more than a bunch of selfish peasants.

So the old boy lost *his* temper. He fetched out his gun and shot the officer dead. They took the cow anyway. And hanged him at the next Assizes." She leans back, adding loudly, "There's no question about it. This soldier means trouble."

I stare from face to face, aching for someone to deny it, for one voice to rise in protest and say she's a foolish old woman who knows nothing. But the only sound is the echoing swifts. Then the women huddle together again, and the hubbub grows like before.

"I've got to go," I say, and start pushing my way out of the crowd.

"Don't be silly," Claudette says. "Ma Malpas *always* makes things up — or makes them seem a hundred times worse than they are."

"Claudie's right," Béatrice adds, taking my arm. "She's just trying to scare you. Stay with us. We'll go swimming."

But my legs are trembling.

In the scream of the swifts I hear the sound our mare made when the soldiers dragged her away last spring. I see the whites of her eyes again, and hear Mother pleading with the sergeant, begging him to leave us our plough horse, screeching at him that we'll break our backs dragging the harrow through the mud without her. I can't bear to think what she'll do if they take our cow as well.

"I'm going," I tell them.

"We'll come with you," Béatrice says.

"And do what?" Claudette puts her hands on her hips.

"Listen, Angie. Bee's right. Come swimming. You need to cool off. You look like a beetroot."

"I can't, Claudie."

"Course you can! Your precious cow isn't going to vanish overnight! Tell her, Bee. Tell her to stop being silly."

But nothing they can say will persuade me to stay.

Running home, I try telling myself Claudette is right. Our cow won't simply disappear. But all the same I have to check she's still safe in her stall.

I find her restless in the heat, swishing at flies with her tail. I ought to take her out to graze, or at least tether her somewhere in the shade, but can't bring myself to do it. I give her fresh hay by way of an apology, then, changing quickly, return to the corn field.

Not that I get much work done. I keep thinking I hear footsteps beneath the endlessly chirring crickets, and have to run to the gate, picturing the scout at the head of a column of trucks.

But the only person I see all afternoon is Mother stumbling, exhausted, down from the woods. She turns into the yard without looking up, and I go back to scything, hour after sweltering hour, telling myself I'm doing this for Pascal. Perhaps he'll eat the loaf I'll bake from the grain I'm cutting right now, or this grain, or this…

I work until the shadows fall. Then, under cover of darkness, I lead the cow along the verges to graze, listening intently to the noises of the night – small scurries, unexplained cracks, the yelping of foxes. Familiar sounds. Yet menacing tonight.

Once the cow is safely back inside, I shoo the hens in behind her, feed King George and the geese, then lock up the little stone barn and bar the threshing barn doors – one rusty padlock and a wormy plank against the might of the Requisition.

I'd laugh if it wasn't pathetic.

A bat flits overhead, a quick scribble in the luminous sky. Napoleon honks in answer to a fox. Breathing in the evening, I begin to calm down at last.

I think about the times Pascal and I sat out here, him with his knife, whittling wood, me shelling peas. Mother would join us sometimes. Never Father, of course.

I think about René as well, wondering if one day I'll leave La Mordue and become his wife. But I'm not ready to think about that. Not yet.

The geese honk again – and finally a smile creeps across my face.

Crossing the yard to the gate to the orchard, I jam it open, then scatter grain about the yard. If that soldier sneaks back tonight – scout for the Requisition or not – he'll find Napoleon waiting.

Seven

Next morning a fiery dawn breaks into my bedroom. Drifting specks of dust seem to burst into flames as shafts of brilliant orange slant through the shutters.

The house creaks as the timbers heat up: the rafters, the eaves, the old window frames.

Every bit of me aches, my arms, shoulders and back especially. The blisters on my hands have burst overnight, and tufts of lint from the sheet stick to yesterday's caked-in dirt.

So what? I mustn't complain. What wouldn't Pascal give to be safe at home in bed?

I hear the creak of Mother's bed through the thin partition wall and gingerly sit up and ease my feet to the floor. The thought of another scorching day in the corn field is awful.

"Angélique?"

Mother knocks on my door.

"Coming."

I wonder if she's still angry with me – or I with her. She was already in bed when I got in last night so we didn't have a chance to talk.

Should I tell her about the scout? She's bound to hear the gossip sooner or later, and I don't want a lie to come between us – not with everything else. But when I come down for breakfast, I see her eyes are red-rimmed. She must have been weeping for Father again. I decide to wait for the right moment. There's no point in worrying her if Madame Malpas was only scaremongering.

Outside, the heat is so fierce that weeds which were green yesterday have shrivelled away in their cracks. I draw water from the well and fill every trough we have for the cow and King George, the hens and the geese, then I follow Mother into the threshing barn.

Father's scythe lies rusted in a corner. I feel guilty about only sharpening Pascal's blade. I knew Mother would need Father's scythe today.

"Let me do that," I say as she reaches for the whetstone, but she brushes me away and bends to the task herself.

A flock of pigeons lifts off the corn field as we open the gate. From the smell I can tell rats and mice have been feasting on our grain, too.

"We need a ratting dog like Pascal's," I say. "You know, like little Poilu."

She glances at me sharply. "You read his letter?"

"Oh. Um..."

I look away, expecting her to scold me, but to my surprise her voice is gentle as she asks, "Did it upset you?"

All of a sudden I want so much to reach out and touch her – my mother, our mother, Pascal's and mine. The real person inside the grieving widow.

Instead I shrug and say, "He seemed different."

"Different?"

"Not like before."

"What did you expect? He's a soldier now."

"I know – but that's just for the war. It's not who he really is."

A sad smile softens her face, and she sighs. "Maybe not."

Grasshoppers leap from under our feet as we walk to the farthest hedge, where the last standing corn trembles in the heat. Sweat is already seeping into my eyes. The air tastes thick and sticky. Carefully, I pat my palms dry on my skirt, and grip the handle of the scythe.

"Ready?" Mother says.

In unison we twist and swing, twist and swing, the corn tumbling at our feet. By mid-morning, the last stems are cut, and we rest briefly under the oak tree, sipping water and nibbling grain, too exhausted to go indoors.

In the sultry quietness, the fox settles into his shady spot under the hedge. I keep an eye on him in case he darts away. Mother notices him too.

"Ah! So that's why you let the geese out," she says

with a wan smile. "I'll fetch your father's gun if I see him in the yard with the hens."

This, I guess, is the moment I ought to tell her about the scout. But she seems a little happier, at last, and we can't do anything about him. Why worry her for no reason? Returning her smile, I say nothing.

We work through the rest of the long, hot day, raking the cut stems into rows. Mother moves slowly, as if in a dream. We hardly speak.

In the evening, while I make us supper, she sits by the empty fireplace, staring sadly at things I can't see – some memory of Father, I guess.

I wonder if she'll ever remember the ogre he truly was.

The third day of the harvest is the hottest yet, the sun a fireball melting the sky.

Mother finishes the raking while I bundle up sheaves by the armful. The stalks scratch my skin, and insects crawl up my sleeves.

By mid-morning the sky is blindingly bright and strangely white. The birds seem stunned into silence, though the sawing of the crickets is maddeningly loud.

Drained by the suffocating heat, we collapse under the oak tree at midday.

Mother falls asleep at once, and it isn't until the dappled shade blurs into one shadow that I finally put two and two together and leap up, electrified by one terrible thought: rain!

Rain now would ruin the lying grain, and if we lose the harvest we'll starve this winter – us and King George and the geese. Sick with fear, I run into the field and look up, just as the watery sun disappears behind the mottled grey clouds.

What in God's name have we done to deserve this?

Tears come, but I drive them away. I have to *think*. At most we'll have a couple of hours to get the corn under cover. How much can we save in that time? Half, perhaps. Less. Livid with fate and dreading what's to come, I run back to Mother and kneel by her side.

"Mmm?" She looks at me vaguely when I touch her arm, then smiles sleepily. "I must have nodded off."

"For a while," I say, then steel myself. "Maman, I think the weather's changing."

For a moment she looks mystified, her face still soft from sleep. Then she sits up and the colour leaves her cheeks. When she looks up, her hands flutter to her throat as if she can't breathe.

"Mon Dieu!"

She staggers to her feet, looking around wildly at the scattered sheaves and rows of lying corn. Then she turns her face to the sky and screams – an animal sound. The fox is gone. Pigeons take off from the trees.

"Maman! There's still time to save ... some of it."

But she sinks to her knees, burying her face in her hands. Through her sobs I hear her crying, "Why, Holy Mary, *why*?"

The clouds thicken. I run to fetch pitchforks and we toss the sheaves into higgledy stooks, like huts with steep roofs. Then, when the first rumble of thunder chases across the eastern sky, we stop and look at each other.

We've no need for words. We knew the worst was coming. Another peal of thunder rattles the air and Mother hurries away to find the handcart and ropes.

I stand in the middle of the field, breathing steadily – in and out, in again and then out – trying to prepare. This is the moment I've dreaded more than any other since the soldiers took our mare.

Adeline, we called her, a chestnut with long black fetlocks. The sergeant said they needed her to pull their cannons into battle and pull injured soldiers out again.

They took our wagon, too.

"Why not?" the sergeant had said as Mother wept. "You don't have a horse to pull it."

The bitter taste of bile fills my mouth as I breathe. In and then out. Alone and afraid.

"I'm sorry, my angel, be brave," Mother says when she comes back.

I try not to look at the rope.

Together we load the handcart with loose stems. Then she says, "It's time."

Under a darkening, crackling sky, I swallow another mouthful of hot, heavy air, then bend forward, bracing, a pack animal awaiting its load.

She ties one sheaf to my back, then ropes another one

to it, and another. I stagger under their weight. My knees buckle. Staring at the ground, I stumble into the lane, with Mother pushing the handcart beside me.

The geese hiss and flap as we totter past the orchard and into the yard.

In the threshing barn, Mother loosens the ropes and I let the sheaves fall onto the empty floor. They look vanishingly small.

We upend the cart and hurry back and forth, time and again, me lurching like a drunk, her face growing crimson, while overhead the clouds glimmer and flash.

At last a fat raindrop strikes me, then another. Seconds later, rain lashes my face and straps my skirt to my legs. The geese honk hysterically as we stagger alongside their fence.

"Keep going," Mother shouts. "Don't stop!"

Her voice is torn away by the wind.

Thunder crashes. Lightning sears the land to the sky. Water streams down my back and the sheaves become sodden, heavier than lead.

Soon I can't raise my head, not even my eyes. All I can see is stubble and mud, and rain hammering down. The flooded field turns into a lake, the lane into a torrent, and I fear if I fall I will drown.

Eight

That night I dream about Pascal.

He's sitting with his back to me on a wide, flat beach. I know we're by the sea because it looks just like the picture we had on the wall of our classroom in school.

Waves lap over my feet. The water weighs down my skirt. I'm running towards him, knowing that he's waiting for me, but my skirt becomes heavier and heavier until I can't move, and when I shout to him, nothing comes out of my mouth.

I wake drenched in sweat and overwhelmed by a sense of despair. Rigid, I stare at the cobwebby rafters, my body throbbing with pain. I can't even clench my blistered fists. I tell myself: how dare you feel sorry for yourself? I try to picture Pascal dancing in the sun with little Poilu, but can't make out my brother's face.

What does he look like now – that stranger in the letter?

Grey daylight seeps through the shutters. I hear the cow mooing to be milked and Mother stifling a cry as she turns over in bed.

"I'll go," I call through the wall and grit my teeth.

As I roll onto my side, pain shoots up my back. I feel giddy and sick, but if I concentrate hard enough I can rise above it.

The yard is a sheet of water reflecting an iron-grey sky. The surface is broken by the tops of a few cobblestones. They look like the dead bodies of fish. Water drips from the eaves – the only sound.

I milk the cow and feed King George, then, with a deep sense of trepidation, open the threshing barn doors.

Mist floats in tendrils above the puddles on the floor. The air is saturated, the sheaves and loose corn sodden. Numb, I stare inside. We haven't saved *any* of the harvest yet. If we can't dry it out, the seeds will sprout and spoil in here, not just in the field!

I break down weeping.

I promised Pascal I'd bring in his harvest. I swore it to myself. I'd believed in myself. What a fool! I shouldn't have started. I should have known the heat would build to a storm.

Even half the harvest might have got us through winter.

Now, because of my wilfulness, we'll likely starve.

I drag myself to the corn field to see if anything can be

salvaged there. The wind-shattered stooks look wretched. Muddy sheaves lie in the clag and half-drowned furrows. I try lifting one, but my back can't take it, nor my swollen, bloody fingers.

I'll just have to try and dry out whatever I can in the barn.

For days we sweep up puddles and air-dry the corn. Each morning, a bleary sun peers through the mist, drawing rich, earthy scents from the soil.

To me, at least, the sun speaks of hope, but Mother seems more broken than ever. She weeps day and night. She can't eat. She brings down the photograph of Father and sits all evening staring at it in her lap.

On the third night, after I've locked both barns securely, I kneel at her feet and say, "I know. Let's pretend Pascal's coming back tomorrow. I'll make him a welcome home feast."

"What will you make him?" she asks in such a sad voice it almost makes me cry.

"Omelettes with wild mushrooms. They'll be out in the woods after that rain. I'll bake potatoes as well, and smother them in butter. I'll start now, shall I? We can have a little taste tonight. You know, just to keep up our strength."

She manages a smile. "Not for me, my angel. I'm really not hungry."

The next evening I try again, pulling up Father's chair and taking her hands in mine.

"Maman, I've been thinking."

"Have you?"

Nodding, I look into her sunken, raw eyes. "I think it *means* something that Pascal survived Verdun. I think it's a sign – a sign he will come home."

"Do you?"

"I do."

Her smile is weak and fades as quickly as it came. I stroke her parchment skin, watching her lose herself in thought again – thoughts I cannot fathom.

"Please, Maman, we've *got* to believe. We can't give up hope. I know it's been horrible this last week, especially for you, but the corn is drying now and the cow's milking well. Things will get better, you'll see. And one day, when Pascal's home, all this will seem like a bad dream."

She draws her hands away from mine and stares at Father's photograph for another long while. Then, quietly, she says, "War is a terrible thing, Angélique. Soldiers *see* terrible things. They *do* terrible things. It changes a man."

"Not deep down. It can't. Pascal is a good person. Whatever he's seen, whatever he's done, we can make it better."

"Are we that clever? Can we mend something that's broken?"

"I don't think we have to be clever. We just have to be here."

She cups my cheek. Her skin feels rough, her blisters still damp, and her smile is so unbearably sad that I know I'll be crying with her soon.

"Hold on to that hope," she says. "Hold on to it with all your strength – for both of us."

Next morning the sunshine is strong and the air feels dry for the first time since the storm. Birds sing and crickets chirr loudly.

As I throw open the threshing barn doors, coils of mist disappear like fleeing ghosts. I could start threshing this morning and then bring in the driest sheaves from the field. Quickly, I let out the hens, tickle King George behind the ear and milk the cow.

But as I'm scattering grain in the orchard to keep the geese out of my way while I'm working, it suddenly occurs to me that today is Friday. Wash day. I glance up at Mother's room.

Her shutters are closed – which is good. She needs her sleep. I can thresh the corn.

All by myself.

While she rests.

I glance up at her room again.

It wouldn't hurt to take *one* morning off. I'll bring her work clothes to the *lavoir* too. They're as filthy as mine.

Quietly, I step inside and go upstairs to listen at her bedroom door, then knock softly and peep in. Her bed is empty.

I call to her, then hurry downstairs, out to the yard,

the little stone barn, the corn field, the yard again, shouting now. With a terrible sinking feeling, I look for the palanche and pails.

They're gone too.

Why?

Why must she *always* go to market? It's not like she buys anything useful with the money she makes! Does she even know we're nearly out of salt and matches? Then I think how she hasn't eaten for days and dash into the lane – the quiet, deserted lane.

Should I follow her? Make sure she's all right? But she'll have left before first light. She always leaves early on market day. I'll never catch up.

Worried – but also exasperated – I go back to the yard, but after a moment I shut the threshing barn doors, go into the kitchen again and fetch the washing basket.

The lane is littered with fallen branches and leaves brought down by the storm. In the village, ladders are propped against walls, and bits of roof tile and chimney pot have been swept to the sides of the streets.

The square is quiet, with just a few old men outside the café and a clutch of women at the *lavoir*. There's no sign of Béatrice – or Madame Malpas – but at least Claudette is there.

"I didn't think anyone was coming," she says as we kiss on both cheeks.

"I needed a break," I tell her. "Where's Bee?"

"Helping her papa. Their chimney came down in that rain."

"Are they all right?"

"They're fine. You?"

I shrug. "We'll survive." I roll up my sleeves, then rummage in my basket for the scrubbing brush.

The women are complaining about the cost of bread and how Madame Faubert is claiming the merchants in Monville are buying up all the flour. No doubt she'll use the storm as an excuse to put up her prices even higher.

No one mentions the scout or the war, which is a relief, though I wish Béatrice would come. I want to tell her about Mother and the harvest.

Claudette chatters away about nothing until she says, "Seen René, have we?"

"Not lately, no."

"You mean he didn't hop along to the farm to rescue you from that storm?"

"Shut up, Claudie."

"Why?" says Béatrice, pushing between us. "What's she said now?"

"Bee!" I hug her tightly, then try to catch her eye as she puts down her washing basket, but she's too busy getting out the family smalls.

"So what are we talking about?" she asks, dropping them into the water.

"René," Claudette says.

"The storm," I add quickly.

"Wasn't it awful?" Béatrice says. "We lost half our roof!"

Claudette mouths, "One chimney pot."

"It was the *whole* chimney." Béatrice turns to me. "I bet your geese loved it. All those puddles! Such fun!"

I give her a half-smile. "They're rather too hungry for fun, Bee."

Claudette laughs. "How can geese be hungry? They eat grass, silly."

"Our orchard's bald as a coot."

"Take them to the water meadow," Béatrice suggests.

I shake my head. "They won't come back. Napoleon bit me last time I tried herding them. Stop laughing, Claudie. It hurt!"

Béatrice says, "You need to hatch a gosling."

"Says the goose expert," Claudette scoffs.

"No, listen, it's easy." Béatrice stops scrubbing. "You just have to be there the moment it hatches. If you're the first thing a gosling sees, it thinks you're its mother and follows you everywhere. Then you can get the other geese to follow the gosling. See? Simple!"

Claudette boggles at her. "How could *you* possibly know that?"

"I bought a book on geese, if you must know. If I'm going to be a farmer's wife I need to learn these things."

Claudette throws back her head and hoots with laughter. "You're actually planning to *marry* Pascal? What will dearest Papa have to say about that?"

"He's a very respectable match," Béatrice replies primly.

"He's a scallywag! That's why you fancy him, Bee. Remember that time he stole René's walking stick and threw it in the duck pond?"

"That was Henri Chevalier," I protest.

"Rubbish," says Claudette. "I was there! You thought Pascal was going to get a proper hiding for it."

"I *never* said that."

"Near enough."

"Did not!"

"Did too!"

"Stop it, both of you," Béatrice breaks in. "René threw the stick away himself. He said he wanted to learn to walk without it. Remember? He told everyone about it."

But I remember that afternoon all too well. How René had lied for Pascal, hoping we'd stop being horrid to him. But we always were horrible to him, calling him names and chasing him, and throwing sticks and stones if he came too close.

Poor René. He never asked to catch polio.

Just then there's a shout from the corner by the bakery, and Madame Malpas sallies into the square, shaking a newspaper in her fist.

"Have you heard the news? It's dreadful!" she cries, then pushes her way through the women at the *lavoir*.

"You know that attack they launched on the Somme to relieve our men at Verdun? Well, listen to this!

"Offensive mired in mud. Early gains lost. Heavy artillery bombardment…"

As she reads the newspaper headlines, Béatrice squeezes my hand.

"Don't worry," she says. "Pascal would have told you if that's where he was."

I manage some kind of distracted smile, but then look away in case my face betrays me, because the Somme is exactly where he'd expected to be sent.

"Seven days of shelling preceded the assault, but the enemy's deadly Maxim guns could not be silenced…"

I plunge Mother's sheet into the water, trying my best not to listen, but the sheet floats to the surface again, buoyed by a pocket of air like a bloated white fish. I push it down again, splashing noisily.

"German defences remained intact along thirty-five kilometres of the Front. When the order was given to advance, the enemy's fearsome weaponry opened fire…"

A flight of swifts shrieks overhead, black against the blue sky. I listen to them instead.

"According to dispatches, the premature detonation of eighteen tons of high explosives…"

Loudly I say, "We're going swimming, right?"

Claudette pulls a face. "Sorry. I've got to pick beans. The storm broke our frames."

"Bee?"

She shakes her head. "Papa needs me to hold the ladder again."

"Oh, come on, you two! We *said*."

Madame Malpas frowns me into silence and then raises her voice.

"According to dispatches, the premature detonation of eighteen tons of high explosives under the Hawthorn Ridge alerted the enemy's gunners to the timing of the attack. Eyewitnesses spoke of the losses being so calamitous that the dead caught on barbed wire resembled fish caught in nets."

Nine

René finds me sitting on the old boathouse jetty by a bend in the river under the willow trees. Fish laze in the shallows and birds pipe in the reeds.

"You've been crying," he says.

I shrug. "It's just something Madame Malpas said."

"You don't want to listen to her."

"I tried not to."

Slowly he sits next to me, easing his bad leg down. His boots dangling over the water look huge next to my bare feet.

"That scout turn up again?" he asks.

I shake my head.

"See? Old Ma Malpas is full of wind," he says. "So what's up?"

I shrug again. "The farm. The harvest. That storm."

"Bad, was it?"

"I don't know how much grain we can save."

I pick a sliver of wood off the jetty and throw it into the river, but it gets stuck in an eddy and spirals around and around.

"Mother's gone to market," I add. "She's taking Pascal's goose eggs to sell."

"And?"

"I need to hatch one to lead the others to graze. They're so hungry."

"Oh."

He throws a stone at my piece of wood, driving it into the current, then peels me off another splinter. This time it drifts off slowly, then picks up speed and hurries away, vanishing amid a raft of yellowing leaves.

"Maybe she missed one," he says.

"I doubt it."

"Did you look?"

I shake my head.

René grins. "Well, wouldn't help much if you did — seeing what you're like with hens' eggs."

"Oi!"

"That's better."

We search the orchard from top to bottom, then the wood-pile and the yard, then every nook and cranny in the barns, and finally the orchard again. Every time I think I've spotted something it turns out to be a patch of sunlight or a fallen leaf.

Luckily, Napoleon is asleep in the orchard with his beak tucked under his wing. But his mate — a little goose snuggled up next to him – watches our every step.

At the bottom hedge we poke about in the under-growth with sticks and find Father's beehives, rotting and empty, and a clutch of cold hens' eggs, but nothing bigger.

At last I straighten up.

"At least we tried," I say.

We walk back up to the gate, glancing one last time into clumps of nettles and the tufts of fresh grass which have sprouted since the rain.

The low afternoon sun makes the ripe plums glow like rubies and the almond cases gleam a soft jade green. From a hidden perch, a blackbird begins his evensong.

"We'll look again if you like," René says as we skirt around Napoleon and his mate. "You know, when your mother's out."

"Thanks. I mean, how could I manage without you?"

I bump his arm. He grins back and looks down.

Then he stops.

The little goose waggles her head at him and honks.

"Let's hurry up, shall we?" I say as Napoleon opens one black, calculating eye.

"Hang on a minute."

"Not a good idea, René!"

But he's peering at the little goose, leaning forward, bobbing his head up and down, then side to side. Napoleon lifts his head.

"Are you mad?" I breathe. "Come away!"

But René continues his strange head-bobbing dance.

Then he points. "I knew it! Look!"

"What? I can't see anything."

"Look closer!"

But the little goose hisses at me and Napoleon eyes us malevolently.

"I still don't—"

At last I see it: a small, shiny dome underneath the goose. An egg!

René crouches, then edges closer to it. Napoleon hisses at him and both geese waggle their heads.

"René, be careful! We can't get it when *he's* there!"

But René flashes me a grin. "Just you watch me."

My legs turn to jelly as — very slowly — he stands, then grows taller, making himself bigger, like a pantomime demon rising through a trapdoor. He forces his bad leg straight and puts his shoulders back, then lifts his chin higher and higher, and sticks out his elbows. Finally, eyes fixed on Napoleon, he takes a heavy step forward.

CLUMP! Then another. *CLUMP!* Just as slowly and even more splendidly, Napoleon lumbers to his feet and flaps his magnificent wings.

"René! Watch out!"

CLUMP!

Napoleon arches his neck into a perfect *S* and gapes his razor-edged beak. Then he stretches out his neck flat to the ground, taut as a pillar of iron, and hisses like a nest full of snakes.

"René!" My voice is a mouse-squeak; my heart pounds

as I wait to see which soft and tender part Napoleon will strike first.

"Get ready," René whispers.

"Ready for what?"

"You'll see."

CLUMP!

In reply, Napoleon smacks one webbed foot on the ground.

SLAP!

Then another.

SLAP. SLAP. SLAP. His barrel-chest rolls as he swaggers towards René.

I'm transfixed – until I hear a hiss behind me.

I spin round. The rest of the flock is approaching, heads down, beaks gaping.

"René! Be *quick*."

"Hold on."

Swallowing, I stand my ground as Napoleon hisses again.

René hisses back.

Napoleon lets out an almighty screech.

René shouts, "Ready? Now!"

He leaps in the air, screaming, thrashing his arms and kicking his legs like a madman. Napoleon wavers for an instant, then charges with outraged shrieks, slapping and flapping and slashing at René's legs.

"Have you got it?" he bellows, then leaps again as Napoleon swipes at his shins.

"Got what?" I shout back as René zigzags crazily left and right, dodging the gander's lightning beak.

"The egg!"

And there it is! Undefended! The little female is on her feet, hissing at René, but now I'm surrounded by the rest of the beak-snapping, wing-beating flock.

"Hurry up!" René yells. Napoleon has him pinned to a tree.

The other geese lash at me, their eyes cunning and hard. I plunge past them. I lunge for the egg in the hollow of a long-rotted tree stump.

"*Got it!*" The little goose pecks madly at my hand.

"Then *RUN!*"

René takes off uphill with Napoleon at his heels. Clutching the egg to my chest, I scramble away, slipping on goose muck, my ankles whipped by beaks.

The egg feels like quicksilver. I almost drop it. I nearly fall. I lose one clog and kick off the other, and dash barefoot towards the gate.

"I'm there!"

I throw myself into the yard, but René is well behind me now, his bad leg trailing, with Napoleon slashing it and blood staining the rips in his trouser legs.

"Come on!" I shout. "You can make it!"

I hold open the gate.

René roars like a bear and spurts forward. Napoleon lands one last ferocious peck on his calf as René throws himself through the gate.

I slam it in Napoleon's face, then collapse beside René, the glittering prize in my hand. A perfect, white, shiny new goose egg.

Ten

We laugh and cry with relief, then inspect our battle scars.

René's trousers are shredded, his legs bruised and bloodied, and his forehead is bleeding from some meeting with a branch.

"Sweet Mary and Joseph," he says, leaning back against the fence. "You could've warned me."

"I did!"

"Then warn me better next time."

As he rubs his shins and dabs at the blood, I check over the egg.

It's warm and smooth, as big as my palm. I cradle it in both hands, examining the shell minutely.

"Any damage?" René asks.

"I don't think so."

"Give us a look."

"Gently!"

I pass it to him and he rolls it from side to side, holding it close to his face and lifting it into the sun.

"Well?" I say.

"Good as new."

I cross my legs and bunch my skirt and René places the egg in my lap, then we gaze at it as if the gosling might hatch any minute.

"Where are you going to keep it?" he asks.

"I hadn't thought. A pocket, maybe?"

"Great plan," he says, rolling his eyes.

"All right. What about a box in the sun? I've got to keep it warm."

"Or cook it."

"Shut up, René."

He grins an exhausted, lopsided grin and then laughs. "How about we sit here till it hatches?"

"That'll take a month!"

"Best get comfy, then."

He shuts his eyes and turns his face to the sun. He looks funny with his nose smeared with muck, and bits of twig and dead leaves stuck in the blood in his hair.

I lean back beside him and close my eyes too, touching the egg with my fingertips, stroking it, feeling its smoothness, its shape, thinking of all the others that never stood a chance of life because Mother took them.

René says, "What d'you reckon? Boy or girl?"

I open my eyes and find his face close to mine.

"You can't tell till they're hatched," I reply, my heart beating a little faster.

"How about Marie-Antoinette for a girl and Louis for a boy?"

I shake my head. "We've already got King George and Napoleon. You can't have three monarchs in one yard."

"True. True." He nods wisely. "What about Juliet and Romeo?"

"How about a happy ending?"

"Angélique and René?"

"Oh. Er..."

I look into his face. It's so tender and hopeful – and silly-looking with all that dirt and blood. I *do* like him – a lot, especially now – and maybe it is more than like. I don't know. But with Pascal away fighting it feels wrong simply to get on with my life, to make plans and fall in love. That would be like a betrayal, a kind of forgetting, as if I'm saying my world is normal and nothing and no one else matters.

I smile. "I-I'm sorry, but I don't think I'm ready...for *that*."

"Is there someone else?"

"No one. I promise."

He nods. "Right. Well. Best be off."

Briefly, our eyes meet again and then he clambers to his feet.

"See you next week?" I ask.

"Maybe." He shrugs. Then, "You need a broody hen for that egg."

"I'll find one. Thanks."

He nods again, then limps off, and I watch him until he disappears.

Eleven

The days shorten as I wait for my gosling to hatch.

Our oldest hen does the sitting, on a nest I make for her at the top of the haystack in the little stone barn. It's a perfect hiding place – Father never found me there.

In the cool of the evenings, I sit outside the door, sharpening Pascal's tools or cleaning his boots – and worry about Mother, who is growing thinner by the day, and more and more sad and silent.

I don't understand it. How could she have loved Father so deeply? Her grief seems... excessive. The only time she rouses herself is on Friday mornings, when the sky is still black. Then she fills her pails with butter and eggs and treks to Monville and back, leaving me to thresh the corn and clean the house, to churn the butter and collect eggs, and milk the cow and feed King George. And, and, and...

Every night I fall into bed exhausted and listen to Mother weep.

Finally, one Saturday morning in early September – after she comes back very late from Monville – she doesn't get up until midday, and even then she just sits by the kitchen fire, staring into space. I ask her what's wrong but – as usual – get no answer.

Losing patience, I ignore her, and spend the afternoon gleaning fallen grain in the corn field. The muddy stooks resemble crumbling fortresses now, and the broken sheaves vanquished warriors scattered across a battlefield.

Smoke trickles from the chimney when I come back hot and tired, and more resentful than ever that she never helps with the harvest. She's banked up the fire and is sitting huddled over it, clutching a shawl.

I'm about to say something sharp about wasting wood, but then notice her face is pale despite the heat. Reluctantly, I fetch more logs from the woodpile and build up the fire till it's roaring.

Still she shivers.

"You're sick," I tell her. "I'm going to Monsieur Lamy's for a cure."

"It's nothing. Just a chill," she replies.

But by the next morning she's burning up with fever.

"You need a doctor," I say as I sit on her bed, mopping sweat off her face.

"We can't afford one," she mumbles.

"But, Maman—"

"Don't argue. Let me rest."

That afternoon she falls into a deep, deep slumber.

I stay with her day and night. At times she cries out, or groans and rambles. Once I hear her begging God to let her die. In her few lucid moments I plead with her to let me fetch help, but she always refuses.

When the cow lows to be milked or King George squeals to be fed, I hurry outside so their noise doesn't disturb her. By the fourth morning I simply tip the milk into King George's trough. I don't have time to churn butter and the milk in the pantry is spoiling.

That night, as I keep watch by her bed, I stare stupidly at the stump of the candle burning in front of the pictures of Father and Pascal and wonder if I should pray too: for her recovery, for Pascal's safe return, that I will still know him...

I'm woken by a soft scuffling in the yard and an odd clucking sound.

Then Napoleon honks.

I jump up.

The hens!

I forgot to put them away!

I take the stairs two at a time and hurl the front door open.

In the moonlight, the fox is sleek and sharp-faced. The white tip of his brush glistens. A hen hangs from his mouth.

He regards me, unmoving, as if he owns the yard at

night and I'm the intruder. Then, like quicksilver, he's up and over the fence and away.

In tears, I track down the other hens. Two lie headless by the well; the rest cower in scrapes and hollows. I carry each trembling bird into the little stone barn, then climb the haystack and anxiously check on my egg.

The old hen clucks her disapproval as I part the hay underneath her.

In the fine blue moonbeams that fall through gaps in the roof, the shell looks like marble – white and perfectly smooth. I hold it to my face, hoping to feel the gosling inside, but the egg is hard as stone.

"Not long now," I whisper, and tuck it safely back into the hay.

Mother wakes later that day, her eyes like dark pools in deep hollows. I help her sit up and feed her thin gruel. She asks me what day it is.

"Um… I've lost track," I say. Which is almost true. I have a suspicion it's Thursday, but don't want her to fret about market day tomorrow.

She mends slowly, eating a little more each day, even smiling sometimes, as if the fever had burnt out her grief, leaving her weak and helpless, but purged and more at peace.

As I step out one evening to pick mint for our potato supper, a shaft of brilliance from the setting sun catches the upstairs windows. They blaze as if the house is on fire, turning the yard a deep lurid orange. Then the sun sinks, leaving behind a bright, jagged scar in the west.

I realize summer is over.

That night the wind rises, rattling the roof and shaking the chimney pots. The rafters creak as if the house is a barge straining at its moorings. I'm jolted awake time and again, heart pounding. Then, out of the blue but with perfect clarity, I remember tomorrow is Friday, and exactly one month since René's battle with Napoleon. My gosling is due to hatch any time now.

Jumping up, I fumble for a candle and matches. The flame spurts and withers in the gusts from under my door. I hunt down an oil lamp instead and step into the gale.

The air is alive with flying leaves and bits of straw and the roaring of the woods, but the little stone barn is quiet, sheltered by the house.

The cow, chewing cud, follows me with her soft brown eyes as I put the lantern on a shelf and bolt the door behind me. In the steady yellow lamplight, the hay gleams like gold.

The hen's wattle eyelids blink open as I climb up to her, but her body doesn't move as I take the egg from beneath her as if she's not really awake.

The shell is warm and smooth. There's not a crack in it, not the tiniest chink. Is the gosling alive?

The hen ruffles her feathers and clucks a complaint when I clamber across her and sit with my back against the rough stone wall, up amongst the cobwebs. I put the egg in my lap.

All night the wind howls and the lamp hisses. King George snuffles and snores. I doze and dream, and pray that Béatrice's book was right and the gosling will follow me – and the rest of the geese will follow it.

When dawn creeps through the holes in the roof, the egg is still perfectly intact.

Outside, feathered clouds scud across a grey sky. Jackdaws tumble above the restless wood.

Throughout the day I wear holes in the haystack, climbing up and down to check on my egg, only to have to tuck it back underneath the old hen, flawless and whole. The hay is ragged by late afternoon and the hen sharp-eyed and cross.

I'm pulling up carrots for dinner when I hear an odd noise in the air. Instantly I think it might be the hen, but the sound is too far away for that. The wind, maybe, or the jackdaws.

I stop to listen – and freeze.

Footsteps.

In the lane.

A picture of the scout leaps into my head. My heart nearly stops as I listen harder, barely breathing, doubting my ears. But I can't fool myself for long. Someone is definitely coming.

No.

More than one person, approaching with slow, deliberate steps.

There's a cough, mutters, the squeak of the gate. I find my legs and run into the yard — then stop dead. The mayor is there — in *our* yard — wearing his sash of office and a black cravat.

At his back, a *gendarme* holds open the gate for half the village widows.

Behind them, in the lane, stand Béatrice, Claudette and René. I stare at them in astonishment until the mayor coughs and the gendarme turns around.

"Mademoiselle Lacroix?" he asks.

A new terror seizes me.

This is how they announce the death of a soldier. I've heard the women talking about it at the *lavoir*. Suddenly the world is spinning. I'm falling. And my voice is shrieking as if from a great distance.

"PASCAL!"

Twelve

I wake with a crowd around me.

The gendarme, his arms outstretched, is trying to keep everyone back. Then Béatrice cries, "She's opening her eyes!" and René pushes forward.

As he helps me sit up, he whispers urgently, "It's about your father, not your brother. All right?" And he looks me in the eye.

I sink against him for an instant as the widows look down on me pityingly. Béatrice and Claudette attempt smiles, and the burly mayor dabs at his forehead with a handkerchief.

The gendarme says, "I'm sorry to have frightened you, mademoiselle. We have the official papers about Monsieur Lacroix, the certificates and so forth. Is your mother home?"

Dizzy and trembling, I nod. "I'll tell her you're here, *messieurs*. Would you like to wait inside?"

When I get to her room, Mother insists we wear full mourning dress, with our faces veiled. I have to help her up. Then we practise walking across the bedroom, her arm around my shoulder and me taking her weight. She stumbles weakly, her face pale in the fading light.

"We could ask the mayor to come upstairs," I suggest, but she shakes her head.

"We must do this properly. For your father's sake."

Very slowly, we manage the stairs.

There are more people in our kitchen than I've ever seen in there before.

The mayor sits at the table – in the middle, I notice, not at the head – with the gendarme standing at his shoulder.

Madame Malpas has taken the chair opposite them, but even she gets to her feet respectfully at Mother's entrance. Béatrice, Claudette and René wait near the pantry door. From behind my veil everyone seems spectral, as if they're the ghosts, not Father.

I lower Mother into the chair vacated by Madame Malpas, then stand behind her – a dark mirror to the mayor and the gendarme. The mayor clears his throat.

He speaks of glory, sacrifice, a grateful nation. Mother listens in silence, perfectly still throughout, even when the other widows start weeping and clutching each other.

My throat tightens too, but I fight the tears. Why mourn him now? Why revisit his life, his death? I'm glad he's gone. I am! But then I think about Pascal's letter.

A direct hit. A great mercy.

It's good that Mother knows he didn't die in pain or in vain. That the mayor and the nation are grateful.

The mayor hands Mother an envelope. He talks about pensions, testaments and the law. Then he stands and bows to her – and to me! The gendarme salutes us both, then makes for the door. I hurry to open it and find Napoleon preening his feathers just beyond the step.

Horrified, I turn to René, appealing to him with my eyes. But of course! He can't see them behind my veil. I flick my head towards Napoleon, then the mayor.

René cocks his head. I nod frantically from side to side, mouthing *help*, even though I know he can't see me. At last he peers round the door.

"Oh. Right. Erm…"

He glances at me, nods and squares his shoulders. But before stepping out, he turns back to the room, signalling to the gendarme to follow him.

Shutting the door behind them, I make a little bow to the mayor and say, "One moment, please, monsieur."

Most of the widows file out behind the mayor, but Madame Malpas and three other crones make themselves comfortable at the table.

I glare at them, then lift my veil and try again, but it does no good. Despite Mother's rigid silence, they stay put, sighing and mopping their eyes with lace handkerchiefs.

I wish Mother would speak instead of sitting like a pillar of black marble.

Béatrice taps my shoulder. "I'm so sorry for your loss," she says.

Claudette kisses me, her cheeks wet with tears.

Awkwardly, René and I shake hands.

"We should go," Béatrice says, hugging me.

"No!" My eyes fly to Madame Malpas. "*Please* stay."

"It's nearly dark," she whispers.

"René will see you home. Won't you?" I put my hand on his arm.

He shrugs. "If you want."

"Thank you," I mouth. Then, "I'll make some refreshment."

"I'll find the kettle," Béatrice says.

"I'll toast some bread," adds Claudette.

Too late I remember there's only one stale loaf left – I'd been saving it for King George – but there's no time to bake anything fresh. They'll just have to make do. With a sigh, I track down a small box of coffee and dust off Mother's best china cups.

Only the ticking clock marks the passage of Father's funeral meal – that and a nerve-racking crunch of old teeth on hard toast. Even spread thickly with butter, it's like concrete.

Madame Malpas places her slice back on her plate and delicately pushes it away.

"Very nice, Angélique," she says, wiping a crumb from the corner of her mouth. Then she turns to Mother. "Such a shame your son couldn't be here – or for the harvest."

Her eyes dart at me as if to say, *I told you so*.

I feel my hackles rise.

"More toast, Madame Malpas?" I say.

Béatrice frowns at me. I shrug, then look at Mother again, trying to see through her veil. I wish she'd drink a little coffee or join us in some way. But she seems lost inside herself and completely alone.

René steps forward. "We'd best go."

Béatrice and Claudette stand immediately. Even the crones scrape their chairs. Only Madame Malpas remains seated.

"Madame Malpas," René says firmly. "Time to go."

She gives him a look as black as her dress, then rises slowly to her feet.

Once they've gone, Mother takes off her veil and lays it across the table like a thin ribbon of night.

"It was good of the mayor to come," she says, looking up at me.

"Yes, it was," I say, surprised at the strength in her voice. "Would you like coffee now, or something to eat?"

"Not yet. Sit with me a minute?"

I pull up a chair and take her hand. And wait.

Two flies land on a piece of discarded toast. I wave them away, but they come straight back, their tiny mouths sucking on the butter. The fire needs stoking. The table lamp smokes, sending greasy coils up to the ceiling and blackening the glass.

I glance at Mother, wondering if she'd mind me trimming the wick, but she's looking into the dark glass as if she can see things in it. I stroke her hand and watch the smoke.

In the stillness, it grows into a column, tall and straight, like a solid, predictable trunk. But then it branches into fantastical patterns, dancing and strange, as if some force in the flame has come alive again.

At last Mother begins to speak.

She tells me about Father, how handsome he was, how strong, skilful, a good shot. Proud of being a father at first, and then...

Silence again.

I brush away the flies and turn down the lamp, then sit quietly in the firelight until she starts talking once more.

She tells me about their wedding day, how happy she was, how Father carried her over the threshold, how he kissed her. How tenderly he treated her on their wedding night.

I shift uncomfortably in my seat. Mother smiles at me.

"I'm sorry, my angel. I shouldn't be telling you about that."

"Um, no, that's all right."

Her smile widens. "René seems nice," she adds.

I look down. "Please, Maman. Not now." I change the subject. "I've got some news for you. Please don't be cross. I hid a goose egg. The gosling's about to hatch."

She touches my face. Her smile is warm now, and for the first time in weeks there's colour in her cheeks.

"Life goes on?" she says.

"Yes. Yes, I think so."

"So you should."

After I've helped Mother to bed — and made sure she's asleep — I take a blanket and a crust of bread to the top of the haystack and prepare for another long vigil. But when I part the hen's belly feathers, she clucks in distress and her blinking white eyelids seem to flash a warning.

"Is it time?" I ask her. "Is it starting?"

Touching the egg, I feel a quiver.

"It *is* time! How *wonderful*."

But what do I do now? Sit up here all night? Hatchings can take days! I wish I'd asked Béatrice exactly what it said in her book.

Risking a peck, I gently lift the egg and inspect it carefully. And there it is — a fingernail-sized hole. The hatching has begun.

Scrabbling across the hay with my blanket, I cross my legs and make a nest of my lap. It's hard to see in the twilight, but I daren't risk bringing a lantern up here in case of fire, so I wait for a moonbeam to find us.

At first, the inner skin seems intact but, as I watch, it's torn apart by a tiny, shiny, pale pink beak.

"Oh, you clever thing!"

I'm beside myself with joy for a long while, but then nothing else happens for hours.

Sometimes I'm afraid the gosling has died because it's

so still, but then it batters the shell again with its hard little beak until, at long, long last, a narrow crack circles the top of the egg. Then the gosling stops moving.

Exhausted, I expect.

I stare at the crack, willing it to open. I want to help, but feel I mustn't. What if the gosling isn't ready to be born? Nature must take its course.

Finally, the struggle begins again. I watch the poor little thing, slimy and dark, wiggling and twitching, constricted in the shell, too weak to break it apart.

"Come on, little one! Don't give up!"

At last, giving in to temptation, I prise open the top of the shell, but I'm frightened of hurting the fragile, formless creature inside. It seems to be nothing but a beak and two blind, bulging eyes. Then there's another spasm of effort, a desperate convulsion, and its head flops onto my lap. Instantly, it seems impossible that such a big head, such a long scrawny neck, could ever have fitted inside the shell.

"Just your feet and body to go," I whisper.

Just? The battle is too hard, the thrashing ceases. I look to the hen, but she's fallen asleep. Clumsily I peel away fragments of shell, chipping them off with my fingernails.

The gosling appears to be glued to the egg, to be part of it still – half born – the head and neck a wormy thing that can't survive alone.

Tremors shake it like death throes, until one outsized webbed foot sticks up out of the shell, crushing the wing against the tiny body. The bird doesn't have the strength to push free. I breathe warm air onto it, stroking the neck with infinite tenderness.

"Fight," I whisper. "It's your life. Fight for it, *please*."

Minutes pass, the tremors increase, then the gosling jerks, arches, the webbed foot paddles, expands and breaks free.

"Come on!"

A claw-like wing jabs up and out. The body spills onto me, a wet, bedraggled ball attached to two gigantic feet. It is the sweetest, silliest, ugliest, most beautiful thing in the world.

Thirteen

I can't believe how fast my gosling grows. Soft and helpless on day one, by day two it's a fluffy, squeaking, bright-eyed imp.

I check the vent. Female. Time to think about a name.

Piggy is one that springs to mind – she eats from dawn till dusk. Within two weeks she's tall and gangly, forever trailing after me.

Luckily, the weather stays fine and most of the time we're outdoors, gleaning in the corn field or wandering along the lane with the cow. Lucky, too, in a way, that Mother is still convalescing in bed or she'd never let her into the house.

One afternoon, in the third week of the gosling's life, we take King George up to the woods to feast on acorns. The two of them root happily in the leaf litter, while I fill a basket with chanterelles, then gather wild marjoram, sorrel and thyme.

The warm October sun draws a sweet dampness from the earth and the yellow leaves on the trees blaze. Strolling home in the burnished glow of the sunset, rose hips and red haws shine like jewels.

I put King George to bed, then, in the gathering dusk, stop by the woodpile to chop logs for the fire. But the gosling gets under my feet, tugging at the hem of my skirt with her beak and squeaking to be picked up.

I'm scared I'll hurt her if Father's heavy axe slips from my hands, so I give up on the idea of chopping wood and sit on the block instead, letting her scramble onto my lap.

There are scuttling sounds in the woodpile, soft scratchings, snuffling in the dark. The moon rises clear of the house, outlining roofs, walls, fence posts like a charcoal sketch.

Beyond lie silver fields and fox-haunted hedgerows: our home, our land – Pascal's and mine – the place where we belong.

I know now that I can't stop time or recapture the years that might have been. It was silly ever to think I could. But no matter what Pascal has seen or done, I can't believe this war will break him. All he'll need is a place to heal – and our love.

I stroke the gosling's downy neck, her stubby wings, her soft back. For all that she's my baby, my darling little thing, tomorrow she'll have to meet the other geese and learn to live with them. And next week, all being well, she'll lead them to graze in the corn field.

We might even go as far as the water meadow one day.

For tonight, I pop her, protesting, into the little stone barn. Then I take my basket into the kitchen and make Mother her supper of wild herbs fried in butter with onion and chanterelles.

In the morning there's a damp chill in the air. Excited to see how the flock will greet my gosling, I dress quickly, but as I pass Mother's room she calls out, "Have you seen my darning needles?" I find her sitting up in bed with a pile of Father's old socks.

"What are you doing?" I ask.

"Mending warm things for your brother," she replies with a smile.

"Winter's a long way off."

"So is he, my angel."

I find her needles and thread. Then more wool. A lamp. A little soup would be nice. Or mushrooms! Last night's were delicious. After breakfast I hurry out of earshot.

Drizzle floats on the air. The gosling trips over her feet to get outside. Squeaking constantly, she sticks to my heels as I fetch a ladder and carry it down through the orchard.

The mouldering plums are full of wasps, slowed by the cold, so I set the ladder against an almond tree and climb up with a basket on my arm, out of reach of Napoleon's beak, but close enough in case of trouble.

The gosling pecks at the base of the ladder, squealing

at me, but at last she settles down to hunt for grubs in the long grass.

Slowly, the other geese approach her, making soft, bubbling sounds. Even Napoleon is curious, though I notice with a touch of sadness that her real mother is no more interested in her than the rest.

After a while, Napoleon honks loudly. I look down, worried that the gosling might be bothering him. But she's still below me while he's waddling along the fence, hissing and stretching his neck. Someone is coming.

The scout? My heart quickens. But then a familiar figure limps into view and I breathe a sigh of relief.

"René! Come quickly! There's someone you've got to meet!" I shin down the ladder and run to the lane, the gosling tripping and flopping behind me. "Look! Isn't she sweet?"

He bends down to pet her and she tugs at his laces.

"She thinks they're worms," I tell him, laughing. "She'll eat anything, that one."

He lets her peck at his fingers, but says nothing.

"Isn't she's lovely?" I ask him again.

"Beautiful," he replies quietly at last.

I put my hand on his arm. "What's wrong?"

It takes him a long time to look up from under his drizzle-dewed fringe. Then, slowly, he stands. "I've come to say goodbye," he says, his voice very soft.

Anxiety tightens my throat.

"Why? Where are you going?"

He meets my gaze calmly.

"I'm going to join the army, Angélique."

My stomach lurches, then twists and constricts. I hear myself gasp. Then I say, "But you can't. You don't have to. They won't make you."

"I know."

"So why…?"

My mind is a blur. Why this sudden decision? It seems… wilful. Crazy. Doesn't he know what *terrible* things are happening out there? This must be some kind of bad joke. A mistake. I shake the confusion out of my head.

"But, René, you're not nineteen yet. You don't *have* to go."

"Yes I do," he replies gently, looking me in the eye.

"No! You *don't*. Ask your mother. She'll tell you."

His smile is kind, as if I'm a foolish child talking about something I don't understand. I reach out and touch his arm.

"Please, René. Have you *really* thought about this?"

He laughs as though I'd told a silly joke.

"Yes, Angélique, I have."

Frightened now, I try pulling myself together – until an image comes into my head of him crawling through barbed wire, with machine guns rattling around him and a sniper's bullet seeking him out. He's going to get himself hurt or maimed or perhaps even—

No! No, he won't. I won't even think about *that*. René *will* come back, just like Pascal will. They must. I wipe my

91

nose with the back of my hand and brush the tears away.

He looks at my other hand which, I suddenly realize, is gripping his arm as if my life depended on it. He puts his own hand over mine and strokes it tenderly with his thumb.

A thrill runs through me like shock or fear or something else entirely. I've no idea what to do or say. I just stand there, staring, mouth open, tears rolling down my face.

René smiles at me again, then looks at the gosling, which is busily untying his laces. When they come undone, she squeals and falls backwards into a rut, her feet sticking into the air. René laughs and kneels to rescue her as rain patters around us.

"There's something else," he says, then hesitates as if lost for words.

"What?" I ask. "You can tell me."

"My mother is…unhappy."

I frown. Of course she's unhappy. Why wouldn't she be?

"She might say something to you," he adds.

"Me? Why?"

He stands, seeming taller somehow. A soldier going to war.

"There's gossip in the village," he says.

I laugh. "So what's new?"

"It's about…us."

"Us? Who's talking about *us*?"

"Madame Malpas mostly."

"Well, there's a surprise! Stupid woman."

He flinches, and at once I regret making light of it.

"What's she saying?" I ask, gently touching his arm again.

He looks at my hand. "She's saying you treated me like the man of the house the other day, when the mayor came." He shrugs, then looks into my eyes from under his fringe. "I didn't want you to think I started the rumour."

"What rumour?" I ask quietly.

"That we agreed…"

"What?"

"You know, to wed. After the war. Not that I mind," he adds quickly. "I just thought you might."

The same tender hope springs into his eyes that I saw when we found the goose egg. My legs weaken, my insides dissolve. I want so much to say something loving to him, to give him a reason to hope.

If only I knew for certain what I felt – like Béatrice knows without a shadow of doubt that she loves Pascal, and always will. But it would be cruel to tell René I love him if I don't. I can't lie to him now of all times.

Rain drips off his fringe and runs down his face, but he doesn't seem to notice. I hear his breathing, my heart beating, the falling rain. Then the gosling squeals. She's stuck in a rut again.

This time I kneel down to pick her up and say to the ground, "It's all right, René. I know you don't gossip about me."

There's silence for a moment, a stillness between us. Then he says, "Right. Well. Must be off." As if I'd just said I wouldn't go swimming with him, or take a walk, or any of the million everyday things we might have done together.

"No," I say. "Please wait."

"Don't tease me, Angélique." His voice shakes with emotion.

"I'm not teasing, I promise. I just need to understand."

He snorts a bitter laugh. "What's to understand?"

"Why fight when you don't have to?"

He shakes his head and shuts his eyes, then turns his face into the rain. When he looks at me again his expression is kinder and sadder, older somehow, and his voice is gentle again.

"I've been called bad names my whole life. You know that. Cripple. Dunce. Hop-along. I'm the stupid baker's boy with one duff leg and two bloody great boots. You called me worse when we were little – you and Pascal. And maybe that is who I am. But I'm not a coward, Angélique. I won't let *anyone* call me that."

He takes my hand and draws me closer. My body trembles. I hold my breath.

He says, "Think what your mother will say if I don't go, or Madame Chevalier. Any of them. What if their sons don't come back, or come back crippled worse than me? What if Pascal comes home without legs? What would you call me then?"

"I wouldn't say anything, René, I promise."

"But you'd think it."

His face is so close to mine that his breath warms my skin. But I can't see him through the tears of self-blame. Is he right? Might I be cruel to him again?

He whispers, "I have to go, Angélique. Don't you see? I couldn't bear you hating me if I don't."

I bite back the tears. It's not fair to bully him with them, not when he cares about me so deeply that he'd rather go to war than risk me thinking him a coward. I can't repay that kind of love with my foolish doubts.

I say, "When will you go?"

"Soon."

"Good luck."

Good luck?

He laughs at that and shakes his head again, and I wish with all my heart that somehow I could magically turn into the sort of person who'd throw her arms around him and kiss him, and tell him that she loves him and will wait for him forever.

A flock of crows lifts off the corn field, cawing noisily, and flaps towards the woods. Frightened, the gosling scuttles under my skirt. René stoops and gently pulls her out.

"A girl, you said?"

I nod.

"Got a name yet?"

I shake my head.

He reaches into my basket, sitting forgotten in the mud, and takes out an almond, then rolls it along the ground. The gosling slips and slides in the puddles as she chases after it.

"We could call her Amandine," he says.

Amandine. Like a dish made with almonds. Perfect.

"Remember me when you play with her," he adds.

Again I nod, my throat too tight to speak.

Fourteen

The clouds thicken all day. By dusk, rain clatters against the roof of the little stone barn.

As I tuck Amandine under a blanket of straw, I'm still cursing myself for all the things I didn't say to René – like *Be careful. I'll miss you. Please write.*

When I come in, Mother is sitting by the kitchen fire, her darning in her lap.

"I managed the stairs on my own," she says proudly. But her smile fades as she sees my face. "Oh, my angel, what is it?"

"Nothing."

"Nothing?"

"René stopped by. That's all."

She pats Father's chair. "Tell me all about it." But I shake my head. My feelings for René are like a tender wound I'm protecting.

That night I lie awake, listening to the rain battering my shutters and trying to decide if I should go to the village tomorrow and talk to him. I ought to explain how I feel. I owe him that much at least.

Drifting into unquiet dreams, I see Pascal walking up the lane with his dog, only I'm frightened of him and don't understand why – until I wake up and realize he was wearing Father's clothes.

As dawn breaks I dress in mourning black, still trying to work out what I'll say to René.

Mother is at her darning again by the fire, bent over her work in the dim light of the flames.

"You need a lamp," I tell her. "I'll fetch one."

"Don't worry. I'll move to the window when it's light."

"But it's cold by the window."

"I've got my shawl."

She looks up and sees my dress. "You're going to the village? Is it Friday?"

I shake my head. "Thursday. Why?"

She avoids my eye. "No reason. I just wondered."

I stand in front of her. "You're not thinking about going to Monville, are you?"

She flutters her hand as if waving my words away.

"Maman! You can't! You just got out of bed!"

"I want to post Pascal's things."

"Monsieur Nicholas will take them!"

"There's lamp oil to buy, and candles and salt…"

"Then I'll go! *Please, Maman!* Promise you won't! You've been ill for weeks!"

She clicks her tongue, irritated, but then sinks back in her chair, looking old and tired and troubled.

"All right. I promise – if you promise you won't go either. Are you going to see René?" she adds after a pause.

Tears spring to my eyes.

"He-he's joining the army," I whisper.

Mother sighs deeply, then nods. "Wish him God's speed from me."

I set off at once, splashing through mud, careless of the dress. Rain sheets down from low, dark clouds. But as I turn the corner to the water meadow, Béatrice and Claudette come into sight, jumping over the puddles, their skirts hitched up, their faces flushed.

I stop dead, overcome by a feeling of dread. He's *gone*. I know it. I'm too late.

Claudette waves when she sees me watching them, and shouts, "Angie! You'll *never* guess what!" She runs the last few steps, her face bright with excitement.

"René's run off to be a soldier! And guess what else? Madame Faubert whacked old Ma Malpas with a baguette!" Her words take a moment to register.

Why would René's mother hit Madame Malpas with a baguette? Perplexed, I stare at her as Béatrice hurries towards us, puffing and panting.

"Are you all right?" she asks as we kiss.

Her eyes are wide with concern, but Claudette elbows her aside.

"Don't tell her *anything*, Bee. I want to!"

But instead of talking, she giggles, then bites her lip, her eyes sparkling.

"What's happened?" I demand. "Stop teasing!"

"It's Madame Faubert," Béatrice begins. "She's—"

"She's told René he can't marry you! What a hoot! As if you would!"

I stare at her again as Béatrice takes my hand and sits me down on a log to explain.

"Madame Malpas has been telling everyone you and René are … more than friends."

"A *lot* more than friends," Claudette sniggers. "And this morning, Madame Faubert gave her what for – right in the middle of the square! *No son of mine is going to marry a peasant!* You know what she's like. So old Ma Malpas calls her an interfering old nag!"

"She didn't," I gasp.

"She did! She said that's why René ran off! So Ma Faubert ups and wops Ma Malpas round the ear! The baguette split in two! You should've *seen* it, Angie. I nearly died laughing."

I look from her to Béatrice, struggling to make sense of it all.

"But *why* would René's mother believe Madame Malpas?" I ask. "Everyone knows she makes things up."

"Ah, but she wasn't making it up, was she, my little

lovebird?" Claudette says. "Go on, Bee, tell her."

Béatrice sighs. "Last week at the *lavoir*, Madame Malpas was talking about the mayor's visit to your farm. How you ... well, fainted into René's arms—"

"I didn't!"

"You did," says Claudette. "You swooned. It was beautiful. And you got him to chase that blasted gander of yours."

"Anyway—" Béatrice begins again.

"Anyway," Claudette breaks in. "Last week, Madame Faubert comes storming out of the bakery and tells Madame Malpas to shut her stupid mouth. She's no business spreading gossip about some strumpet farm girl who's putting her hooks into *her* darling son!"

"But I didn't—"

"You want to hear the story or not?" Claudette says.

I fall silent and let her go on.

"So out comes René, shouting at his ma to shut up. Because you're not a strumpet, you're the love of his life! And he'll marry whoever he wants! Isn't that *delicious*, Angie? As if you'd ever marry *him*!"

I gape at her, shocked beyond belief. René *had* proposed to me. Sort of – in his own sweet, shy way. And I'd turned him down. More or less.

"Claudie, be quiet," Béatrice snaps as Claudette's laughter rings out like a bell. "Can't you see this isn't funny?"

"Yes it is! It's hilarious!"

"No it's not," I tell her.

"How would you know? You weren't there."

"René came to see me before he left," I say quietly.

"Oo-oo! Did he now?" Claudette squashes up next to me on the log. "Tell us *all* about it." They both look at me expectantly, their lips parted.

What should I tell them? I don't want to betray René or shame him. I know whatever I say will get back to the village.

"Has he gone?" I ask at last.

Béatrice nods. "Last night."

He must have walked past the farm.

I shut my eyes, trying to calm the storm of guilt and regret and confusion. He must be in Monville by now, or perhaps on a train or in some recruiting office. I offer up a small prayer of safekeeping, then say, "He told me he wanted to be a soldier."

"Good for him," Béatrice says. "I think he's very brave."

"Shut up," Claudette says. "Come on, Angie. What did he *really* say?"

I look down at my hands.

"He said he didn't want me to think he'd started the rumour."

"About the wedding?" Béatrice asks.

"But there isn't going to be a wedding!"

"So you turned him down?" Claudette says.

"No! Yes. Well, maybe. I don't know."

Claudette's face becomes a picture of disbelief. "You

don't know if you said yes or no to René Faubert's proposal of marriage? Oh, Angie! You're *hopeless*!" And she throws back her head and shrieks with laughter.

Fifteen

Amandine squeals in excitement when she sees me through the orchard fence, but she's shivering and soaking wet. Of course! Her downy feathers aren't waterproof yet.

I pick her up and hug her, whispering, "I'm sorry. So very, very sorry."

She stays close all day, as if chiding me for leaving her behind this morning. Each time she falls over or pulls at a thread on my hem, I'm reminded of René. I try to imagine him in uniform with a rifle slung over his shoulder, but can't make the picture seem real.

That evening I bring Amandine into the kitchen to warm by the fire. Mother says nothing at first, but as we lay the table she tells me to put her outside.

"I'll take her out later," I say.

Mother opens her mouth as if to argue, then just purses her lips.

As we eat our boiled potatoes she asks about René. When I tell her he left last night she pats my hand and says, "Go to Mass. Light him a candle."

But her candles didn't save Father.

I toss and turn all night, wondering where René is sleeping – and Pascal. Are they safe in some warm hayloft or out in the cold, wet night? The idea that they might be suffering while I'm comfy in bed haunts my dreams, and I wake in the small hours.

Quietly, I get out of bed, dress in the warmest clothes I own and tiptoe downstairs.

The night is black and spitting with rain. Taking a lantern from the kitchen, I creep across to the threshing barn to find Mother's palanche and pails.

There aren't any eggs to sell, the hens have hardly been laying since the fox's visit. Instead, I fill both pails with butter from the well and set out at once, before I have time to change my mind.

The long walk to Monville will be my penance for the cruel words I said to René when we were children, the weight of the palanche my punishment for the loving words I never said.

In the lane, the wind tries to extinguish my lantern. The flame gutters and leaps. But in the woods, the trees banish the wind and rain as if they, too, are trespassers here.

Shadows in the branches make faces at me. I knew they would. But still I shy from them – gnarled, menacing phantoms springing from my lantern, the outlines of wolves and bears.

My feet snap twigs, alerting hidden watchers. They flee. *It's just a fox*, I tell myself, *a deer or a hare*. But the trees seem to gather, rustling, listening. Soft mud sucks at my clogs.

Once, I trip over and the leaping shadows become goblins, witches, ghouls. If the lantern blows out I'll be helpless, lost in the nothingness of night. I conjure pictures of Béatrice, Mother, even Claudette laughing at me. Then I think about Pascal and René; nothing I can imagine could ever be worse than the things they'll see.

An owl hoots, another answers. Then quiet returns.

In the dark my nose twitches, scenting earth, rotting leaves, fungus, a fox. Dawn is a pale promise at first, a glimmer between the trunks. Finally, branches take shape and birds begin to sing. I stop by a stream when there's enough light to blow the lantern out, and ease the palanche off my shoulders, then kneel to drink and wash my face.

On the far side of the woods, the road to Monville snakes along the bottom of a wide, green valley. Figures crawl along it, some of them balancing palanches like me, others herding sheep, ducks, geese or a pig.

On the road, old men and women carry trussed-up chickens upside down. Hawkers push handcarts. A lorry goes by. Then there are buildings, tall and grand, with women beating rugs on cast-iron balconies and pigeons gliding between the sweeping grey rooftops. The bustle of traders guides me through the alleyways to the market square.

A dozen dairy maids have set up their wares on the pavement outside the doors of a church. There are buckets of milk and baskets of eggs, and pails of butter like mine. When they see me they fold their arms and glare, resentful of the competition.

I have to explain that I'm Angélique Lacroix, daughter of Madame Lacroix from La Mordue farm, who's been selling our butter and eggs here for years.

Grudgingly, they make a small space for me.

Trade is brisk. Housewives and merchants pack the square. Soon my skirt pocket jingles with coins and my first pail is nearly empty.

I notice a thin, ragged girl watching me and smile at her, but she quickly disappears into the crowd.

My second bucket is half empty when I see her again. I wonder if I can afford to pay her to show me a shop selling lamp oil. But she's gone already – and a hush is falling. I look around, then up, into a scarred and brutish face.

The man is a giant with hard, dirt-creased eyes. His crooked nose is veined purple and his pock-marked neck erupts like a boil from his coat.

I step back. My eyes drop to his knuckles, calloused and yellow as horn. He's a bull of a man. I half expect him to snort. Instead he just stares down at me.

Summoning what little courage I can, I ask, "What do you want?"

"You the Lacroix girl?"

"Why?"

"Are you?"

When I nod, he bends stiffly and extends a fist towards one of my pails.

"What are you doing?" I cry as he up-ends it. "You can't!"

My last pats of butter flump onto the pavement.

"Stop it!" I scream as he lifts his boot and crushes the overturned pail, grinding it into splinters. My heart racing, I appeal to the other dairy maids with raised hands, but they look away.

"But...but..." In stunned disbelief, I watch the man crush my second pail under his boot. Remnants of butter ooze along the gaps between the cobblestones. "I-I don't understand."

His hand shoots out again, this time grabbing my wrist, forcing me onto my knees. His coat reeks of tobacco, his breath of wine.

"You're hurting me," I whimper.

Wordlessly, he pulls me up, wrenching my shoulder. Then he dips his other hand into my pocket, his knuckles grinding against my thigh.

"Not my money! You can't!"

But his fingers fish and probe.

"Please, monsieur. I have to buy oil and candles and salt for my mother. She's been sick."

But his face remains implacable as he withdraws his hand from my skirt and drops my coins, jangling, into his own coat pocket. Then he drops me and I crumple at his feet.

"But...*why*?" I whisper. "By what right?"

"Lacroix?" he says. "From La Mordue?"

"Yes! So?"

He walks away without a backward glance.

Sixteen

I stare after the brute of a man, the noise of the market remote. When he's gone, I look at the frightened faces around me.

"Who was he?" I ask, shaking.

But no one will admit to knowing him, and when I start shouting, "Who was he? Why did he steal my money?" the dairy maids back away as if I have some contagious disease.

A skinny white cat laps the spilt butter at my feet, its shoulder blades sticking up through its fur like spikes. In floods of tears, I pick up the palanche and my lantern and leave.

The journey home seems endless, the questions more endless still. Why? By what right? Why did he ask my name and where I lived?

Sore-footed and faint with hunger, I stop at last under

the eaves of the wood and look down into our valley. Smoke from our chimney drifts across the stubble. The sprouting green stooks look like islands in the grey.

What will I tell Mother? What will I ask her? I feel lost and alone, afraid to go home.

Afraid too, perhaps, to hear her answers.

She runs into the yard as soon as I open the gate, as though she'd been watching for me. She stares at the empty hooks on the ends of the palanche and turns pale.

"Come inside. Come quickly."

Putting her arm around me, she looks up the lane as if scared that I might have been followed. She refuses to answer my questions. She tells me I shouldn't have gone.

"Going to market is *my* job. *Always.* I told you that!"

Later, after we've eaten, she asks if the man hurt me. When I shrug, her eyes fill with tears.

"I'm sorry, my angel. I never meant for this to happen."

"So tell me what did happen."

"When you're older, I promise."

"I'm not a child!"

"I know. Trust me. And promise you won't ever go to Monville again."

When she's finally gone to bed, I run outside and bring Amandine back into the kitchen, settling her on my lap beside the dying fire. I had hoped she'd calm my pain and confusion, but all I do is fret over this man and wonder what dark secrets Mother is hiding about him.

Perhaps I should write to Pascal's regiment and beg

them to grant him leave. He ought to know that some thug is stealing from his sister and mother.

But what if they refuse? Pascal will worry – or, worse still, defy their orders and come home anyway. No. He can't know anything about this.

Stroking Amandine, I think maybe Béatrice could help me, or her father, perhaps. But Mother is such a private person; she'd hate any gossip getting out. And Claudette always prises secrets out of Béatrice. She's hopeless like that.

I prod the embers of the fire, sending a flurry of ash whirling across the hearth. From the last glowing log, a tiny blue flame begins to pulse.

Watching it, I think about René. I could have trusted him with my fears, and told him how badly that man had frightened me and how much Mother's secretiveness hurts.

The blue flame fizzes and spurts, each little jet igniting the amber heart of the fire. I expect the flame to die any minute. But it doesn't.

I glance at the darkest corner of the kitchen, an idea forming. It would mean going into *his* room, sitting at *that* desk. So what? He's dead and gone. I don't have to be afraid any more. Holding Amandine close, I stand.

A heavy, brown curtain covers the archway to the passage. I take the table lamp and walk towards it. The lamplight wavers as I kick the curtain aside and a cold draft hits me.

I could swear the air still smells of his tobacco.

Don't be silly. He's dead. He's gone.

But my palms sweat and my skin crawls as I open the door to his study. There it is — his desk, the one he bent Pascal and me over to thrash us.

I force myself to look at it. The old-fashioned legs, the scuffed leather inlay. I stride towards it, telling Amandine she's allowed to play on it now. There's no one to stop her.

I sit in his chair and search the drawers for ink, pen and paper. Then, with Amandine nibbling at the inlaid leather, I write a long letter to my Uncle Gustav in faraway Étaples.

Seventeen

Days of waiting for a reply turn into weeks. I almost give up hope. What if my letter got lost on the way? Étaples is hundreds of kilometres from here. And will Uncle Gustav realize that, although I didn't say as much, I'm actually begging him to come?

As November's rain turns into sleet, and the water-logged ground freezes over, I watch the lane anxiously and keep my fingers crossed.

Happily, Amandine's adult feathers grow, so at least the wet weather bounces off her.

But the fallen grain in the corn field becomes iced into the earth, so there's no point in her leading the flock out to graze.

Instead I feed them and King George on the grain that went mouldy before I threshed it, which upsets the pig's stomach and requires a great deal of mucking out.

I sit with him through the long winter evenings, with Amandine and the cow for company, and the plump brown hens asleep in the rafters, and my lantern guttering.

I don't tell Mother about my letter, and she never mentions the thug in Monville, but as she grows stronger she churns butter each day and searches for eggs, and one Friday morning I wake to find her gone.

Anxiously, I wait for her to return, picturing the thug and the ragged girl, and the thin white cat lapping our butter off the cobblestones.

Dusk seems to arrive before daylight gets going. Wind howls in the chimney and hail rattles on the roof. I take a candle out to King George. It flickers in the icy drafts, sending shadows dancing across the stone walls.

I'm almost asleep when Napoleon suddenly screeches in the yard. My heart leaps. It can't be Mother. He never shrieks at her. The scout? Surely fate couldn't be that cruel. But as I snatch up the candle and reach for the door, I hear a man shout.

"Ruddy bird! Get off!"

"Uncle Gustav!"

The relief is like a waterfall of pure joy. I dash outside and bury my face in his greatcoat.

"Ma petite!"

His voice booms louder than the wind. His arms wrap around me, scooping me up. His coat is rough and sodden, spattered with mud, but I want to stay pressed against it forever.

"Uncle! I thought you weren't coming!"

"I'll always come. You know that."

He kisses my hair and cradles my head and I feel his chest vibrate as he chuckles.

"My word, you've grown. I can't call you ma petite any more."

"Yes, you can, Uncle Gustav. You always can."

"Then I shall. Ma petite."

His dark eyes crinkle as he smiles down at me, and his splendid white moustache tickles as he kisses my forehead.

"Let's get out of this weather," he says. "And if that ruddy gander pecks my backside one more time, I swear I'll put him in the pot."

When Mother gets home she scolds me for bothering Uncle Gustav with our troubles, but she can't hide the smile behind her tears.

Soon he has her laughing, and while I build up the fire he tells us tales of his journey and Aunt Mathilde's health. Then we talk about Father, Pascal, the war – everything except the man in Monville.

"What about you, Brigitte?" he asks Mother. "Angélique said you've been under the weather." He holds her hands as we tell him about her fever.

"Poor girl! How terrible for you both."

At last he leans back and stretches out his legs towards the fire.

"So, ma petite, what delicious thing are you going to prepare for our supper?"

"Potato soup?"

"My favourite! And tomorrow it's my turn to cook. The only thing I'll need is your father's hunting gun."

I find him the rifle next morning. He walks to the woods and brings back five pigeons, two rabbits and a duck. I help him pluck and skin them while Mother rests upstairs.

"Fine woods you've got there," he tells me. "You should set snares."

"Father and Pascal used to, but I don't know how."

"I'll teach you," he says with a smile. "Now," he adds, lowering his voice. "Have you managed to winkle anything more out of your mother about this fellow at the market?"

I shake my head.

"And he knew your name and the name of the farm?"

"Yes."

He frowns. Then winks. "A mystery to be sure – and a bad business – but we'll get to the bottom of it. We can't have Pascal coming home to a pickle."

He gives me a crinkled smile, then looks down at the plucked birds. "So, ma petite, what's your fancy for tonight? Duck, pigeon – or both?"

After dinner I leave him talking with Mother beside a crackling fire.

At first, I eavesdrop through the floorboards, but it's cold lying there, so I hop into bed, listening for her footsteps on the stairs, meaning to sneak down again and talk to Uncle Gustav. But the next thing I know, an axe is thumping outside and grey light is seeping through my shutters. Dressing quickly, I hurry outside and find him swinging Father's axe against the stump of a big, old walnut tree which has been lying at the back of the wood-pile for years.

"Mind out!" he cries as splinters fly. Then he puts a finger to his lips and nods towards the vegetable patch where Mother is digging potatoes.

"Is there somewhere we can talk?" he asks.

I lead him to the little stone barn. Amandine rushes out to meet us. So does the stink of King George. His straw is thick with his muck.

"How long has he been like this?" Uncle Gustav asks as he squats beside the sty.

"A week, maybe longer."

I expect a scolding, but Uncle Gustav just scratches King George's ear.

"*Ma pauvre petite.* What a rotten time you've been having."

Then he picks up Amandine, who's slipped on a patch of ice and landed on her face.

"What did Maman say last night?" I ask, taking the gosling from him.

"Not a lot. She's a stubborn woman."

"What can we do?"

"I'm not too sure, to be honest. We'll have to give it some time."

"You mean you're staying?"

"A little while, yes."

He laughs as I hug him in delight.

"I can't leave your aunt for too long," he adds. "But she'll understand if I'm away for a week or two."

Two weeks! I sigh with gratitude and rest my head against his chest. He kisses my hair, then gently pushes me away.

"Right! To work," he says. "Let's clean up this pig and talk tactics about how to get the truth out of your mother."

For a fortnight, Uncle Gustav mends fences and fixes roof tiles. He teaches me how to set snares and shoot woodcocks and pigeons for the pot, and he chops enough wood for us to have fires until Christmas.

In the evenings we sit up late, talking and laughing. No one mentions the man in Monville — at least, not within my hearing.

Then, at the end of November, snow falls overnight.

Snow. We hardly ever get it this far south, but now the valley is pearly white and the low clouds sag with the weight of more. Thrilled, I run to Pascal's bedroom to wake Uncle Gustav — but his bed is cold.

I throw open the window and listen for his footsteps or the thud of the axe, then run downstairs. Mother is darning by a blazing fire. Her back is straight. Her needle stabs a brown woollen sock.

"Where's Uncle Gustav?" I ask her.

She looks up sharply. "Where do you think? It is Friday."

Market day. I'd completely lost track of time over the past few weeks.

I swallow hard, frightened for him. I can't bear to think of him trudging alone through the woods in this terrible cold, and the long road to Monville, and that man at the end of it…

"Will he be all right?" I ask, still dithering at the bottom of the stairs.

"You should have thought about that before."

Stung by her coldness, I answer back without thinking. "And if you'd told him the truth, he wouldn't have to go and find it out for himself!"

Mother's face hardens. "If I'd wanted help I would have asked for it. No good will come of this, child. Mark my words."

Child. She hasn't called me that in years. I stumble outside with tears in my eyes, knowing she's right. If Uncle Gustav is hurt by that man, it will be my fault.

The frozen air turns my fingers blue as I milk the cow, then break the ice on all the drinking troughs. I daren't let Amandine outside for fear she'll freeze to death. I'd bring her into the house if I thought for a moment that Mother would let her stay.

Briefly, I consider taking her with me to the village – not to the *lavoir*; the water will be solid ice – just to hear Béatrice's friendly voice, or even Claudette laughing at me. But I can't be away when Uncle Gustav gets back.

Reluctantly, I return to the kitchen fire to thaw out my hands.

Mother's gaze remains steadfastly on her sewing. The cheerful crackle of the logs somehow makes her silence crueller. It's as if all of Uncle Gustav's kindness counts for naught.

"I was only trying to help," I say miserably.

"And now you can face the consequences."

The waiting is torture, the quiet deafening. At last I say, "Why won't you tell me about this man in the market? Uncle Gustav will find out, anyway. Why don't you talk to me first?"

"If I'd meant to tell you, you'd know by now."

"But why is it such a terrible secret?"

She pauses in her work and looks into the flames, her face unreadable. She's still for so long that I almost hope she will explain, but in the end she bends to her needle again and says, "There are things children shouldn't know."

"I'm not a child."

"But I am your parent. And so was your father."

"He's dead." I spit out the words.

Mother eyes me levelly. "Remember I loved him, Angélique, even if you never did."

121

"You *loved* him? After what he—"

She raises her hand, her face pinched and forbidding. "He was a good husband, a hard worker. He put food on the table and kept a roof over our heads."

"He *beat* your children."

"As was his right."

"His *right*? He enjoyed it! He was cruel!"

"How *dare* you say that to my face!"

Our eyes lock, hers unforgiving, mine stinging with tears of frustration.

"He was a monster and you know it," I say through gritted teeth.

Her mouth turns down at the corners. "Get out of my sight, Angélique. I don't want to see you right now."

I snatch up a shawl, my heart thundering, and run from the house into the bitter cold. Flurries of snow fall on the yard. Icy puddles crack underfoot. Frozen ruts trip me.

How could she *ever* have loved that devil? Why didn't she protect Pascal and me? Doesn't she love us?

As I race up the hill, I have no idea where I'm going. Nor do I care. Slush and mud splash up my legs, the falling snow thickens. Then I'm beneath the snow-bent branches of the wood, scrabbling between stark, frosted trunks.

My breath steams, and the steam freezes on my face. My skin feels raw, my body like ice and fire, at war with itself. But still I run.

Where to? Monville? That's absurd. I'll never make it.

And besides, Uncle Gustav won't want me there.

At last I slow to a walk, my heart *thump, thump, thump*ing. A deer barks. There's a yelp. A fox, perhaps, or some poor creature caught in the fox's jaws – or in one of my snares. I stop to catch my breath.

Thump. Thump. Thump. My blood is loud in my ears. The air is utterly still, utterly silent. The weight of the snow-darkened sky bears down on the land.

Thump, thump, thump.

I seem to hear an echoing heartbeat, somewhere deep in the woods, a steadier rhythm. I quieten my breathing, slow my heart. Listen.

Tramp, tramp, tramp.

The sound grows louder, clearer.

Tramp. Tramp. Tramp.

My pulse quickens again. What is it? What's coming?

Don't be stupid. You know perfectly well.

But still I hold my breath, hoping against hope that I'm wrong. I wait for the stillness to return, to be lost in silence again.

TRAMP. TRAMP. TRAMP.

Holy Mother of God! I see them. There! Through the trees. Soldiers in blue. My hand flies to my mouth. I can't breathe. I'm rooted to the spot like a petrified woodland creature.

Then, as if a trap had been sprung, I leap away and pelt through the snow, splashing, scrambling, my soaking skirt heavier than lead. I haul it up away from my legs and race downhill into the yard, screaming at the top of my voice, *"Maman!"*

Napoleon shrieks at me, then attacks.

Good.

I wave my arms to rile him up. I chase him about the yard, yelling meaningless noises. He flees in panic, flapping and slapping.

"What is it?" Mother stands in the doorway.

"The Requisition!"

I see her stagger. See her clutch at the door.

"Mon Dieu! What are we going to do?"

"Hide the cow!" I shout. "They'll take her!"

"They can't."

She dithers, hands fluttering. I tear into the little stone barn and drag the cow from her stall, pulling at her halter, tugging her to the door. But she fights back, stamping and snorting, the whites of her eyes like crescent moons.

Alarmed, Amandine scurries under my skirt.

"Not now!" I scream at her, putting my shoulder to the cow's back end and shoving her outside.

The hens scatter under my feet. Amandine squawks in protest. Desperately, I try to think where to hide the cow. The back of the woodpile? They'll see her! I drag her around the side of the house with Napoleon snapping at my ankles. I kick him away and bellow at Mother, "Help me!"

But then, from the lane, *Tramp, tramp, tramp.*

A man barks, "Halt!"

Napoleon knocks me sideways as he charges the gate, screeching and beating his wings.

Scrabbling to my feet, I see him plunging his long neck through the gate, lashing wildly at the nearest soldier with his beak.

"Call the gander off or I'll shoot!"

The man's voice is hard as iron. I see braid on his cap, brass on his collar. Five more soldiers stand in line beside him, each with a rifle at his shoulder. The braided man shouts, "One!"

"No! Don't hurt him."

I push the cow into the vegetable patch.

"Two!"

I dash for the gate.

"Three!"

BANG!

"Noooooo!"

I fling myself across Napoleon's body. His head whips round. He slashes my eyes. I grab his neck and thrust him down. He thrashes and shrieks underneath me. Then I hear, "Put the gun down, madame."

Terrified, I roll over. Mother is aiming Father's gun at the gate. The barrel is smoking. I look back at the soldiers. Their rifles are pointing at her!

"Put the gun down!" I scream.

"I won't tell you again, madame."

"Maman! They'll shoot!"

"Ready..."

"Please! Think of Pascal!"

"Aim..."

"Maman, no!"

For unbearable seconds, the soldiers stand stock still. Mother is a statue. Only Napoleon writhes and hisses beneath me.

"Please," I cry, "don't leave me alone."

At last she drops the gun and, like a rag doll, falls weeping to the ground.

Eighteen

Sobbing, shaking, I carry Napoleon into the orchard and shut him inside, then run to Mother, shielding her against the gaze of the soldiers with my body.

She seems to be in a trance, moaning and rocking as she sits crumpled in the doorway.

As the braided officer marches past he snarls at me under his breath, "Shut her up. She's upsetting my men."

I gawp at him.

"You think we wanted this job?" he says.

For an instant I see a flicker of sympathy on his broad, unshaven face, but then it's gone and he's saying, "Don't go spreading rumours we're here."

Two of his men hold the cow by her halter. They're stroking her neck, calming her down. Placidly, she stands and waits as they tie a rope to the halter.

"Maman, come inside," I whisper.

But as I put my shoulder under her arm to lift her, two more soldiers walk into the yard, each with a hen hanging limply in either hand.

I gag with disbelief. "You can't! That's stealing!" I let Mother go and leap up, but the officer steps in front of me, his hand raised in a warning.

"We've a right to take everything," he growls. "Everything! Understand? The army has to eat. It's the law."

"But my brother's a soldier! He fought at Verdun! This is *his* farm."

"Quiet," barks the officer, but his men shoot troubled glances my way.

I appeal to them with my eyes, reaching out as if to touch them.

"Please," I beg them. "My father is *Mort pour la France*. We have the certificate to prove it. I'll fetch it. I'll show you!"

But one by one they turn away.

Then the fifth soldier rounds the corner of the house. He's a putty-nosed man with a long length of rope in his hand. Attached to the other end is poor, stumbling King George.

"No! Not our pig as well!"

My legs give way. I clutch the wall. "He's sick. He's been ill. There's no meat on him." I step towards the officer, palms outstretched.

Frowning, he turns to the putty-nosed man and asks, "Is the animal sick?"

The man looks King George up and down. He rubs his chin, then pulls a face and spits on the ground. "Nah. He just needs fattenin' up. It's these peasant women. They don't know how to keep pigs."

When they're gone, Mother and I sit in the dimness of the kitchen, too stunned to light a lamp or stoke the fire. She holds her head in her hands, weeping silently.

I feel too shocked for tears. I can't see our future any more. I can't imagine the farm without the cow or King George or the hens. When at last Napoleon honks and I hear Uncle Gustav in the yard, I run out to meet him. Alarm springs to his face.

"What is it, *ma petite*? What's happened?"

I fall into his arms, sobbing. "The Requisition came."

"Mon Dieu!"

He holds me tightly as I cry uncontrollably against his chest. Then, sweeping me up, he almost carries me inside.

"Brigitte," he says to Mother. "I'm sorry. I should've been here."

She looks up with a wan smile as if she's gone beyond despair. Her eyes stray around the kitchen as if seeing it for the first time, then she says, "Angélique, would you light the lamps, please?"

A knot tightens in my stomach. Her voice is weirdly calm, as if she's already buried what happened in some recess of her mind.

Uncle Gustav and I exchange glances. Then I run to

find the matches while he empties the pockets of his great-coat onto the table.

He's bought us candles, bonbons, buttons, wool, nails, tins of kerosene, a new whetstone, salt.

"Put the kettle on," he tells me, producing one last package – a fancy box with a picture of coffee beans on the label. I kneel at the hearth and remake the fire, then we sit at the table and talk.

Uncle Gustav explains how he found the man in the market and talked to his employer. Mother sighs and nods, and when he's finished she smiles at me with such infinite sorrow that I'm afraid the Requisition has broken her mind.

She says, "I never wanted you to hear this, my angel. I only ever wanted to protect you and Pascal. But I never could, could I?"

"You did," I say, though I see in her eyes that she, too, knows it's a lie.

I listen intently as she finally admits the truth about Father. He was a drunk and a gambler who mortgaged the farm to pay off his gambling debts.

"The butter and eggs paid the interest – almost – but now…"

She lifts her hands in that fluttering way of hers, like two little birds too thin and weak to fly. Then she makes a sound almost like a laugh. I stare at her, unable to comprehend her strange resignation.

"So that's why you always went to market," I say. "To pay off his debts?"

She nods. "But I could only pay off the interest. When I was ill and couldn't go, I fell behind with the payments."

Uncle Gustav leans forward and rests his hand on mine. "That's why the moneylender set his thug on you. It was a warning to your mother to pay up."

"So what are we going to do?" I force my voice to stay steady, even though panic is gripping my chest. "Maman? Uncle? What do we do next?"

Uncle Gustav shakes his head. "I'm sorry, ma petite. The moneylender is going to send in the bailiffs. They'll come for the furniture first."

"And then?" I look from him to Mother, but she's staring into the fire again, her eyes far away.

"Uncle Gustav? What then?"

"Then they'll come for the farm."

His words sound dull and distant, like the slamming of a door. But I can't really make sense of them or understand why there are tears on his cheeks, just like Mother's.

I say, "I didn't mean what are *they* going to do? I meant, what are *we* going to do? *Us*. Not them."

His sigh is long and deep. His eyebrows rise slowly, then fall. He leans across the table to take my hand, but I draw back, alert all of a sudden, my eyes flicking about the room.

"Of course," I say. "Silly me. We'll have to sell things to pay him off. I knew that."

I look at the dresser, then the pantry door.

"There's our china, and the butter churn. We'll have to

buy a new one when we can afford it. And the farm tools must be worth a lot. And Pascal's bed can go. You'll have to have mine, Uncle Gustav, for the moment."

"Ma petite—"

"No!" I pull my hand away from him. "We've got to think this through. It's important!"

"Hush, Angélique," he says. "Things will work out. You'll see."

"I know they will. They have to. This is *Pascal's* farm. We can't lose it. They can't take it away."

His face creases with concern. "Perhaps after the war we might find the money..."

"No!" I glare at him. "No!"

His face is worn down and hopeless. Mother has buried her head in her hands again. I jump up and pace the floor. I fling open the door and let the cold air shock me.

Napoleon hisses from the dark. I picture Amandine and the oldest hen alone in the little stone barn: one too small, the other too scrawny to bother taking away. And the rest of the geese – left by the Requisition out of respect for Father.

Respect?

Respect?

He doesn't deserve respect! He's contemptible. Hateful. Unforgiveable. The land belongs to Pascal and me, and one day it will belong to his and Béatrice's children, and to their children and theirs and theirs. Father had no right to steal their future, to gamble it away, to snatch our hopes and dreams from beyond the grave.

"Damn you!" I scream into the night. "Damn you to hell, *Father*!"

"*Ma petite!*"

"*My angel!*"

There is hurt in their voices, as well as shock, to hear how I truly feel about him at last.

I turn to the kitchen again, to the smouldering fire and smoking lantern, the steaming kettle and coffee pot. I can almost see Pascal sitting there between Mother and Uncle Gustav, elbows on the table, his hands cupped around his coffee.

He will sit there again. He *will*. I know it because I will make it happen. I take a deep breath and wipe my tears away.

Then I say, "We'll sell the geese. We have to. Pascal will understand."

Nineteen

Uncle Gustav frowns. "I'm sorry," he says. "They'll never fetch enough."

"How can they not?" I demand. "Butter and eggs used to be enough. Geese are worth far more than that."

He gives me his warmest, crinkliest smile. "Come in. Sit down. I'll make more coffee and try to explain."

I make one last stubborn effort to stand in the doorway, but then, with a shiver, shut the door and sit at the table again.

Uncle Gustav tells me how much Father borrowed and how much the moneylender is charging in interest. He takes a stubby pencil from his pocket and scribbles numbers on a scrap of paper.

"See? That's how much your mother owes."

I stare at the paper, but don't see at all. I don't understand any of it. I look him in the eye.

"But, Uncle, what is Pascal fighting for, if not his home and land?"

He opens his mouth, then shuts it. He rubs the back of his neck and looks at the scrap of paper. Then he picks up the pencil again.

"How many geese do you have?"

"Gustav, don't." Mother turns from the fire, her face exhausted but her eyes less far away. "You mustn't raise her hopes like that."

"Twenty-nine," I say quickly. "Plus Amandine."

Uncle Gustav bends over his calculations once more, like a schoolboy in class.

Mother purses her lips. "I know the price of geese, Gustav."

"In Monville, certainly," he replies, without looking up. "But there's Paris, Amiens – and Étaples, of course. Prices are already sky-high near the Front, and the Christmas markets are coming."

"You can't herd the geese to the Front," she says with a sigh.

"But you can buy them a railway ticket," he replies.

He rubs his forehead, then taps his pencil on the table, staring at the squiggles that now blacken his scrap of paper. He drains his coffee and then starts calculating again.

Watching him from the edge of my seat, my stomach turns somersaults. He believes in me. This is possible – whatever Mother says. I smile at her hopefully, but she's staring into the flames again.

Finally Uncle Gustav leans back, his eyes darting up and down the columns of numbers. Then he puts the paper down and pinches the bridge of his nose.

"Well?" I ask.

He sighs.

"I told you," Mother says. "There's no hope. There never was, not from the day this war broke out."

But I snatch the piece of paper off the table and stare at it.

"It *has* to work! It must!"

"I'm sorry, ma petite. Your mother is right. I was wrong."

"What about the Christmas markets? And there's the pension. Remember, Mother? The mayor told us about it."

"A *pension*?" Uncle Gustav leaps up. "How much?"

"I don't know," Mother says.

"Then find out!"

He strides up and down the kitchen as she searches through drawers and pockets for the envelope the mayor gave her. When at last she finds it and empties it onto the table, there's money inside – one hundred and fifty francs – and a letter promising more.

I hug her and then Uncle Gustav, crying, "That'll do it! Won't it? That and the geese. That'll be enough!"

He rubs a hand down his face, then his eyes dart over the calculations again.

"It might, possibly, at a pinch. We'll have to be lucky, and get top money for those birds…"

Suddenly he stops speaking and a twinkle appears in his eyes.

"What?" I say.

He chuckles. "Top brass, that's what we need – rich officers with more money than sense."

"Where do we find them?" I ask, my heart thumping against my ribs.

"Étaples is full of 'em. But the richest pickings of all might well be at Frévent."

"Why? What's there?"

"The field headquarters of His Excellency General Foch."

"Who?"

"Really, ma petite! Have you never heard of the general? He's a very important man. Commander-in-chief of the Battle of the Somme."

"The Somme!"

That's where Pascal was going. A spark of hope ignites within me. Perhaps this general will know where Pascal is. Perhaps he'll let me see him.

"Will he pay a lot for a goose?" I ask.

"From what I hear, only the very best is good enough for His Excellency's table."

"And our geese are very fine, aren't they, Uncle Gustav?"

"The finest in all of France."

"Then *that's* what we'll do. We'll sell Pascal's geese to General Foch at Frévent!"

Twenty

Next morning, home has never seemed so sweet. Each familiar object is precious. I dress slowly, capturing every detail.

Mother knocks on my door and brings in a bundle of clothes: a pair of Pascal's trousers, his thickest woollen vest, socks, a shirt, his sheepskin jacket and his stout walking boots.

"For me?"

I'm surprised – and still angry with her for keeping Father's debts a secret, and for arguing against selling the geese – but she's my mother and I love her, and don't want us to part on bad terms.

"It's safer to travel as a boy," she says.

"Thank you," I reply and smile.

I change quickly, then strut about like a man, thrilled to be tall and broad shouldered like Pascal. I march into Mother's room and pose in front of her mirror.

"You look just like him," she says with a sigh. Then she stands behind me, gazing over my shoulder at our reflection. I notice for the first time that I've grown taller than her – or perhaps she's shrunk.

"Would you brush my hair like you used to?" I ask.

Smiling, she fetches her brush.

I feel the same comforting tingle I did when I was little and she brushed my hair every night. She ties it into a ponytail and tucks it under one of Pascal's caps.

The transformation is complete. Tears well in her eyes. She squeezes my arm and whispers, "Please try to understand. Your father didn't mean to gamble. It was the drink, and then when he lost, he grew angry..."

And came home and beat Pascal. I know. I remember.

I shrug her off and look at myself one last time in the mirror. I am him now. I am my brother. Saving the farm is my job, not hers. And unlike her I won't let Pascal down.

In the kitchen, Uncle Gustav claps me on the shoulder. "My word! You make a fine fellow!"

I blush and giggle, and then kiss him on the cheek.

We eat bread and cheese standing up while Mother retrieves baked potatoes from the fire. I put two in my pockets, their heat seeping through the rough material of my trousers. Then we step outside.

Icy puddles crunch underfoot. Our breath smokes in the freezing air, but a robin is singing his wistful song and the sky is a washed-out blue.

While Mother rounds up the geese from the orchard, Uncle Gustav and I fill small sacks with grain for them, tie them with rope and hook them over our shoulders, like haversacks. Then we open the little stone barn. Amandine trots out without a backward glance at the empty pigsty or the cow's silent byre.

"Ready?" Uncle Gustav puts a hand on my shoulder. I nod. "Good."

Suddenly feeling shy – and wishing I'd practised herding the geese before – I lead Amandine into the lane, then wait for the rest of the flock to follow. But they settle down to preen or feed on fallen seed.

"Come up!" I call as if they were horses.

"Go on!" Uncle Gustav shouts, waving his arms.

The geese take no notice at all.

Feeling foolish, I scatter a trail of grain out of the gate and click my tongue the way I coax the hens in at night – or rather, the way I used to coax them in. But Amandine gobbles up the seed and tugs at my trousers for more while the rest of the flock continues to ignore me.

"Let's try shooing them out," Uncle Gustav suggests, and he and Mother circle behind them. She moves quietly, holding out her arms, but he sweeps his hands forward, shouting, "Get up!" until Napoleon hisses at him – and holds his ground.

"I'll get a stick," Uncle Gustav mutters, and hurries into the orchard.

As I wait, Amandine wanders along the verge, nibbling

on frosted tussocks and pecking at patches of snow, calling to me all the while with a gentle murmuring sound like a running brook. In the quiet, I hear replies from the yard: a bubbling conversation.

"Wait," I say as Uncle Gustav approaches Napoleon with a long, whippy stick. "Look!"

Amandine's mother is in the gateway, stretching out her neck. She looks from right to left, then waddles into the lane. Another goose follows her, waggling her tail, then they both stop to feed. One by one, the whole flock files slowly into the lane, with Napoleon lumbering out last. Mother shuts the gate behind him. Uncle Gustav takes up his position at the rear. I lead Amandine forward and, with a wave of farewell to Mother, we set off to cross France at the pace of a snail.

It's bitingly cold. No matter how much we stamp our feet and rub our arms, the chill grinds into our bones. And no matter how much we harry and cajole the geese, they walk not one jot faster.

Napoleon is the slowest of all, his great chest too heavy for his legs to carry him far without a rest. Whenever he flops into a puddle or plumps down on a mossy knoll, the other geese scatter in search of grass.

At midday we're still in the woods and Uncle Gustav's face is red.

"By all the Saints!" he shouts as Amandine slips into a ditch – again.

"We could stop for lunch," I suggest. "They'll go faster after a rest."

"*Faster?* Any slower and we'll be going backwards! Are they always like this?"

"Um, well, actually, I've never herded them before."

He raises his eyes to the sky.

We eat cold potatoes in a glade a short way off the track. It had looked inviting in the slanting winter sunlight – dappled green and filled with chirping birds, with a glint of bright water further on – but the cold is penetrating. Within minutes we're shivering and eager to leave. Except that the geese have found a pond. They refuse to come out until we throw stones at them. And pine cones and sticks.

As we chivvy them back to the lane, I ask, "Do you think we'll reach Monville tonight?"

Uncle Gustav gives me a look. It was a stupid question. At this rate we won't even be there by tomorrow.

Throughout the short, bleak afternoon, a clinging mist closes in, bringing the day to a premature end. I wrack my brains for somewhere to stay the night. We'll freeze to death in our sleep if we can't find shelter before dark.

At last, at a fork in the road, I remember the Chevaliers' farm.

"Henri was Pascal's best friend," I explain as we peer into the gloom. "They did everything together before the war."

"Are they good people, the parents?"

"Why wouldn't they be?"

Uncle Gustav rubs his moustache. "And there's nowhere else you can think of? An empty barn? An abandoned farm?"

"No. Why?"

"No reason. I'm sure it'll be fine."

The track to the Chevaliers' soon narrows to a broken stone path, running along a ridge between stunted oak trees and looming stands of dark pines. In the silence of the freezing fog, our footsteps sound loud. Peering ahead, all is vague and uncertain. Behind me, the geese huddle together.

"How much further?" Uncle Gustav asks as owls start to call.

"Um."

"Never mind. Let's press on."

Without warning, a pair of iron gates materializes from the gloom, then timber sheds and the solid stone doorway of a low thatched house. We stop in the fog and listen. There's not a bleat of a sheep or a grunt from a pigsty, nor does any light spill under the door or from the deep-set windows.

"Maybe they left," I say, my vision of a warm bed and a bright fire rapidly dissolving.

"Maybe." He almost sounds relieved.

I look at him, wondering what worries him about the Chevaliers.

"We could sleep rough if you think that's best," I say.

"Not tonight, ma petite. We need to get indoors."

In answer to our knocking, a thin man finally opens the door – just a crack, enough to peer out. His face is pinched, more beard than skin, and his head is dwarfed by a big woollen hat.

"Monsieur Chevalier?" Uncle Gustav asks.

"Who's asking?"

Quickly, I explain who we are.

Monsieur Chevalier opens the door a little wider, enough to stick his head outside. His eyes boggle when he sees the flock, and he turns to the room behind him and shouts, "We have company, ma cherie! Friends of Henri lost in the fog with their geese! Come in! And welcome!"

He opens the door wide this time.

I pick up Amandine, meaning to bring her in with me, but Monsieur Chevalier whisks her out of my arms and sets her down on the ground.

"But it's so cold," I say. "She'll freeze outside."

"Don't worry, little mademoiselle. We know how to look after geese."

The house is dimly lit by an open fire. Smoke trickles through the blackened thatch and threadbare rugs cover the earthen floor. Blocking every window and door are thick, greasy curtains.

Madame Chevalier sits, propped up by pillows, in a large four-poster bed. She looks a lot older than her husband, with wild, white hair sticking out from her cap like so many spiders.

"Madame." Uncle Gustav bows to her. But she's staring at me.

"Henri?" Her voice quavers, thinly.

"No, ma cherie," says Monsieur Chevalier. "He's gone soldiering. Remember?"

But Madame Chevalier grins at me with a mouth half-filled with brown, broken teeth. Monsieur Chevalier bends over her and kisses her forehead tenderly. Then he turns to Uncle Gustav with moist eyes.

"You have my seat by the fire, monsieur," he says. "We'll leave the girls to natter."

Dismayed, I watch him usher Uncle Gustav into a high-backed settle.

"Our geese, monsieur," Uncle Gustav reminds him. "They'll need shelter."

"Of course! Of course. Just sit yourself down. I'll see to them."

"Um… I'll come too. If you don't mind."

I think I see a shadow crossing Monsieur Chevalier's face, but he just says, "This way, then. Mind your head."

I make a move to follow them, but Madame Chevalier reaches out pitiably. "Henri? You're leaving?"

Monsieur Chevalier looks at me sharply. "There's soup in the pot. Help my wife to some as well."

Uncle Gustav smiles at me encouragingly before they both disappear.

The soup is thin, but at least it's hot. Madame Chevalier slurps hers noisily while I sit beside her on a rickety chair.

In the firelight, I see a narrow bed tucked into an

alcove – Henri's, perhaps. It's cluttered with newspapers, gramophone records and dog-eared magazines. The gramophone player stands on a bow-legged table.

"Shall we dance, Henri?" Madame Chevalier says, following my gaze.

"Let me take your bowl if you've finished."

Her watery eyes fill with tears. "You never dance with me any more."

"I'm not your son, madame. My brother is a friend of his. Pascal Lacroix? He used to visit you often."

She just smiles.

There's a draft from the door, and Monsieur Chevalier stamps inside with mud on his boots and frost in his beard.

"Terrible weather," he says. "I can't remember worse."

As Uncle Gustav follows him inside, he gives me a reassuring smile.

"All's well," he says. "The geese are tucked up with Monsieur Chevalier's sheep."

He hangs up his coat and takes off his boots, then carries them across to the fire and sits down on the settle, where both he and Monsieur Chevalier are hidden from view.

I'd love to toast my toes too, or curl up in bed, but Madame Chevalier is saying, "Read me one of your letters, Henri. Your writing's so small. You know my eyes aren't what they were."

"I'll fetch you a lamp."

"No! Read to me, naughty boy."

Her voice is high with complaint. Monsieur Chevalier

sticks his head around the side of the settle and frowns. I sigh.

"All right."

As she fusses under her pillow for her son's letters, I listen to the sizzling of a new log on the fire, the clinking of glasses and the clank of a ladle against the iron pot.

Henri's letters are strange. He writes about the red roofs of Verdun vanishing in the cannons' fog and bark stripped from trees by starving horses.

He describes coloured fountains of mud rising into the air – grey fountains when the shells explode in stone villages, brown from fields and pink when they hit...

My stomach lurches and my chest hurts. I tell Madame Chevalier I can't make out the next word.

I glance through another letter and read on. "The noise is like a giant forge and the daylight is grey with ash." I look up. "Are you sure you want me to read this?"

"Tell me about the food. Is there enough?"

I glance down again. She gave me his letters in no particular order. He seems to have spent more time away from Verdun than Pascal, but he also complains that no one got leave.

I read aloud: "'They call them communication trenches, but I've dug deeper ditches in a morning. We have to move at night, and lay up in the day, even when we're lost. The stench of the dead is so dreadful you hardly mind the gas...'"

I shift in my chair and skip a horrible passage about

horses caught in a gas attack, and another about how he rolled a dead friend up in canvas and tipped him into a shell hole for a grave. In another letter he writes, "They tell us our mission is sacrifice. It is our sacred duty to hold fast or fall. And when we've fallen, more men will stand on our bones. We are lambs to the slaughter. Any day now whole battalions will bleat."

I stop reading. Poor Henri. And Pascal. And René. I glance at Madame Chevalier, whose eyes are far away now, staring at nothing, yet somehow more focused than before.

It would be cruel to go on, so quietly I pack the letters away and gather them in my lap, thinking it must be a comfort to believe her son is safely at home.

She hardly seems to notice I've fallen silent, but when I stand she grabs my wrist with snakelike speed and snaps, "Where are you going?"

The whine in her voice is gone, and the light in her eyes is bright.

"Madame?" I stare at her. She doesn't seem the least bit mad any more.

She gives a slight shrug and lets my arm go, the lines of her mouth hard and bitter. And suddenly I realize I've been deceived. She's not a crazy old woman at all.

But why pretend?

Mon Dieu! The geese!

"Uncle Gustav?"

But the only sound is the hissing of the fire.

I jump up and run to the settle. Uncle Gustav is alone, fast asleep, his face flushed and his breathing heavy, an empty glass in his hand.

I shake him hard. "Wake up!" I turn on Madame Chevalier and shout, "What did your husband give him?"

"Food and drink, like he asked."

"What drink?"

She chuckles. "As if I'd tell you. You'd only make me drink it too."

I glare at her. "How *could* you? You *used* Henri to trick me."

"He might as well be some use now he's blind."

"Blind?"

"Mustard gas. Our own. The wind changed direction. It ruined his lungs, too. So you see, he won't be no good on the farm."

I gape at her. "But–but…" I look around. "That doesn't make it right to steal our geese. That's what he's doing, isn't it? That's where Monsieur Chevalier's gone?"

Madame Chevalier leans back into her pillows. "It's a dog-eat-dog world. Your uncle should've told you that." She glances at me almost pityingly. "Sit down. Stay here, where it's nice and warm. We'll talk about it all night if you like."

But I won't be fooled again.

Grabbing Pascal's jacket and cap, I run into the night.

Twenty-one

Fog lingers under the trees, but the yard is moonlit – a ghostly world of drifting mists and white ice. I hold my breath, listening. Monsieur Chevalier can't be far.

Now I'm here, alone in the frozen silence, I've no idea what to do. How can I defeat a determined man? It's only my desperation that keeps me outside, shivering.

Before slipping into the shadows, I wedge a piece of wood under the door handle to stop Madame Chevalier escaping or shouting a warning, and pray that the windows have been iced shut.

Frost lies thick on every roof, every empty outhouse. In the moonlight I see ploughs and harnesses, axes and snares, but no sheep in any of the sheds. And no geese.

Then a spectral figure emerges from the fog: Monsieur Chevalier walking softly out of the woods. I slide back into the darkness – and step on a twig.

He stops, cocks his head, walks on slowly.

Standing stiller than the night, I watch him disappear around the side of the house. A latch clicks. A hinge creaks. Then silence. I creep forward.

His footsteps have worn a dark path in the ice. It leads between two tall pillars in a high stone wall. Peering through the gap, I see a wide timber door in the side of the house.

The sheep barn must be part of the house. I guess Monsieur Chevalier is taking the geese from there and hiding them in the woods. I'll have to follow him to find them. Perhaps when they're all there, I could hide them somewhere else until Uncle Gustav finds us. I shrink into the darkness and wait.

A shaft of yellow light falls across the white mist as Monsieur Chevalier opens the door again. He's holding something tightly under one arm: a sack.

A ripple of fear, but also excitement, goes through me. There must be a goose inside it, perhaps more than one. He's trying to keep them quiet. My biggest worry now is that Monsieur Chevalier will hear my galloping heart.

But then the moonlight glints off something long and metallic under his other arm.

A gun!

A long hunting rifle.

Mon Dieu. I can't defeat a man with a gun! As the fog swallows him up, disbelief edges towards despair.

Trembling, I steal into the sheep barn. Napoleon hisses

at me. But the brief satisfaction of picturing Monsieur Chevalier trying to put *him* in a sack is swept aside by the thought of a bullet. Napoleon will be as valuable to them dead as alive.

Amandine scrambles towards me, squeaking. I pick her up and hold her close as I move quietly among the few scraggy sheep, counting my geese.

Seventeen, including Amandine and Napoleon. He's hidden thirteen already.

I want to take Amandine with me but daren't risk Monsieur Chevalier noticing her gone. It breaks my heart to hear her pecking on the inside of the door as I shut it behind me.

An idea is forming. Not a nice idea, to be sure. I'm shocked it's even occurred to me. But there it is – and nothing else comes to mind. I can't wait, not with a gun pointing at Napoleon's head. Silently, quickly, I return to one of the outhouses I searched before.

Behind a large wooden chopping block, hung on pegs in the wall, is a row of wire snares. I select a long one, big enough to catch a deer. The metal is cold, but not brittle: brass, perhaps, supple and strong.

Am I *really* going to do this? Dare I? What if it doesn't work, or backfires? What is the worst Monsieur Chevalier could do to me?

Putting the thought of his rifle out of my head, I return to my waiting game – hiding in the shadows, breathing onto my fingers to stop them from freezing. It seems to take forever for Monsieur Chevalier to return.

When he does, the rifle is in his hand, the empty sack under his arm.

I count how long he's inside. Thirty seconds. One minute. Two. Two and a half. Three. Then another poor goose is carted into the woods.

Can I do this? Have I time? *Should* I do it? Snares are cruel.

Holy Mother. Grant me the courage to do this — then forgive me for doing it.

For Pascal and the farm I set my trap, twining the long end of the wire around the base of a pillar, fastening it like Uncle Gustav taught me to.

I practise propping open the hooped end on the path with sticks, worried that the wire might break. Or will he see it before he trips? But I'm out of time. I hear him moving in the woods. I hide the hoop out of sight. His hands must be full when he falls.

Twenty-two

Striding out of the barn through the narrow gateway between the pillars, Monsieur Chevalier's foot catches in the snare and he crashes down full-length as if pole-axed.

The goose squawks madly in its sack and the rifle falls from his hand.

Before I know it, I've snatched the gun and am backing away, shocked and amazed at what I've done.

Sprawled on his face in the dirt, the old man groans in pain. I have to remind myself he deserves it. I grab the sack before the goose escapes and retreat once again out of his reach.

He lifts his head. His face is smeared with mud. Blood trickles from his nose.

"Don't touch the snare," I warn him, my voice shaking. "It'll tighten if you struggle."

Through gritted teeth, he says, "Get it off me."

"No! You stole my geese. You can stay there till my uncle wakes."

"Or what? You'll kill me?"

"I'm aiming at your foot, actually. But I should warn you, I'm a terrible shot."

He snorts a bitter laugh, then clambers to his knees and crawls to the pillar, propping himself up. After inspecting the snare, he eyes me up and down, a sneer on his face.

"Go on, shoot. Put me out of my misery. Kill Madame Chevalier too. Then you can steal our sheep. I'll wager that's what you planned all along."

I square my shoulders. "Then you would lose your bet, monsieur. We came in good faith."

"And yet here you are – a whisker away from shooting a man."

I glower at him, almost tempted to throw the rifle away, but I'm sure this is just another trick. He brought this on himself.

"I'm only trying to save my home," I say.

"And I'm saving mine! You've seen my wife. A lifetime's hard work and we're *starving*. Now our boy's blind! We'll have to feed him the rest of his life. On what, hey? Tell me that. On what?"

"I-I'm sorry."

"Not sorry enough to put that gun down, I'll be bound."

I stare at him, torn between doubt and regret. Then the goose squirms in the sack and I rest it down gently.

Amandine's mother waddles out, honking loudly. I hear replies from the shed, but nothing from the woods.

"Where are my geese?" I demand.

"Why should I tell you?"

"We'll get this over quicker."

"I've got all night."

"Then we wait."

Monsieur Chevalier looks at me darkly. "I should've drugged you as well as your uncle – or shut the door in your face as soon as you said your name."

"Angélique?"

"Lacroix."

"Don't say that! We're good people!"

"Says the girl with the gun."

He leans back against the pillar, wincing in pain. "Next time you're feeling high and mighty, ask your uncle about Metz. Ask how many good people got out of that."

I ignore him, refusing to ask him what some town in the east could possibly have to do with the name of Lacroix. He's just trying to confuse me.

But as we wait in the moonlight, our teeth chattering, our fingers turning blue, I ache for Uncle Gustav to wake up and take the gun out of my hands, and tell me that what I'm doing had to be done for the good of the farm.

At last Uncle Gustav roars out of the house like a force of nature. He barges open the door and bellows my name.

"Over here!" I scream and he charges towards me – then

stops dead, his mouth falling open, his face aghast.

"Ma petite? What on earth…?"

He looks from Monsieur Chevalier to the rifle, then me.

"He was stealing our geese," I say quickly. "I did it for Pascal."

I search his face for sympathy and understanding but find only shock and pain.

Quickly, he kneels and loosens the snare, asking anxiously, "Are you all right, monsieur? Can you hear me?"

But the old man is so cold he's barely able to nod. Tearful now, and deeply ashamed, I set down the rifle and help Uncle Gustav carry Monsieur Chevalier inside.

Madame Chevalier shrieks at us.

"What have you done? Is he dead? Oh, you wicked, wicked people!"

She struggles to get out of bed, but only succeeds in dragging her blankets off. I notice her legs are withered.

A snare and a gun? Against an old man and an invalid? What was I thinking?

Uncle Gustav says, "Stay there, madame, where it's warm." As we lay Monsieur Chevalier on the hearth rug by the fire, he adds, "Get him blankets, Angélique, and something hot to drink."

"What about the geese?" I ask timidly.

"I'll find them."

He pauses, his face still creased with care.

I whisper, "I'm sorry."

He manages a half-smile.

"Warm yourself, too," he says. Then he's gone.

And I'm left alone with the Chevaliers.

Madame Chevalier carps constantly as I heat up last night's soup.

"You'll pay dearly if he dies!" she wails, even though Monsieur Chevalier is already sitting up.

I help him hold the steaming bowl steady in his shaking hands. Yet still Madame Chevalier complains.

"How would I have survived alone? Did you ever think about that?"

I feel like telling her I know they must have planned the theft − or something like it − but the pitiful state of Monsieur Chevalier keeps my lips sealed.

Poor man. He could so easily have frozen to death. What would have happened then? I'd have been sent to prison, or worse. The farm would have been lost and his life on my conscience forever. I shudder to think how narrow the path is that I'm treading.

When he's finished his soup, I help Monsieur Chevalier into bed beside his wife, then build up the fire and doze on the settle until I hear honking outside. Then I dash into the yard and help Uncle Gustav herd the stolen geese back into the sheep shed.

Not one is hurt, none lost. They preen and feed on the grain that we scatter as if nothing had happened.

As we watch them, Uncle Gustav says quietly, "Should

we let the Chevaliers have one bird, ma petite? They are wretchedly poor."

I hesitate for a moment and then shake my head. "Let's leave them a goose and a gander. They'll have goslings and eggs that way too."

He smiles. "We can't actually afford two birds."

"I know. But what if it was Pascal coming home blinded by gas?"

Twenty-three

We leave at first light, eager to reach Monville by nightfall, and promising each other the fog will soon lift.

The woods are white with frost and eerily beautiful, every twig furred with spreading crystals of ice. In the shimmering boughs of one giant oak, roosting crows look like black lanterns, as if the ancient tree was the site of some magical ritual.

We scour the path for the fork to the track we left last night but somehow never find it. Instead the path widens into a cart track, paved with stones and gnarled tree roots.

"Should we turn back?" I ask.

Uncle Gustav shakes his head. "We'll end up walking in circles."

Soon a low stone wall rises to our right. It keeps us company for the rest of the morning. By the time the fog thins we're in an unknown country of wild, hilly grasslands, where the geese graze greedily on the frosted tussocks as they waddle slowly along.

Across a steep valley, ancient houses cling to the spine of a ridge. Two tall, windowless keeps guard the village rooftops like broken dragon's teeth. A church bell chimes midday.

"Lunchtime!" Uncle Gustav rubs his belly. My stomach is rumbling too.

We herd the geese into the narrow street which divides the village in two. Half-timbered houses lean against each other, their low roofs patchworked moss and ivy.

From every door, smells of fresh bread and roasted meat tantalize our noses, but the street remains empty until a little boy with pudding-basin hair tugs at Uncle Gustav's sleeve and points to a woman standing in a doorway with folded arms.

"Bonjour," says Uncle Gustav with a small bow.

"You want food?" she asks bluntly.

"We can't pay you much, I'm afraid."

"Two francs and a goose for two bowls of soup."

His eyebrows shoot up. "But each goose is worth a cauldron of soup!"

"Beggars can't be choosers," she says.

"We aren't beggars, madame."

She pulls the boy inside and closes the door in our faces.

We try the café at the base of the first crumbling keep, but a surly waitress tells us the tables are already full. "Come back tomorrow before midday. And don't bring them geese!"

Beyond the second keep an old stone church watches over a run-down market hall – just six rickety pillars holding up a slate-tiled roof. In one corner there's a covered well with a pail on a rope and an inscription requesting one *sous* per bucketful of water.

"At least we won't go thirsty," Uncle Gustav says with a sigh. He digs a handful of coins out from his pocket and pays.

I fill little depressions in the ground so the geese can drink, and lay small piles of grain on the dry cobbles for them to eat. Then we cup our hands and drink the sour water straight from the bucket.

"Nectar," says Uncle Gustav, smacking his lips. "Let's take the weight off our feet."

We sit on a cold stone bench, nibbling the last lumps of hard cheese from home and sharing a stale crust of bread. Amandine scrambles onto my lap, demanding her share.

We must have nodded off because the next thing I know, the church bells are chiming and a small bald man in a cassock is standing in front of us. I think perhaps he's a monk because he doesn't speak. He just hands me a loaf of warm bread and a small flagon of wine.

"*Merci beaucoup!* Thank you very much!"

Smiling, he makes the sign of the cross, then turns to leave.

"Monsieur," I say quickly. "Are we on the right road to

Monville?" He points towards the far end of the village, where the street falls away into a sea of fog.

"Will we get there before nightfall?" I ask. He lifts his hands and shrugs, then smiles again and hurries off. Gently I prod Uncle Gustav awake.

He takes half the loaf gladly, but ruefully refuses the wine.

"If I'd been less willing to accept a drink from a stranger, then last night would have gone better for us," he says.

"You weren't to know," I tell him.

"But I had my suspicions. Then, well…" He sighs. "I always want to see the good in people, but that's not necessarily wise."

I pause, then ask, "Uncle, are we good people? My family, I mean."

"The best! Why?"

I look down, then lean my shoulder against him. "It was just something Monsieur Chevalier said. He told me to ask you about Metz."

"I see." He sighs again – more deeply this time – then pats my hand. "Don't worry. No doubt he was angry with you. You did humiliate him."

"But what happened at Metz?"

He hesitates before replying. "It was in the last war. There was a siege, a terrible business: disease, dysentery, starvation. When our forces surrendered, people said it cost us victory, that the Prussians couldn't have defeated our army in the Loire if the garrison at Metz hadn't capitulated."

"Was my father there?"

"It was long before his time. But I believe his father was."

"My grandfather was a soldier?"

"And a prisoner of war, which can be a very bad thing if it breaks a man's spirit. However..." He swallows his last mouthful of bread and stands. "We have a long way to go. Are you ready? Good. Then *allons-y*!"

We descend into the fog and the cold, penetrating damp. The gloom is depressing, and our clothes are soon heavy and dank.

The geese graze constantly on grassy tussocks that grow between the cartwheel tracks. At times they walk so slowly that it seems we're actually going backwards, as the fine water droplets overtake us and swirl before our eyes.

Twilight sets in before we've found anywhere to spend the night. As we trudge on and on, into the grey nothingness of a fog-bound winter's night, a conviction grows deep in my heart that we're well and truly lost.

At last a yellow pinprick punctures the murk and we stop.

"Maybe it's a farm," I say, "or an auberge with stables and a fire."

"Wouldn't that be nice," Uncle Gustav replies, sounding unconvinced.

We urge the geese onward, watching the dim light grow.

Sometimes it seems to float, sometimes to darken again. We're almost upon it before I'm sure we're seeing the flames of a fire. Then, out of the darkness, a wagon looms. A sack-of-bones mule is tethered to a thorn tree at the corner of a crossing track.

I make the sign of the cross, then pick up Amandine, remembering the village tales of ghosts haunting crossroads and faerie people using them as gateways to our world.

Uncle Gustav peers towards the shifting flames. Finally, I see why they're moving. A figure is tending the fire, reaching across it to poke at the carcass of some creature on a spit. The smell of its charred flesh penetrates the fog.

"Good evening, madame!" Uncle Gustav calls before I'm even certain it's a woman.

As we approach, I see that her clothes are ragged and her cheeks hollow. In the firelight, her knuckles look more gnarled than old tree roots.

"A dirty night," Uncle Gustav says when we're almost upon her.

Still she doesn't look up; she just prods at the rabbit on her spit.

Taking another step closer, I say, "We're going to Monville, madame. Is this the right way?"

Uncle Gustav sucks his teeth. The woman's head snaps up. I stifle a cry.

Her face is sunken, shrunk by time, sucked dry. She

doesn't have eyes, just shadowed sockets, and yet when I back away, clutching Amandine, her empty gaze follows me.

"Tell your fortune, my angel?"

My angel? How does she know my name?

"It's written in the stars," she says, as if reading my mind.

She turns a ghastly smile on me – a black gash in her ravaged face. I gape at her in horror, certain that somehow she sees me. No. Worse. She sees *through* me. To the darkness inside – the cruel instinct that made me hurt Monsieur Chevalier, the meanness that stopped me saying a kinder goodbye to Mother...

The old woman claws at the smoke of her fire as if parting the mists, and when I look up I see the night sky, and cry out, terrified that she'll foresee my end in the stars, that she'll tell me I'll lose the farm and that Pascal won't ever come home...

"Come away!" I tug at Uncle Gustav's sleeve. "She's a witch!"

"Hush, ma petite. It's just the fog lifting."

Then, louder, "Good night, madame, and *bon appétit.*"

But as we hurry the geese away, I can't shake a terrible sense of dread.

Twenty-four

The road begins to climb, a long, steady pull. Above us, a stiffening breeze tears the fog apart. Then a full moon rises, revealing a wild, wide heath of wind-twisted shrubs and weirdly contorted shadows. Narrow mires reflect the sky, silver and flat.

I'd never imagined we could travel this far without finding a farmstead or seeing the lights of a town. "I'm sorry, Uncle," I say. He seems to jolt awake.

"What's that, ma petite?"

"We should've stopped at that crossroads. If I hadn't been so scared…"

"Never mind. That rabbit would hardly have stretched to three." He smiles at me but his eyes are puffy, as if he really had been asleep on his feet.

The geese, I notice, have started to wander off. I hurry after them to herd them back onto the road, but they waddle away even faster, heading straight for a mire. One by one they launch themselves into the water, honking loudly.

As we watch them splashing and dipping their heads, and paddling happily now that the weight is finally off their feet, the wind sends icy fingers under our clothes, numbing our tired bodies. We rub our arms and stamp our aching feet, and I look around the heath in despair.

"What's that?" I point to the top of a distant ridge.

"Hmm?"

"Over there."

An odd bulky shape is silhouetted against the sky. Peering harder, I can just make out what looks like an *X* set against some kind of tower, and realize it must be a windmill. The *X* will be the wooden frame of the sails. Uncle Gustav lets out a whistle of relief.

"Well spotted," he says. "That'll do just fine for tonight! Now, how do we get the geese up there?"

It takes us an age, shouting at them and luring them out with grass and grain. We have to shoo them on from behind and chase stragglers out from under bushes where they've settled down. When at last the windmill is in plain sight, we give up.

"Napoleon will see off any foxes," Uncle Gustav says wearily.

I scoop Amandine out from a tussock and carry her with me as we force our legs into one final effort.

* * *

We collect firewood as we go, furze especially: it blazes brightest and hottest. As we climb the last hundred metres I expect to see the lights of distant houses, or some sign of the people who use the mill.

But there's nothing but the windmill — a lonely stone giant outlined against the stars, its vast tethered sail-arms creaking and straining in the wind.

When we stand beneath them, looking back, the whole world seems to fall away at our feet. The silver mires sparkle, and the voices of our geese carry on the wind.

"Will they be all right?" I ask.

"They'll be fine."

I lean against him, trusting him completely, knowing that whatever my hopes and fears, he will never let me down. Together we put our shoulders against the mill's stout door and shove.

Our furze fire soon makes a circle of warmth and brightness, though the heat brings out the stink of rats. Before we eat, I make Amandine a cage out of a wooden crate I find in a corner to keep her safe from their jaws.

Uncle Gustav produces one last baked potato he'd saved from before. We warm it in the fire, then singe the hairs on the backs of our hands when we knock it out from the flames.

"Ouch!" we cry and our laughter echoes in the rafters. Along with a crust of bread, half a hot potato seems like a feast.

Afterwards, we make mattresses from old, floury sacks and find more for blankets, then lay down on either side of the embers. I expect Uncle Gustav to fall asleep at once, but his eyes remain glittering in the half light.

"Uncle," I begin, still troubled by the strangeness of the day and that sudden dread I'd felt at the thought of having my fortune read. "Do you blame the garrison at Metz for losing us the last war?"

"What an odd question, ma petite."

"I know. But was it their fault?"

"Marshal Bazaine thought he was doing the right thing. He did save his men."

"But people still blamed them?"

"People like the Chevaliers?"

I shrug, then add quietly, "I could've killed him – Monsieur Chevalier, I mean."

"I know."

"I wouldn't have meant to."

"I know that, too, ma petite."

I wake at some frozen hour of the night. Amandine blinks at me from her crate, her eyes reflecting the dying embers. I stare into the rafters, trying to remember the dream that woke me. But it's gone.

Then the stillness strikes me, and the quiet. The wind must have died if the great sail-arms aren't moving. I realize Uncle Gustav isn't snoring either. Panicked, I sit up. His bed is empty. Perhaps he's gone for more firewood.

I get up as quickly as my stiff legs will let me.

Outside, the silence is profound. Frost shrouds the ground. Above me, the ice-ringed moon peers down like an eye.

"Careful you don't catch your death, ma petite."

I jump as Uncle Gustav appears from the shadows. I run to him and hug him. He kisses my hair, then folds his great coat about me.

"Look!" He points to where our geese have gathered near the windmill.

"They found us!"

"Shh. Watch."

The geese are standing close together, staring at the sky, a forest of necks and gaping beaks. Following their gaze, I see great skeins of birds, high up, wave upon wave of them, like endless flights of arrows.

"What are they?" I ask.

"Wild geese from the north. They come south with the cold."

Mesmerized, I watch our geese watching the wild birds draw nearer. They grow restless, honking and flapping. Napoleon spreads his wings – wide, wider, as wide as he can reach. He beats them powerfully and runs a few clumsy steps, trying to take off, wanting to be with them...

My heart bleeds for him. I wish he could fly just this once, and wheel freely in the glittering heavens, soaring weightlessly as birds are meant to do. But he's too heavy for that. His big webbed feet can't ever leave the ground.

As if he knows it, he lets out a mournful cry. The other geese join in, and from afar there comes an eerie whistle – the wild geese are calling back.

One phalanx breaks off and circles the moon. They fly lower, lower, towards us.

More birds break ranks, then more and more, until an almighty host is swirling about us, a riotous, honking, feathery mass. Dark bodies seethe across the heath. Our geese vanish beneath them as if overwhelmed by the sea.

"Aren't they extraordinary?" Uncle Gustav shouts above the noise.

"Amazing!"

I step away from him and whirl my arms about, spinning like the earth and the stars, feeling as if this heath were the very centre of our chaotic universe, knowing that I'll never see the likes of these wild geese again.

We wait for the last skein to land, then walk among them, searching for our geese. We find them crowded together, with Napoleon honking loudly in their midst.

Slowly, even he settles down to graze peaceably side by side with this vast wild flock. Looking across their teeming backs, rippling in the moonlight, it seems as if the land itself is alive.

"Do you think they know they're far from home?" I ask.

"The wild geese?"

"Ours too."

Uncle Gustav considers for a moment, then says, "Perhaps for them home is wherever they're together. The flock is their home."

"I like that," I say, resting my head against his great coat. "It's nice."

"Let's hope it's true, then. Come on. We ought to get some sleep."

The wild geese are gone by dawn, leaving the heath bleak and empty. I count our birds just in case any of them flew away too. I don't know that the females can fly, but I can't remember the last time Mother clipped their wings.

To my surprise I find tears in my eyes when I'm certain they're all safe and sound. It's as if my strange moods of yesterday have left me on edge.

I feel weepy again when I stumble across the body of a wild goose frozen solid under a bush. It looks so beautiful, with its sculpted black feathers etched by the pale winter light. I think perhaps I ought to take it back to the wind mill so Uncle Gustav can cook it for later, but I can't bear the idea of plucking such a lovely creature.

Returning with an armful of furze for the fire, I find Uncle Gustav making a griddle from an old piece of metal. He'd discovered a sack of flour at first light and set to at once, preparing flat bread for breakfast and to eat on the way.

"We'd better find Monville soon," he says glumly, staring down at the grey, unappetizing dough. "I think on the whole I'd rather eat grass."

As soon as the bread is ready, we share one piece between us, save the rest, then herd the flock down off the ridge, retracing our steps to the road.

Now and then I spot another wild goose that didn't survive the night. Some lie half-hidden off the path, others float belly up in the mires. I bend down to pick one up to show it to Uncle Gustav, but he stops my hand.

"Best not, ma petite."

"Why not? They died of the cold, didn't they, or tiredness? You said they'd come a long way."

"Um…" He scratches his ear, looking worried, then squats down to examine the body.

Panic flutters unexpectedly in my chest.

"What's wrong? Was it sick? Could it be catching?"

Unbidden, a picture of my geese lying stiff on the ground forms in my head. Yesterday's dread seeps through me again, and a moan escapes from my throat.

Uncle Gustav looks up. My face must betray me because his forehead furrows at once. He stands, his eyes filled with concern, and takes me in his arms.

"Oh, ma petite. There's nothing to worry about. I'm just fussing. It's an old man's vice."

But I notice he's careful to steer our geese away from the next dead bird we see.

Twenty-five

The geese show no sign of ailing as we hurry them down to the road, then turn north, guided by a low, watery sun. If anything they're quicker than before, as if getting into their stride, but it still takes us most of the morning to leave the heath behind.

At midday we stop in farmland to rest the geese and let them graze to their hearts' content while we wash Uncle Gustav's flat bread down with water from a stream. It's mid-afternoon before we see a pale road snaking its way along the bottom of a wide green valley.

"That's it!" I cry. "That's the Monville road!"

Uncle Gustav does a little dance of triumph and the geese honk at him in alarm. We lead them down to the roadside verge, then let them rest and preen.

A feeling of calm settles on me as the afternoon air fills with their bubbling conversations and splashing sounds from the ditch where Amandine is playing. It's as if we've already arrived at our journey's end.

Uncle Gustav sits on a broken stone wall beside the verge and stretches out his legs. I hunt through my pockets for any last crumbs, but have to be content with tightening my belt.

"We'll buy something delicious in town," Uncle Gustav says as I perch next to him.

A donkey cart trundles by, then a farm boy appears with a pig on a lead.

"Is this the way to Monville?" I call out to him.

"Course," he grunts and walks on.

Soon Uncle Gustav's head is nodding. I feel drowsy too. Idly, I watch a girl about my age grazing her cow on the verge. There's a lad with her, his hands in his pockets, his boots scuffing the ground. I wish she'd smile at him just once, or let him hold her hand.

Looking away, I wonder where René is now.

I must write to him as soon as I'm home and explain how I feel about him and why I never said anything before. Madame Faubert is bound to know what regiment he's in. If she still hasn't forgiven me for René being in love with me, I'll get Béatrice to ask her.

With a sigh, I get up and fetch Amandine out of the ditch and dry her feathers on the sleeve of my jacket. Shivering, she settles down for a nap. It's interrupted by an odd clattering sound, like machinery.

At first I don't take much notice of it, but when the

noise grows louder I squint up the road. Only the lad, the girl and her cow are visible through the afternoon haze. Like me, they're looking towards the rattling sound, which grows louder and more insistent, like hammering. Napoleon raises his head. I look down at Uncle Gustav, but don't want to wake him.

Not yet.

The lad climbs onto the wall. I peer up the road. Then all of a sudden the girl shouts and snatches up the cow's halter. The lad leaps off the wall and throws open a field gate. Together they haul the cow into the water meadow.

My mouth goes dry. They're *hiding* the cow.

"Uncle Gustav!" I scream it. He sits up, dazed.

"There's a lorry coming," I yell. "An *army* lorry!"

"Are you sure?"

"Yes!"

With a curse, he jumps up. I spin around. Our geese are scattered. There's no hope of hiding them quickly.

"Perhaps they won't see us," I say. But even to my ears I don't sound convinced.

Frowning, Uncle Gustav rubs his face. He seems at a loss. But Napoleon has made up his mind. He's marching towards the oncoming noise, neck out, beak open, hissing. The other geese flap and honk.

"Hide as many as you can. Behind that wall," Uncle Gustav says.

"What about Napoleon?"

"I'll deal with him."

Heart pounding, I grab Amandine and another pro-testing goose and drop them out of sight while Uncle Gustav rushes Napoleon and battles him into the ditch.

As I round up more geese, the hammering fills my head; the sound is maddening. Then I see it in the dis-tance: a sludge-green truck with a flapping canvas top, hurtling towards us at breakneck speed.

Please, God, don't let them see us.

I crouch behind the wall with half the flock beside me, hoping against hope that the others will hide from the noise, and praying that the truck is going too fast to stop, that its brakes are useless, that it'll end up in the ditch...

The truck flashes past. Two soldiers sit bolt upright in an open cab at the front, a driver wearing goggles and a passenger in a splendid red cap. Both men stare straight ahead until...

Until...

There's a squeal of rubber and the lorry swerves to a halt.

Uncle Gustav sets Napoleon down, then clambers out of the ditch. He stands in the middle of the road, legs apart, hands on hips. Napoleon hisses at the soldiers as they climb out of the cab.

"Monsieur," says the officer in the red cap.

"Monsieur," says Uncle Gustav.

Neither man touches his hat.

"Splendid bird," the officer adds, eyeing Napoleon. "Off to market with him, are you?"

"That's no one's business but mine," Uncle Gustav replies.

"Mind your manners," growls the driver. "You're talking to a colonel."

"That's all right, Barras," the colonel says with a small gesture of his gloved hand.

He smiles at Uncle Gustav, who frowns.

More geese slap towards them, their necks level and low. When they honk, the geese I'm hiding behind the wall do as well.

"Ah," says the colonel. "What have we here? You weren't trying to conceal your flock from me, were you, monsieur? That would be... naughty."

Uncle Gustav bristles. "We were trying to stop you running them over with that contraption," he snorts.

The colonel chuckles. "A reasonable explanation, I'm sure."

But the driver mutters, "They're hoarders, the lot of 'em, *mon colonel*. Damn peasants." Then to me, "Come out, boy, where I can see you. Stop lurking."

Boy? I'd almost forgotten I was dressed like Pascal.

Reluctantly, I join Uncle Gustav in the road.

"And who have we here, Barras?" the colonel asks, peering at me.

"A shirker, mon colonel. A shirker shirking his duty, I'll be bound."

"I'm not shirking," I mutter, scowling at him.

The colonel's eyes open wide. "A girl, no less, Barras.

And one who talks back! Whatever next?" He chucks my chin and I pull my face away.

"Take care," Uncle Gustav growls. "My niece is a respectable girl."

The colonel's smile is lazy and self-satisfied. His eyes twinkle as he gestures towards the geese.

"Then perhaps mademoiselle will tell me where you're taking these fine birds."

I feel my cheeks growing hot. He has no right to tease me. His army has hurt us enough.

"Speak up, *girl*," the driver orders. "The colonel asked you a question."

I shoot him a look, then square my shoulders and meet the colonel's gaze.

"North," I tell him flatly. "We're taking them north."

The colonel smiles again. "An evasive answer, Barras. I do believe the young lady is teasing us."

"I'm not the one who's teasing," I snap, knowing my cheeks are blazing red now.

Uncle Gustav puts a hand on my arm.

"Hush, Angélique," he says. "Let me handle this."

But the colonel raises a finger.

"No, no, monsieur. These days the ladies are entitled to be heard. It's the new fashion, you know." He bends towards me, chuckling. "So, my dear, tell me, are these birds yours?"

"My brother's, monsieur."

"Another shirker, no doubt," the driver sneers.

"Hoarders and shirkers. The countryside's plagued with 'em, mon colonel."

I glare at him briefly, then draw myself up and look the colonel in the eye.

"My brother is a soldier, monsieur. An artilleryman in the thirty-fifth regiment of field artillery, serving at the Somme."

The colonel smiles. "The Somme? Good for him. Barras, remind me to write to the colonel of the thirty-fifth RFA and thank him for my supper."

"Your supper? *Yours?* You can't *steal* food! You've no right!"

"Angélique! That's enough!" Uncle Gustav sounds angry.

The driver scowls and even the colonel looks shocked.

But I stand my ground, daring the colonel to deny it.

"Come, come, mademoiselle," he says, forcing a laugh. "The Requisition doesn't steal. It's our duty! How else would your brother eat if the army didn't feed him?"

"You could buy food," I say. "Not bankrupt poor farmers!"

"That is a very serious charge, indeed."

"Well, it's true," I reply, faltering now, frightened of going too far.

The colonel sighs. "You see, Barras? Deep down these people understand we're right."

His words sting me to the core. How dare he talk about *these people*? The pompous fool! The army is meant to be fighting for us, the people of France, for *our* land. This war isn't about *them*.

From some hidden well of my proud peasant's soul, a place I didn't even know existed, words arrive which I never dreamt I'd have the courage to say, certainly not to a man festooned with brass buttons and gold braid.

With flaming cheeks, I plant my feet apart.

"The Requisition has been to my home twice, monsieur. They took everything we own except these geese. And now *I'm* selling them. Me. Angélique Lacroix! I'm taking them to General Foch himself, and I'm going to get as much money for them as I possibly can because I need it to save my brother's farm. I *need* the money. Do you understand? This is *my* duty, monsieur, and I'll not let anyone stand in my way!"

The colonel goggles at me, his mouth open. Uncle Gustav looks thunderstruck. The driver appears to be choking. I imagine the colonel will order his driver to fetch his cane any second and then thrash me for impudence. Like Father would.

My legs turn to water. Long seconds pass. Uncle Gustav grips my arm so tightly it hurts. But then the colonel throws back his head and *laughs*. A deep belly laugh.

"Well said, mademoiselle! That's the spirit! Barras! Fetch me my satchel at once!"

Stunned, I watch his driver run to the truck and hurry back with a leather case.

The colonel pulls a fat notebook from it. He opens the

notebook with a flourish and writes something down, then tears off the piece of paper and hands it to Uncle Gustav.

"Monsieur." The colonel inclines his head. "Mademoiselle."

He chucks me under the chin, his eyes twinkling once more. I just stand there gawping as he turns on his heels and marches back to the cab. The driver scurries after him and they're gone, disappearing in a farting cloud of fug.

Speechless, I stare at Uncle Gustav, who stares at the piece of paper, moving his lips as he reads it.

"What does it say?" I ask in a whisper.

He sits down heavily.

"What is it?"

There are tears in his eyes. He rakes his fingers through his hair.

"Uncle Gustav! What did he write?"

I snatch the paper from him. It's covered in fancy scrolls and headed with ornate printed words: Liberty. Equality. Fraternity.

"*Mon Dieu!* It's a Requisition chit!"

"Read what he wrote, ma petite."

I make out each word with difficulty. The colonel's writing is flowery with twirls and underlining, but in the end I work it out.

Gasping, I read it again.

"Read it out loud," Uncle Gustav says, "so I can believe it."

Blinking away tears of relief, I clear my throat.

"By Order of the Government of France, the Geese in Possession of Mademoiselle A. Lacroix are in Transit to His Excellency General Ferdinand Foch. Priority Passage Requested."

Uncle Gustav starts laughing. I do too. He leaps up and punches the air. I dance a jig in the middle of the road. Then he grabs my hands and we're twirling, twirling, and Napoleon is honking, Amandine is squeaking, and the world is such a wonderful place to be.

"They can't stop us now, Uncle Gustav! No one can stop us now!"

Twenty-six

We march into Monville in triumph. Shop windows glitter. Street lanterns shine. Motor cars honk and tram bells jangle. I feel like laughing out loud.

The grand station building stands at the top of a wide boulevard, its steps bustling with women and soldiers. Ragged children hold out grubby hands to passers-by.

We herd the geese round the side of the building and into the sprawling marshalling yard. Pigs squeal. Crates of hens leak feathers. Every holding pen seems full.

At the far end of the platform, a monstrous locomotive is spewing smoke and grit. An acrid fog of black soot hangs in the air.

"Is that our train?" I call over the noise. "Should we go straight on?"

"I need to get permissions first! And food! It's a long way to Paris," Uncle Gustav shouts back.

We find a pen set back from the platform. The geese hiss angrily as we herd them inside. I can't blame them. The concrete floor is slick with cow muck. The Requisition must have been here.

"I'll stay with them!" I call to Uncle Gustav.

He nods. "I'll be back in a minute."

I feel sadder when he's gone. Less excited. Nervous now I'm surrounded by strangers. I watch two herders poke their pigs with sticks and whack their backsides as they force them onto the platform. The pigs respond with frantic squeals, setting off the geese in a chorus of panicky honking.

"That gander's something special."

I turn around to find a tall, handsome man with a florid face eyeing Napoleon.

"I'll give you a fair price for him here and now," he says. "Save you the trouble of getting him on the train."

"No," I say. Then, "Thank you. I'm waiting for my uncle."

He gives me a brief, puzzled look, and I realize he must have thought I was a boy.

"Tell me if you change your mind," he says, then turns to his handcart, which is packed with miserable-looking turkeys. He lifts his birds one by one into the next-door pen.

I crane my neck, searching for Uncle Gustav, but the platform is packed. Guards check passengers' tickets and point to carriages, while railway officials in dark uniforms tour the marshalling yard asking for documents.

"My uncle has a transit chit," I tell one when he stops by the geese.

He looks over my boy's clothing, then grunts. "Where are you going?"

"Paris. Then north."

"Loading begins in five minutes. Pen nine. Truck twelve. Move up now."

"I'm meant to wait," I say, but he's already moved on.

I glance into the cattle wagon painted with the number twelve. It stands empty, near the back of the train. Anxious, I look for Uncle Gustav again, but the air is even fuggier now that a second train is shunting in, pumping out more clouds of soot.

"You want help moving them?" the florid man asks me when he comes back from loading his turkeys.

I shake my head. "I'll wait."

"Rather you than me. Lose your place in this queue and you'll be here all night."

"Really?"

I stand on tiptoe, peering over carts laden with poultry crates and trollies loaded with vegetables. A thick-set man with cages of partridges in the pen behind mine shouts, "What's the hold-up? Get a move on!"

The pigs squeal again as they're prodded up a wooden ramp into a soot-blackened wagon. Then the train whistles, a long, drawn-out shriek, and Napoleon batters his wings against the sides of the pen, shrieking back.

"He'll hurt hisself like that," says the partridge man,

pushing past me with his cages. "Shouldn't have birds if you can't control 'em."

Ignoring him, I peer every which way for Uncle Gustav.

Then, up and down the platform, guards shout, "All aboard for Paris!" and a tide of people surges forward with luggage and carts and crates.

"Uncle! Uncle Gustav!" I yell at the top of my voice, but the tumult drowns me out.

Then a third train thunders into the station, billowing blackness, and the people pause for a moment – passengers and guards – and watch grim-faced as it screeches to a halt in a siding.

"A hospital train!" shouts the florid man above the noise. "Poor devils. Come on. I'll give you a hand."

"But I have to wait," I protest, though he's already opening the gate to my pen.

As he shoos the geese forward – a hissing, seething mass of writhing necks and gaping beaks – bells clang in the road outside, then two omnibuses slew round the corner and skid to a halt in the yard.

"Ambulances! Come on! We can't get in their way!" the florid man yells.

"I–I don't think we're in their way!" I shout back, but he's hustling the geese on, driving them towards the partridge man and the pig herders, who've formed a corridor to the wagon with outstretched arms.

"No, stop!" I shout, but above the clanging, the yells and slamming of doors, no one seems to hear me.

Hurrying after my geese, I stop at the top of the ramp and desperately look back for Uncle Gustav, but all I see are more ambulances and nurses in white uniforms, orderlies with stretchers, then the wounded hobbling off the train: dark-faced men in loose, muddy jackets and baggy trousers, some with one leg empty, or an arm strapped up, or a dangling sleeve.

I feel sick.

And dreadfully worried.

"I've got to take the geese off till my uncle's here," I tell the pig herders as they jump down from the ramp. But just then, with a flood of relief, I spot Uncle Gustav running out of the station building.

I wave and shout, then jump down too – just as the guards start blowing their whistles. More and more doors slam. Women wave goodbye. Children hang on to soldiers' legs.

Faintly I hear Uncle Gustav bellow along the platform, "Are the geese loaded?"

"Yes!" I yell back.

"Then get on with them! Go back! I'll find you!"

"No! We've got to go together!"

"Go back now, Angélique! Go on! *Go!*"

I hesitate a split second, then hurtle back to the wagon, throwing myself inside just as a guard is rolling the great door shut. I scramble back to my feet and jam my boot in the doorway to keep it open a crack.

"Wait!" I scream at the guard. "My uncle's here! Give him a second."

I shove the door open and stick out my head. Uncle Gustav is by an open carriage door, one foot lifted, his hand on the handle.

"Thank God," I breathe, but in that instant the train lurches. He stumbles, then recovers himself, lifting his foot again, but now a guard on the platform is pulling him back, wrenching the door handle from his hand.

"No!" I shriek. "Stop the train!"

Uncle Gustav waves madly at me, but already the train is grinding forward. The guard keeps a grip on his shoulder.

I scream, "This way! Come on!"

He turns. Shakes off the guard. Runs alongside the grumbling wagons.

"Uncle Gustav!"

"Ma petite!"

I clutch the frame of the door and stretch out. Further. Further. He's almost there. Almost. But we're going too fast. He can't catch my hand.

Red-faced, he shouts, "Meet me in Paris! At the station! Under the—"

But a piercing whistle cuts him off.

"I didn't hear you!" I scream, overwhelmed by a desire to leap off the train.

"I'll get off at the next stop!" I yell. "I'll wait for you there!"

But I've no idea if he heard me or not.

Twenty-seven

Frozen to the spot, I watch the lights of the station vanish into the smog. The ground spins away beneath me. Smoke and grit whip my face, but I can't shut the door. I have to go back. I must find Uncle Gustav no matter what.

"I'll close this for you, shall I?"

It's the red-faced man with the turkeys, shouting in my ear above the clatter of the train. I stare at him stupidly; I'd forgotten he was there.

"You'd best sit down," he says. "You look done in."

In tears of desperation, I slide to the floor, blinded by the darkness that falls the moment he shuts the heavy door.

The wagon judders and clanks. Ice-cold wind slices through gaps in the slatted walls. I bury my face in my hands. I feel powerless and lost. I can't go on alone.

"There! That's better," says the man, striking a match. "We might as well get comfy."

Comfy? He deliberately put my geese on the train when I told him not to! For a second, anger flares inside me and I glare at him, but he smiles back at me, rueful and apologetic.

"I thought he'd make it," he says with a shrug. "Honestly, I did. Would you, um, mind holding this for me?"

Numb with shock, I stare at the candle he's holding out to me until the match goes out.

"Oops," he says. "Never mind. Here we go."

He lights another match and offers me the candle again. This time I take it with shaking hands. He lights the wick, then melts the base of the candle and sticks it to a floorboard. The flame wobbles and gutters, slowly spreading a blanket of yellow around us.

The man smiles again.

"Your uncle, was it, the chap who missed the train?"

When I don't answer, he shrugs again, then leans back against the pen, where my geese have already settled down next to his turkeys.

"Hungry?" he asks, pulling an apple from his great coat.

I shake my head, despite the aching emptiness of my stomach.

"No? Well, it's here if you want it."

He places the apple next to the candle. It rolls around in the dirt until Amandine wriggles out from the pen and chases it. The man grins at her. I pick her up.

After a while I pick up the apple too.

* * *

The train slows half an hour later, sooner than I'd expected. Clambering to my feet, I peer between the slats at the flat, dark countryside sliding past us.

"Monville-Gare," the man says as the train rattles and wheezes to a halt. I edge the door open and peep out.

A derelict shed casts a broken shadow in the moonlight. A frosted waste ground stands silent and empty beyond it. There isn't even a proper platform, just gravel held back by a line of rotten sleepers.

"It used to be busy," the man says gloomily.

"What happened?"

"The war. Half the farms I visit are abandoned these days." He sighs deeply. "No one can keep body and soul together on rations. Not with all these shortages. But I guess you know that." He glances at my geese and then winks. "You want a hand getting them down?"

"Why would I?" I ask suspiciously.

His eyes widen. "Sorry, I thought you said you'd meet your uncle here. Rather you than me. *Brr!* It's freezing!"

He jumps down and I peer out again, hoping to see lights or houses. But there's nothing and no one. What a place to spend the night, alone and unprotected. And what if Uncle Gustav didn't hear me? What will I do then?

"Tell you what," says the man, seeing me hesitate. "There's a tap by the station house, and they always keep a bucket handy. I'm going to get my birds a drink. I'll fetch yours some too, if you like."

"Is there time?"

"If I'm quick." He looks into the shed and sighs. "I was hoping to find some straw to block up those blasted holes. Never mind."

His breath smokes as he hurries away.

In the stillness, laughter filters from the carriages nearer to the locomotive. Muted conversations come from the wagons nearby, along with the smells of tobacco and pigs. The candle in our wagon shines steadily now that we've stopped.

Should I wake the geese? Stay with them out here until the next train – whenever that might be? Even Amandine is fast asleep now, tucked up inside Pascal's jacket. I kiss her head, then wrap my arms about her.

The man returns with two buckets. He sets one down on the gravel and passes the other up to me.

"Better hurry if you're getting off," he says, throwing me a worried look.

"Is something wrong?" I ask him.

"No! It's nothing. Really." He glances back along the moon-silvered tracks, then adds, "Well, since you asked, the thing is, you can't rely on timetables these days. Everything's topsy-turvy. You never know where the next train's going to stop."

I stare at him blankly.

"The next Paris train, for instance. Who knows if it's going to stop here?"

My heart sinks. I could wait here all night and still not find Uncle Gustav.

He smiles at me sadly. "Did I hear your uncle suggest-ing you meet in Paris?" I nod. "Your decision, of course," he says. "Shall I leave your water out here?"

I hesitate for a moment, then shake my head.

The train stops and starts all night, clanking into silent towns and idling in lonely sidings.

Sometimes other locomotives thunder past us, pulling a hospital train, I imagine, or perhaps a military train filled with soldiers bound for the Front.

Dozing, I dream about Pascal and René, and when I wake I think of Uncle Gustav and how happy he'll be when we find each other again.

Once when I wake I find the man looking at me intently, and when I sit up, he comes over to sit beside me.

"Cheese?" he asks and I accept a piece gratefully.

"I'll be honest," he says as I eat it, "I want to buy your geese."

Alarmed, I sit up straighter, wishing I wasn't famished, or tired, cold and lonely.

"They're not for sale," I reply.

"You're taking them north for their health?"

"I didn't say that!"

"I know. I'm sorry." He grins. "Tell you what, you name whatever price you like for that gander and I'll pay it."

I swallow hard. I've no idea how much I want for Napoleon. I don't even want to sell him, though I know I'll have to eventually.

"My uncle deals with that side of things," I tell him.

"Ah, yes, your uncle. Now, how do I put this? Um. You're not all that likely to find him in Paris."

"But you said I've only got to wait at the station!"

"That's the problem, I'm afraid, right there in a nut-shell. *The* station. But which one? It could be Le Bourget or the Gare de l'Est. No. I tell a lie. From Monville it might be the Gare d'Orléans. At least I think it is…"

His forehead wrinkles. Then he shrugs.

"Anyhow, I'm not trying to cheat you," he continues. "I'll pay a good price. You'll go home with money in your pocket, and I'll turn a nice little profit in Paris. What's fairer than that?"

"Me turning a nice little profit in Paris, for a start!"

"Looking like that?" He looks pointedly at my sooty, mucky, crumpled clothes. "They'll say you stole them, you know. It's a suspicious old world out there."

He pulls a face, then stands up and returns to his place by the pen.

I wake again to the delicious smell of coffee.

The man is squatting over a miniature stove with a tiny pot balanced on top of a quivering blue flame – another treasure from his bulging great coat pockets, I expect.

"Morning," he says cheerfully.

Thin ribbons of grey fall across the slimy floorboards. Beyond the slats a thick fog rolls past.

"Here we go." He pours coffee into two little cups and

hands one to me. The steam warms my nose and the cup thaws my frozen fingers.

I feel his eyes on me as I drink. When I've finished he says, "Tell me. Why are you selling those marvellous geese of yours?"

"That's none of your business," I reply, eyeing him doubtfully.

"True. But let me speculate…"

He leans back, arms folded, and looks into nothing as if thinking deeply. "You said you're heading north of Paris…"

"No I didn't."

"You did. I heard you. In Monville station."

"You shouldn't have been listening!"

He grins. "You can't blame a chap for being interested when a boy with a flock of very fine geese turns out to be a girl on a remarkably long journey. So I said to myself, *Ah-ha! What's going on here, then?* And you know what I told myself?"

I frown but say nothing.

"I told myself that you're after richer pickings than Paris. Me," he goes on, scratching the growth on his chin, "I never go past Amiens. That's near enough to the fighting for me. But you, where are you going, I wonder. Prices aren't that much better till you get *dangerously* close to the Front. It's a brave girl who'd travel that road alone, with half the people starving and the other half looking for a chance to make a quick profit."

His eyes are bright now. He pins them on me. "Those birds are worth a great deal of money. Did you know that?

How are you going to get them north? Do you know the way to the Gare du Nord? Can you herd them across Paris on your own? Have you thought about that?"

He shakes his head and sighs. "I'm sure your uncle would agree with me. The best thing you can do is sell them to me. Think about it. And drink up. There's another cup in the pot."

All morning his words bother me like flies buzzing inside my head. What if it's another trick, like Monsieur Chevalier's, and he's pretending to be friendly when he's not?

Maybe the next Paris train is faster than ours. Uncle Gustav might already be there, waiting for me in the Gare de l'Est.

Or Le Bourget.

Or that other station he mentioned.

As I chew my dirty fingernails, fretting about what to do, the train grinds slowly on through muddy countryside, stopping now and then at towns wreathed in smoke.

At midday I feed the geese a miserly handful of grain, then sit Amandine in my lap. She's restless and won't settle. The man stares through the slats, seeming out of sorts.

"This war," he moans. "This war!"

"Were you a soldier?" I ask him.

He beats his chest. "Weak heart. Damn shame. A man should fight."

He takes a swig from a bottle and the vinegary smell of red wine fills the wagon.

A city looms into view. Warehouses. Factories. I press my eye to a hole in the slats, searching for the Eiffel Tower, gripped by excitement – and fear.

"Are we here?" I ask, wondering how on earth I'll keep the geese together at the station and how long I'll have to wait for Uncle Gustav to arrive.

The man crawls to another hole on his hands and knees, then collapses against the slats, clutching his bottle tightly.

"We're way off yet," he says morosely, taking another long swig.

"Are you sure?" I ask, nervous about being confined in a small wagon with a drunk.

"I've done thiz journey a thousand times," he slurs, then shuts his eyes.

I look down at him, dismayed that he's become this drunk this quickly, but also a little disappointed that in his cups he seems to have forgotten about the geese.

If he doesn't want to buy them, then everything is down to me. But if I can't find Uncle Gustav, how can I possibly find the Gare du Nord, let alone Frévent, on my own? It's impossible. I simply can't do it.

"D'you know who profits from thiz war?" the man says suddenly, his tone angry. "Politicians! Thaz who! And arms manufacturerz. And they have the cheek, the absolute *cheek* to call *us* profiteers!"

He looks up at me, bleary-eyed. "You and me! You. And. Me! You wanna know why?"

I shake my head, alarmed by his vehemence.

"Becuz we deal in food. Thaz all! No other reason!"

He shakes his head. "Why, hey? Why are you a profiteer when you've got *every* right t'zell your birds for *whatever* price you like! Iz not illegal. Well, it shouldn't be illegal, anyhow."

"I'm not a profiteer," I say cautiously.

"Try telling *them* that! The women screeching *peasant* at you. Men zwearing." He leans forward, the smell of wine heavy on his breath. "They get their kids to throw stones at us. Like we wuz dogs! When we're doin' 'em a favour. A *favour*, I tell you!"

He hiccups and waves his hand in the air. "Go north, mademoiselle. Forget Paris. And Amiens. Stinking, ztupid places."

"So you don't want to buy my geese?" I ask, trying not to picture people shouting at me in the streets and boys throwing stones at the geese.

"You wanna sell them?" he asks, sounding surprised as if he'd forgotten.

"Maybe. For the right price."

He wipes his mouth on the back of his hand, and tries to focus his eyes on the pen. Just then, the whistle sounds and the train rumbles to a halt.

I press my eye to the hole in the slats again.

We've stopped by a vast marshalling yard. It's crammed with crates and rolls of barbed wire, and row upon row of artillery shells vanishing into the fog.

I gasp at the size of it — boxes beyond count, giant metal shells. All that death and destruction waiting to be sent to the battlefield.

All that noise and terror.

All those fountains of grey and brown and pink mud that Henri Chevalier wrote about…

"*Sacre bleu!*" The man slaps his forehead and leaps up unsteadily. "Mademoiselle! Tell me you have zat travel chit for your geese!"

"My uncle has it. Why?"

"*Mon Dieu!* No!"

The sudden panic in his voice terrifies me. My stomach churns.

"Why? What's wrong?" I ask him.

"You've never heard of z'Requisition?"

"The Requisition?" I clutch at the wall of the pen.

"Look!" He grabs my shoulders and spins me around so I'm looking outside again. "There! Barracks! Cannons! It's an army camp."

But I can't make them out. I turn to him, my heart thumping.

"What can we do? I can't let them take them, not when I've come this far! Help me! Please!"

"Hold on! Hold on!" He drags a hand through his hair. "Lemme think."

But almost at once there's a rap on the door and a shout.

"Papers, messieurs! Open up!"

"*Please,*" I whimper. "You've got to help me."

"Shhhhhh! Maybe...? No. That won't work."

"What won't work?"

"A ztupid idea."

"Tell me!" Already the wagon door is rolling open.

The man seizes my hand and whispers in my ear, "I travel thiz line all the time. I've got papers, documents..."

"So?"

"If we zay the geese are mine, I bought 'em, they might believe me."

"You really think so?"

"Iz worth a try, no?"

"What's the hold up, messieurs?" a uniformed railway guard asks sharply as he clambers into the wagon.

"Zorry," the man replies, looking me in the eye.

I haven't the faintest idea what else to do, so I nod furtively, then shrink into the shadows, my blood pounding, my head filled with terror that I might lose the geese.

The man blinks at me and smiles ever so slightly, then rummages through his pockets, pulls out a greasy wallet filled with worn-out papers and shows them to the guard, who walks over to the turkeys' pen without even glancing at me.

The guard checks the man's papers again, then says, "What about the geese? They're not on here."

My heart leaps into my mouth. The man's eyes dart towards me, then back to the guard.

"I, um, bought 'em at Monville-Gare. Off some peasant family. The station house was shut, so..." He jerks his chin at me. "The lad saw me buy them. He can confirm it."

Finally the guard looks at me.

I lick my lips, torn about lying about the geese, yet ter-rified at the sight of the marshalling yard and the unseen barracks of the Requisition.

"Well?" the guard asks. I nod quickly. The guard grunts, then makes a mark on the man's papers and gives them back to him.

The man smiles.

"Cost me a fortune, them geese," he says, his voice cheerful as he carefully folds the papers and puts them back in his wallet. "Cleaned me out, they did. Damned peasants. No better than thieves, hey?"

Oddly, his drunken slur has disappeared completely.

The guard turns to me. "Right, lad. Ticket, please."
I swallow hard.

The man laughs. "You'll be lucky. That one's been scrounging food off me since Monville."

My jaw drops. "But you said…"

The man steps back, smirking over the guard's shoul-der as the guard plants himself in front of me, scowling.

Twenty-eight

"Ticket," the guard repeats.

"I-I…"

My head whirls as I try to force what just happened into a shape that makes sense. If I admit I don't have a ticket, I'll get thrown off the train – without my geese, which is unthinkable. And yet I have to think it.

"They're mine! The geese."

As I blurt it out, my hand reaches towards the guard's arm, but he backs away from me, a look of distaste on his face. I, too, see how filthy I am. Soot-stained, and worse.

The man laughs. "As if *you* could afford such birds! You scruffy little urchin. Go on! Clear off before he calls the police."

"The police?" I stare at the guard, then point at the man. "But *he's* the thief."

The guard's frown deepens. "I asked for your ticket."

"My uncle's got it," I say, thinking quickly.

"And where's he?" the guard asks.

The man nudges him. "You'll enjoy this. He's got a store of nonsensical stories, this one. Been boring me with 'em for hours. Haven't you, lad? Still, you can't blame him for trying. Just not on my time, hey? Things to do. Places to go..."

The guard keeps his eyes fixed on me.

I take a deep breath. "My uncle is in Monville, monsieur. Or possibly Paris by now. Or on a train..."

The man chuckles. "Get your story straight, lad."

"I'm not a lad! And you know it!"

As I tear off Pascal's cap, the guard's look of surprise quickly turns to mistrust and suspicion. I see myself in his eyes – a homeless waif, stealing a ride to heaven knows where, making up stories as I go along. Claiming to own a flock of the finest Toulouse geese must seem crazy to him.

"Well, I never," says the man, grinning at me behind the guard's back.

The guard shoots him a look, then turns to me.

"Complain to the gendarmes about that," he says. "*After* you get off my train."

"But they won't believe me! Any more than you do. Please, monsieur. I'm going to Frévent to sell the geese to General Foch. We've got a chit from the army to say we can go there!"

The man snorts. "This gets better and better! She'd never heard of Frévent till I told her about the fat profits people are making there."

"You never said any such thing! I told you that!"

The man rolls his eyes. "Now she wants to be a profiteer! Shame on you! Don't you know there's a war?"

The guard frowns at him. "That's enough," he growls. "This war's cruel enough to orphans. But you have to get off the train, mademoiselle. No ticket, no travel. That's the rule."

"And my geese?"

He puffs out his cheeks and shrugs.

Tears of frustration well in my eyes. I feel desperate and cornered. Instinctively, I move towards the geese, but the guard grabs my arm as I pass and propels me towards the door.

On the platform, I burst into tears.

How could I have been so stupid? *Tell the guard the geese are mine*, the man had said. And I fell for it! What an idiot! Now I've lost everything. The geese. The farm. Uncle Gustav.

Bitterly angry with myself, I smear the useless tears off my face as the guard climbs down behind me and begins to roll shut the door.

"But my geese," I plead, pulling at his sleeve. "They're mine, I tell you. Mine!"

"Sing another song!" the man calls from the wagon.

"All right, then. How many geese have you got? How many ganders?"

"I buy and sell 'em. That's all."

"Sixteen geese, eleven ganders and a female gosling," I tell the guard. "Check their vents. But mind the big gander or he'll bite your nose off!"

"Give it up," says the man. "Know when you're beaten."

I push myself between the guard and the wagon. "Ask him what the people looked like who sold him the geese. He won't be able to tell you, because there wasn't anyone at Monville-Gare. I'd have got off if there was – with *my* geese. You've got to believe me, monsieur. That man pretended to be my friend. He tricked me."

"Liar!" The man's voice issues from the darkness at the back of the wagon.

"You're the liar!" I shout back. "I hope you burn in Hell!"

"Now, now," the guard mutters. "There's no call for that."

"*No call?* He just ruined my family! My mother's at home right now, waiting for the bailiffs. My brother won't *ever* be able to come home again. Never!"

Beside myself with fury now, I scream at the man at the top of my voice, "*Never!* You hear me? You've destroyed my brother's *life!*"

Hearing me shriek, Amandine squeaks in alarm and squeezes out from under the pen. Jumping back into the wagon, I push past the man and run to her and pick her up, cradling her close to me.

"Put it down, mademoiselle," the guard says, "and come on out here."

"She's not an it. Look!" I thrust Amandine's backside into his face.

"Oh, let her have her pet," the man says wearily.

"Her *pet*?" The guard looks closely at the man – who hesitates.

"Well, what else would you call it? Scrawny little thing. It's no good to me."

"I'll take the rest of my property too, then, shall I?"

I've no idea how I managed to say it so calmly. Maybe I didn't want to shout and frighten Amandine, or maybe it was the man's split-second hesitation, but whatever gave me the courage to glare at him now, I definitely saw the first glimmer of doubt in his eyes.

I turn to the guard again. "My brother's name is Pascal Lacroix. He's an artilleryman, serving on the Somme. At least I think he's there. That's why I've got to find General Foch – to ask him where he is. We haven't seen him for years, you see. Harvest leave was cancelled twice."

"I heard," the guard replies quietly.

"I thought, maybe, if I gave His Excellency my best gander, he might let Pascal come home, you know, for a few days at Christmas."

"Home for Christmas, hey?" the man sneers. "I told you she spun a good yarn."

I bite my tongue, refusing to be baited again. Instead I look the man up and down. His arms are folded over his great coat – a coat exactly like Uncle Gustav's.

Was that really all it took to fool me? A coat?

I turn back to the guard, "I've never been on my own before, monsieur. I thought my uncle would always be with me, and when he wasn't..." I shrug.

"You have no father?"

I shake my head.

"The war?" he asks.

"Verdun."

"My brother fell there, too."

"I'm sorry for your loss, monsieur."

"Thank you."

The guard lets out a long breath, then, rubbing his chin, looks at Amandine nestled in my arms.

"I hatched her," I tell him. "She follows me everywhere, and the other geese follow her – sort of. They're terribly slow. I'll show you – if you'll let me."

Frozen seconds pass.

"No tricks?" the guard says at last.

"None. I promise."

Another long moment.

Then he nods.

Together, we slide a plank from the wagon to the platform so the geese can walk down it, and then he steps back. For once the geese behave beautifully, shuffling out of the pen as soon as I open the gate, then waddling after Amandine the moment I put her down. When they're all clustered around me on the platform, the man shrugs.

"Like I said, you can't blame a chap for trying," he says.

"You-you...rogue!" The guard's face turns scarlet

with outrage. "You should prosecute him, mademoiselle."

"Yes, yes," the man says dismissively. He kicks the end of the plank onto the platform, then rolls the wagon door shut in our faces.

The guard is beside himself. He says he'll call the gendarmes for me. He promises to be a witness. We'll get a message to Uncle Gustav. But then he admits the court procedure could take months, and my geese would be impounded in the meantime.

"I'm sorry, monsieur, but I can't afford that much time. The bailiffs, you understand."

Looking deeply troubled, he stares at the wagon's closed doors, but then nods sadly and sighs. He blows his whistle and raises his flag. The train clatters off, belching smoke and grit.

"What will you do now?" he asks me as we watch it departing into the morning haze.

"Find my uncle in Paris. Though I don't know which station he'll come into."

The guard's face brightens. "I can help you with that. This way!"

He hurries off towards the station's grimy entrance hall, and I lead the geese after him.

"The Gare d'Orléans," he says. "All last night's trains from Monville stop there. I'm sorry I can't buy you a ticket. It's against railway policy. You know, to pay for vagrants…"

"Of course — and thank you. You've done so much already."

We stand awkwardly for another moment, then he says, "Here. My wife would want you to have this." He gives me a small brown paper parcel. "Ham and a little cheese. My lunch."

"Oh! That's so kind!"

He smiles. "Go left outside the station. That'll take you straight to the main Paris road. And mademoiselle…"

"Yes?"

"You might want to put on your cap."

Outside the station, the air tastes acrid, as if laced with chemicals. A narrow cobbled alleyway runs between high, soot-blackened brick walls, which are topped with barbed wire and broken glass — protection for the marshalling yards, I suppose.

The geese bunch together, agitated by this ugly, alien world. Even the weeds growing at the base of the walls are caked in filth. The geese quickly stop grazing on them.

I walk behind them, urging them on, feeling anxious and small, and wishing with all my heart that I wasn't alone.

Under the railway arches, we pass by a café with grease-grimed windows. It's crowded with soldiers sitting with their womenfolk. Heads turn as the geese waddle into view. A few smiles appear among the looks of surprise, but not many. I half expect someone to shout *"Peasant!"* or *"Profiteer!"*

At the corner by the main road, I stop by a horse trough with an ornate cast iron tap and wash my face and hands, then brush as much soot and muck off my clothes as I can. I eat a handful of the guard's ham as well, hiding it under my jacket whenever anyone emerges from the thickening fog. Mostly they're women, drably dressed in greys and browns, with shawls held tightly against the cold. In their thin, pinched faces I think I see hunger…

I scold myself for being a coward. Uncle Gustav wouldn't stand on a street corner, lost and confused, quaking at the sight of half-starved women. Nor would Pascal or René.

Be bold, I tell myself. *Be a man!* I'm dressed like Pascal so I have to become him.

Tucking a loose strand of hair out of sight, I ask the next passer-by to point me in the direction of Paris.

I'm sent through a maze of streets that crouch at the bottom of massive walls. Huge chimneys soar into the smog, and the clanging of metalwork issues from behind factory gates.

A long line of women with baskets on their arms wait outside a bakery. As the geese approach, a nudge ripples along the queue and someone shouts, "A franc for that gander!"

There's laughter.

I wonder if I should laugh too, or smile, at least. But the eyes that meet mine are hostile as well as hungry. I put my hands in my pockets and look down as the laughter turns to catcalls.

"Come 'ere, darlin'. We won't bite."

"A kiss for a goose! A grope for a gander!"

I try hurrying the geese on, but four girls in shiny boots and skirts halfway to their knees run across the road and stand in my way, swishing their skirts from side to side, grinning.

"Aw, look," says the shortest girl. "He's got a lickle one in 'is jacket. Your pet, is it, darlin'?" She reaches for Amandine.

Instinctively, I pull her back.

"That's not very friendly," the girl pouts, and the others crowd around me, laughing.

My eye runs the gauntlet of the breadline. Only one person smiles at me – a girl about my age, skeleton-thin, with eyes too big for her wasted face. I look away and try again to drive the geese past the four girls, but my birds are skittish, frightened and slippery.

"Get lost," I say gruffly, keeping my voice deep.

"Or what?" the short girl says.

"I'll call the gendarmes. That's what."

The tallest girl shouts to the breadline, "'E's gonna call the police!"

"No 'e ain't," someone shouts back.

A tough-looking, broad-shouldered woman with wiry grey hair gestures to me to be off. "Get out of 'ere. We've got trouble enough as it is."

But a hand is snaking over my shoulder. The tallest girl plucks Amandine from under my jacket, to shrieks of delight from the others.

"Stop it!" I yell. "You'll hurt her!"

I pull off Pascal's cap and a murmur runs up and down the queue. But the four girls dance about me, taunting me, the tallest one holding Amandine high above her head.

"Put her down!" I shout, afraid to grab her in case I hurt her.

Napoleon advances on the girls, neck out, honking, flanked by the rest of the flock. Amandine poos in fright down the girl's arm.

"Eeew!" she shrieks – and drops her.

I lunge forward, but the short girl is closer.

"Give her back!" I scream as she tears off with Amandine under her arm.

"Come and get her, goose girl!"

Without thinking, I start after her, but stop almost at once as two huge horses clomp around the corner, pulling a loaded dray. The horses' great hooves strike the cobbles like hammers. Just one stamp could break a person's back – or squash a goose flat.

I freeze. But Napoleon waddles towards the horses, shrieking his outrage. I have a split second to decide which one to rescue – him or Amandine – but my feet remain rooted to the spot. Then the skeletal girl darts into the road, running towards the horses too, waving her tiny hands in their blinkered faces. She stands in their path, like a fluttering sparrow trying to stop a relentless train.

The wire-haired woman screams, "No! Thérèse! Stop!" Then to me, "Get that bleedin' bird under control! You're gonna get 'er killed!" And she runs towards the dray too, shouting at the driver to wake up.

At last he lifts his head and hauls on the reins, pouring curses on the two women, who stand centimetres from the horses' tossing heads and their enormous stamping hooves.

Napoleon screeches at them and beats his wings as I look back for Amandine, feeling utterly lost without her, as if part of me is being held hostage by those girls.

The short girl's grin is pure malice. She squeezes Amandine, who squeaks in alarm. The other geese honk aimlessly and rush back and forth, panicking and out of control.

The horses snort, the driver swears. But the skeletal girl smiles happily at Napoleon – an open, innocent smile, revealing two rows of chipped yellow teeth.

My heart goes out to her. She's clearly sick, starving too, yet she risked her life under those hooves to save Napoleon. A smile of thanks is not enough, but it's all I've got to give her. That and a nod. She gives me a little wave.

Quickly, I shoo Amandine's mother towards Napoleon, hoping she'll calm him down. But how can I get Amandine back? I can see she's being choked, her fragile body crushed against the short girl's shabby dress. Her feet paddle frantically to escape.

I look about for help. But the wire-haired woman

scowls at me and the driver shouts, "Get that bird out the way!" The women in the bread queue purse their lips and the four girls smirk at me. Turning to the skeletal girl, I smile at her again.

"I like your gander," she says, smiling back. "He's naughty. Does he have a name?"

"Napoleon," I say, then point out Amandine's mother and Amandine herself. "I need the gosling to herd them," I tell her – loudly enough for everyone to hear. "They follow her."

"She was in yer jacket," the short girl mocks.

"She gets cold. She's only little."

"So you don't actually *need* 'er," the short girl says.

"I bet she don't need none of 'em!" someone else shouts.

Looking round, I see nothing but contempt in their eyes. They despise me. Despite my clothes, they think I'm rich! With a rising sense of panic, I appeal to the starving girl.

"I love her. I hatched her. She's mine."

"Don't be fooled, Thérèse," the wire-haired woman says. "Them birds ain't pets. They're money under the mattress for the likes of 'er."

"The money isn't going under a mattress! I *need* it!"

Too late, I recognize my mistake. Up and down the breadline, arms fold and expressions harden. I hear them mutter.

"Crafty little madam…"

"Teasing Thérèse like that..."

Then come the dreaded words:

"Profiteer!"

"They're all the same, these peasants."

"None of 'em does an honest day's work."

"I work as hard as you do," I reply – earning jeers from the women and a snort of derision from the drayman. The wire-haired woman puts her arm around Thérèse's thin shoulder and narrows her eyes.

"Eleven hours a day she works, thirteen days straight, no break. That's workin'," she growls. "And they say she ain't worth one franc an hour? It's a disgrace!"

I look at the starving girl with pity. She smiles back, but the wire-haired woman glares at me as if I'm the owner of whatever sweatshop they work in.

"We should take 'er to the factory!" a voice shouts from the breadline. "See what Madame Zenon reckons to some lyin' peasant havin' all them geese!"

Dark looks flash among the women. A few cast sharp glances at me. Then the short girl steps forward with Amandine held above her head.

"We'll hold one of our special courts!" she shouts. "Liberty, equality, sisterhood! The goslin' or 'er geese."

"That's stealing!" I shout back, my heart racing and my legs weak.

"Property is theft," she replies. "Ask Madame Zenon."

"Quiet, you," the wire-haired woman orders, glancing about.

The short girl laughs. "There ain't no informers 'ere. They wouldn't dare!" Then she turns to Thérèse. "You'll defend 'er, won't you, sweetie? Seein' how you're best friends."

Thérèse's face lights up. She claps her hands and turns her innocent smile on me. "I'll defend her, yes!"

Twenty-nine

The women take control of the geese, herding me ahead of them, the four girls in front with Amandine held high. Their mascot.

I'm trapped, powerless, swept along, struck dumb with apprehension. Bewildered, I listen to Thérèse's endless chattering.

The wire-haired woman is Madame Villeneuve, the short girl, Marie-Gabrielle Séché, a relation of Madame Zenon.

Thérèse lives on the third floor of a tenement on rue des Poissonniers with five sisters, four brothers, her mother and twenty cats, only the cats live in the dustbins and are very greedy.

"Do you like cats?" she asks, pausing for breath.

I shake my head, then add, "My brother's got a dog."

"That's nice." She takes my hand. "Don't worry.

Madame Zenon's very fair. She thinks everyone should get the same – same money, same food, same everything, really."

Ahead, the four girls swing into another high-walled street, the stamping of their boots echoing off the blackened bricks. We bunch to a halt outside a pair of solid wooden gates with *Usine Saint-Laurent* painted on them in white.

"Here we are," Thérèse says happily, as if we've arrived at her home.

The gates creak open.

Inside, giant sheds with corrugated sides line a straight road scored by tramlines. It's like another town within the town, the chemical stink heavy in the air. I can't imagine working in such a place.

But I have to imagine it. I can't be a country girl weeping for her gosling, or her brother, demanding his property back. Other rules apply here. Madame Zenon's rules. Equality. Sisterhood. But liberty?

As the gates clang shut behind us, my fists hurt from clenching them so hard.

The factory is dimly lit and eerily silent, the great machinery idle. The chemical reek is so strong in here it catches in my throat.

Metal workbenches are littered with hideous masks, like elongated canvas heads with goggle eyes: gas masks.

"This isn't a *gas* factory, is it?" I ask Thérèse. "That's not *toxic* gas I can smell?"

She nods. "The empty shells come up by river. We make the canisters to fill them. We make these too. Look! I did this one." She shows me the neat seam on a gas mask as if it's a sampler for an apron.

"But gas is *deadly*," I say, my hand over my mouth.

She shrugs. "It makes everybody sick. That's what's wrong with me."

"You're not ... *very* ill are you?"

Sadly, she smiles.

"Oh, Thérèse! That's *terrible*."

"It's why I'm careful with these."

She strokes the seam of the mask she made, then lays it carefully on the workbench again and falls silent. With tears in my eyes, I look away.

Most of the women are making a barricade of tables to pen the geese behind, but a few have taken out knitting and sit talking — with evident satisfaction — under a large sign which says No SITTING. No TALKING. No STRIKING.

Marie-Gabrielle stands with her friends in a doorway next to a grimy glass window. It reflects the machinery like a dark mirror.

Behind the glass, shadows move.

I'm seized by the urge to run away, fetch the police and demand my property back. But then one of the shadows stops and something tells me it's Madame Zenon, watching me.

I shudder, imagining a mad-eyed revolutionary dressed in rags like the pictures from the Reign of Terror. But the woman who steps out is small and neat, with tightly waved grey hair and penetrating eyes.

The women stop whatever they're doing and watch us watching one another. Slowly Madame Zenon nods.

Should I nod back? Acknowledge that battle is joined? The fight seems so unequal with her battalions around us.

"Have you been told why we're on strike?" she asks me.

"I didn't know you were on strike," I say.

"They cut our wages by ten sous to pay for a crèche. They want the mothers to work longer shifts."

"That's not fair. To make you pay for it."

"I'm glad you understand."

Madame Zenon gestures and Marie-Gabrielle puts Amandine down on a table. At once, she slithers to the floor and scurries over to me.

I pick her up, looking at Madame Zenon, who nods slowly again, then sits at a workbench, facing me.

Thérèse sits on her left and Madame Villeneuve on her right. All around chairs scrape as the rest of the women take their seats too.

With horror I realize the court is now in session.

I take deep breaths. If Madame Zenon is fair like Thérèse said, then she'll see my side of things. All I have to do is be calm and reasonable – and not say anything stupid.

"You are accused of war profiteering, a crime against the people of France," Madame Zenon says. "If found guilty, your geese will be forfeit."

Her words chill me. It's as if I'm on trial for my life.

"I'm not a criminal," I say, standing tall, "and you've no right to judge me."

Despite my best effort, my voice sounds small and weak.

Madame Villeneuve looks at me severely. "We *are* the people of France," she says. "We've got every right to judge what's right and wrong."

"Just tell the truth," Thérèse says sweetly. "Tell us you aren't going to ask a silly price for your geese. That's all we want to hear."

My mouth goes dry. I lick my lips, buying a moment of silence.

"The geese are mine. That's the truth. There's nothing else to say."

Madame Zenon leans forward. "You know, of course, that this is a time of war?"

I look at her. "Ye-es."

"We have men at the Front – husbands, sons, brothers, sweethearts. Perhaps you do too?"

I nod, afraid of where this is going but unable to stop it.

"Should they pay for their food," Madame Zenon goes on, "their weapons, their uniforms? Should the doctors and nurses charge to treat their wounds?"

I shake my head.

"And isn't our work just as important to the war? We have families to feed, coal, clothes and medicines to buy. Have we no right to these things?"

"But ... you're paid for working here."

"Soldiers are paid for workin' in the trenches," Madame

Villeneuve replies. "They're still fed for free."

"Only because the Requisition steals their food from us!" I cry.

"And you believe that's right and fair?" Madame Zenon asks me.

I open my mouth. And close it again. I can't tell her I hate the Requisition with a passion. But I can't lie to her, either. She'd see it in my eyes. Looking down, I shrug.

"See," Thérèse says brightly. "She agrees with us. The war isn't fair. No one thinks it is."

Madame Villeneuve glances at her. Then she asks me, "Say I wanted to buy thcm geese off you, how much would you charge me?"

"I-I don't know exactly."

"But a sensible price, right? One a workin' woman can afford."

My heart beats faster and my face grows hot.

Marie-Gabrielle sniggers.

I turn on her. "But I'm not profiteering! I'm not going to hide the money under a mattress!" I look back at Madame Zenon. "The bailiffs are coming. My family's farm is bankrupt!"

"So you're protectin' your property," Madame Villeneuve says.

"I'm saving my home!"

"But not your life?"

"A goose dinner won't save our lives either," Thérèse says quietly.

Madame Villeneuve inclines her head.

I take another deep breath, then say, "My brother's in the artillery. I'd hate him to starve. But farm work is hard without our horse. Pulling a horse-plough through mud is horrible. It's like being an animal. And now they've taken our cow and pig. We've nothing left except the geese. Please let me keep them. They're my only hope."

"So we can't afford 'em," Madame Villeneuve replies. "That's what you're sayin'."

"I *need* the money."

"And bad luck us, hey? We can starve?" Madame Villeneuve says.

I look at her steadily. "My father was a violent drunk and a gambler who died in debt. You're asking my brother to pay for *his* mistakes? And me and my mother. How's that fair? How's that right?"

Madame Villeneuve fixes me with a stare. "For the last time I'm askin'. Will you sell them geese at a fair price or send our children hungry to bed?"

"I-I can't sell you them. It's not my choice! I've *got* to get as much for them as I can."

Around me tongues click and heads shake. Thérèse looks at me sadly. Madame Villeneuve turns to Madame Zenon.

With a sigh, Madame Zenon nods. Then she says, "Take her to my office, Thérèse. We'll let you know what we decide."

* * *

I sit in the dingy room behind the plate glass window and bury my head in my hands, overwhelmed by guilt and regret.

After all these years blaming Father for every bad thing in our lives – and hating Mother for being too weak to protect us – I'm the one who has let Pascal down worst of all.

I've lost him everything. Not them, me. I start to cry. Heaving, bitter sobs.

I abandon myself to them, knowing I can't blame these women for what they're about to do. It's what I tried to do – protect my family – but today they will succeed and I'll fail.

"They'll let you keep the gosling," Thérèse says quietly, sitting beside me, her arm around me. "What's her name? Amandine? It's pretty."

After a while she adds, "I'm sorry I didn't defend you very well."

I shake my head. "It's not your fault. I think I lost them days ago, really."

It's true. I let myself get bullied and tricked. I panicked and relied on other people when all I had to do was wait for Uncle Gustav in Monville station – something any child could do.

And I thought Mother was useless! No wonder she dressed me up like Pascal. I never, ever want to get married if I'm going to let my own children down like this.

Softly, Thérèse says, "It's time."

I feel a draught on my face. The door is open. Beyond it, the end of the world as I know it.

"Is there anything you wish to say?" Madame Zenon asks as I face her again.

Beside me, Thérèse whispers, "Go on. It might help."

Can I think of any last words? I look down, thinking of Pascal and Béatrice – the lives they might have led. And René and me – not to be. Never to be, perhaps.

And Mother, waiting for the bailiffs.

"I think my brother's going mad," I say at last. "He's living with dead people. He *breathes* corpses. How could anyone not go mad after that?"

"They all live with the dead," Madame Zenon replies. "Many of our men will come home damaged or broken beyond repair."

"But you'd heal them if you could! You'd save them. Our land isn't just a farm. It's part of us, him and me. When he touches it, when he breathes the clean air, the corpses will leave him. I know they will. *Please* let me save him."

Madame Zenon sighs. "Because of your troubles your geese are not forfeit. But—"

She frowns at me as I let out a small cry. "You are guilty as charged. You intended to sell your flock for the highest price possible while others starve. However, you also believe your reasons are good. For that, we will pay you one hundred and eight francs for these birds, that's four hours' wages for each, except the gosling. You may keep that. This sum is for us a considerable sacrifice."

A fair price, no doubt.

But nowhere near enough to save La Mordue.

My knees give way. The factory spins, the benches and machines.

Swift hands soften the blow as I fall.

Thirty

There's a thudding in my ears as I come round. It grows louder: a clanging of metal on metal. I stare up at the corrugated ceiling, unable to make sense of my surroundings until Thérèse cries, "Wake up! Please! Get up now!" Her withered little face fills my vision.

"What?" I ask weakly.

"Police! They're breaking down the doors! Get up!"

I struggle to sit.

Madame Villeneuve is already hustling Madame Zenon into her office. Women are covering the window with gas masks and coats; others wait to block the door with a bench.

"Please, Madame Zenon," Thérèse calls after her. "Let her keep her geese! They'll take them! The police won't let us have them!"

Madame Zenon pauses.

"We have to go," Madame Villeneuve insists, pushing her forward. On the threshold, Madame Zenon glances back at me, then nods curtly to Thérèse. "Perhaps Émile—"

But there's a loud crash and the sound of splintering, and Madame Villeneuve pushes Madame Zenon into her office and slams the door.

Thérèse grabs my arm and tugs me to my feet. My legs are shaking, my vision blurred. I feel weak with shock. But I can't afford to be weak. Not now.

More clangs reverberate around the cavernous factory as we break open a gap in the furniture barricade. The geese are edgy and hard to control with all the noise. They hiss and huddle together.

"Why are the police breaking in?" I ask as we herd them into the gloom at the back of the factory.

"We're not allowed to occupy the factory. We're not even allowed to strike."

She pulls a tarpaulin off a machine and cold air flows out from a passage hidden behind it. As we stretch out our arms and funnel the geese towards this secret entrance, Marie-Gabrielle and her friends push past us.

Thérèse scowls at them, but they just laugh and run on.

When the geese are inside, we disguise the entrance with the tarpaulin again, then grope our way forward in the darkness, listening for danger.

In the blackness ahead I hear Marie-Gabrielle whisper, "We'll get you next time, goose girl."

"We could get her now," another girl mutters.

"I'll tell," Thérèse hisses. "Madame Zenon said she can go!"

"Creep," Marie-Gabrielle replies.

A greyish-orange light silhouettes the girls and the geese. Outside, a gas lamp barely penetrates the fog.

Marie-Gabrielle and her friends are huddled around a doorway, which opens onto an alley that runs between the backs of the factory sheds and the perimeter wall.

We listen for voices, but hear only dripping silence.

"I'm off," says Marie-Gabrielle.

"No," Thérèse whispers. "They'll search the yard if they see you. Let her go first."

But Marie-Gabrielle laughs, and the four girls slip into the night.

Thérèse shrugs an apology. "Put your cap on. They're looking for girls, not boys." She helps me tuck my hair out of sight, then we hug.

"Thank you for defending me," I say.

She giggles. "I've never done it before."

"You were brilliant. Really. You saved my life."

Her eyes shine.

Quickly, before I can change my mind, I pick up a gander without a mate and thrust him into her arms.

"For me? How lovely!" She holds him close and strokes his chest. He looks huge in her tiny arms. But then she kisses him and gives him back. "You keep him. The police will only take him – or Marie-Gabrielle."

"Why is she so mean?"

"It's just her way. She hates anyone who's got anything she hasn't."

We linger another moment, then I say, "I should go. Come with me?"

She shakes her head. "They know I'm a striker. You're safer without me. Ask at the wharves for Émile. They like Madame Zenon down there. If he's suspicious, say you've heard our foreman should be sent to the Front with a big white circle on his chest and another on the back of his head. He'll know we trust you then."

I laugh. "You don't like him much!"

"He's the worst!"

We kiss and hug again, then she says, "Don't be frightened of Émile."

"Why would I be?"

"You'll see."

The fog muffles the tread of my boots and the small sounds the geese make. I avoid the murky circles of light cast by the gas lamps in case there are police informers about and stick to the dark spaces in-between.

The geese are almost invisible – no more than shadows with pale white rumps. I have to prod the stragglers forward. Poor things, they're exhausted. I'll need to find them somewhere to sleep very soon.

A gantry looms overhead, then a crane. There's a slapping sound of water on wood, and the creaking of ropes.

When a curlew calls, plain and clear, Napoleon lifts his head. The wharves which Thérèse told me about must be on a river.

And if curlews are feeding there, it must have mudflats and marshes.

The geese will love that.

My heart leaps into my mouth. Mudflats and marshes? A river! I'll never get the geese out if they reach the water before me! But if I walk in front of them, I'll never spot any lost stragglers on this blind, foggy night.

I run past them and bring them to a halt, desperately trying to think up a plan.

I need some kind of pen, a shipping crate, perhaps. Then I could go and find this Émile and ask for his help. And if I can't find him? I'll have to go back, find that station again, and sneak the geese on board a Paris-bound train. Somehow.

As I dither, a lone figure appears, skirting the lamplight, like us. A night watchman, perhaps. I have to take a chance.

"I'm looking for Émile," I call out. "Do you know him?"

"Never 'eard of 'im."

The shape of the man merges again with the fog, and with a jolt I realize he hadn't been in the alleyway. We must be at the entrance to some wider, more open space. I'll never keep the geese together out there.

At a loss what to do, I sink down on my haunches.

Something cracks in my pocket: a fragment of Uncle Gustav's flat bread gone brittle and hard. The windmill and the heath seem like paradise compared to this! I tell myself off. Things could be so much worse. The geese are alive – and all mine – not stiff and cold like those poor frozen wild birds.

I scatter a handful of grain on the cobbles, hoping it will distract the geese from the tempting river sounds. Then I rest my back against the damp, mossy perimeter wall, stretch out my legs, and fetch out the last of the railway guard's lunch.

Amandine climbs onto my lap as I eat and tucks her beak under her wing. In seconds she's asleep. Half the flock settles down as well, but I know that if I nod off, the other half will be heading for the river in no time.

Another shape takes form in the fog, a tall figure in a long overcoat, seemingly with an outsized head. Napoleon hisses a warning. I stand up, my pulse quickening, any thoughts of sleep banished.

"You the one askin' about Émile?" the man asks.

"I am."

"Why d'you want 'im?"

"A friend said he might be able to help me."

"What friend?"

"Thérèse. She works in the gas mask factory."

I wave, pointlessly, into the fog.

"The factory's shut," he says. "They're on strike. You're lyin'."

"They occupied the factory. But the police just broke in."

I wonder if I should tell him that Thérèse helped me escape, but that might get her in trouble if this man is a police informer. I lick my lips, my mouth dry, unsure what to say next.

The man takes a step closer, near enough for me to make out a thick scarf wrapped around his head.

"So why's she strikin', this Thérèse?" he asks.

"They want more money."

"Everybody wants more money."

I think quickly. Thérèse said the dockworkers like Madame Zenon, so perhaps this man is one of them, not an informer. Maybe he's protecting Émile.

I say, "They want the money back that was stopped for the crèche. They don't think it's fair to have to pay for it."

"So you've talked to 'em. So have others – police informers and the like."

There's a challenge in his voice, as if this is a test to prove I'm a friend of the strikers – or a trick to discover if I'm their accomplice.

I chew my lip, wondering if it's an offence to say the foreman of the factory should be sent to the Front with a target on his back and another on his head.

Squaring my shoulders, I say, "How do I know you're not the informer?"

"Mebbe I am. Or mebbe you're a troublemaker what'll get himself sent to the Front."

He puts his head to one side.

Now I'm sure this is a test. He wants to know if I know

the tale about the foreman. Perhaps it's some kind of code between the strikers and dockers.

Crossing my fingers that I've judged him right, I step forward to meet him and take off my cap. I lift up my face so he can see I'm a girl and say, "Like that foreman, who should be sent to the Front with a white circle on his chest and another on the back of his head?"

At last he comes into the light. He takes off his scarf, revealing a scarred and brutally disfigured face. His nose and right eye are missing. He has no cheekbone on the right side, either, just cruelly distorted flesh.

I swallow a gasp of shock.

"You're Émile," I say, willing my voice to stay calm.

"And you know Madame Zenon."

He demands my full story and only drops his guard after I tell him Madame Zenon would have bought the geese if the police hadn't come.

"What did she offer?"

"Four francs for each of them."

"And you accepted?"

"I didn't have much choice."

He snorts a laugh, then looks at me closely. I try not to flinch.

"Warned you about me, did they?" He points at his face.

I shake my head. "Thérèse just said I shouldn't be frightened."

"Are you?"

"A bit." A raise my eyes until I'm looking straight at him. "What happened?"

"Shrapnel bomb. And yeah, I saw the shell comin'."

We fall silent a moment, but the geese are growing restless with the water so close. Soon he says, "Right. Let's get out of 'ere before them police come sniffin' around."

We herd the geese into the fog.

They're eager now, honking with excitement as we draw near the river. The water seethes and sloshes around wooden pilings and half-seen hulks. It's hard to keep them away from the edge. We stop beside a barge and stand either side of its ramp as the geese waddle off the dock and into the hold.

At one end is a warm, smoky cabin, lit by oil lamps, with a coal-fired stove, thick rugs and a wooden bunk built into the curve of the hull. To me it looks like heaven, a sanctuary. Words of gratitude fail me. I smile through tears and offer him my hand.

He looks at it.

"There's food in the cupboard an' crumbs for the geese. Take the bunk. I'll sleep in the wheelhouse. We'll talk again in the mornin'."

The slow throbbing of the engine wakes me and the slapping of water on the hull. Hours might have passed, or minutes or days. I'd been so deeply asleep I can't tell.

I lie still, picturing Uncle Gustav waiting for me, believing in me, trusting that I will find him.

Then I think of Émile, and his horror at watching that

shrapnel shell screaming towards him. Does he still see it in his dreams? A shiver runs through me, and a twinge of guilt: I've never really wondered before whether Father saw the missile that killed him.

Maybe that's why Mother wanted me to forgive him: not because of what he'd done to us, but because of the things he'd seen on the battlefield.

Poor Mother. She must have known how much I hated him. I never tried to hide it. Did she guess that part me hated her too, for not protecting Pascal from him? That I hated the idea of being like her – too weak to protect her children?

Another dark thought scurries into my head, a sad and foolish one. If I'm scared of growing up like her, maybe I'm frightened of growing up at all, and that's why I couldn't tell René I love him.

I sigh. If he were here now I'd tell him. I'd promise to wait for him too, and to be there for him always.

I lie still another short while, then climb out of the bunk and kneel on the planking. I close my eyes and bow my head, and put my hands together. I pray for Pascal and René, for Mother's forgiveness. For Uncle Gustav. Émile. Madame Zenon. Thérèse. The guard at the station. The soldiers, the strikers, the dead.

And I pray that one day I'll find it in my heart to forgive my father too.

Thirty-one

The daylight is full by the time I climb onto the deck and discover we're underway. The river is wide and turbulent, spanned by iron bridges. Wharves and warehouses rise out of the mist, and white birds fly alongside us. Running to the wheelhouse, I ask Émile where we are.

"On the Seine," he says, his eyes on the water ahead.

"Where are we going?"

"That depends."

"On what?"

"Where you want to go."

His eye flicks towards me, then he looks straight ahead. The clear morning light picks out his scars cruelly. They're yellowish white in places, red raw in others.

"I told you last night," I remind him. "I need to get to Paris, the Gare d'Orléans. My uncle's waiting for me."

Émile grunts but says nothing more until we reach

the next bridge. Then he points out a channel marker and names the canal that's joining the river, and the different gulls keeping pace with us. On the right-hand bank tall buildings appear – seven, eight, nine stories high. I stare at them, amazed.

"Is this Paris?"

He nods.

"Oh, Émile! Thank you! Thank you!"

I run from side to side in the wheelhouse, gasping at every new sight. The river is busy with barges, and the quays bustle with people and horse-drawn cabs.

Horses! I haven't seen one in ages. I hurry onto the deck and lean against the rail, shouting out to Émile whenever I see some new and marvellous thing.

Soon a fantastical church appears underneath the arches of an ornate stone bridge. It has the most delicate filigree buttresses I've ever seen, carved stonework that glows in the first glimmering of winter sunshine, and a stark black spire that pierces the sky.

"How beautiful!" I cry. "What church is it?"

"The cathedral of Notre Dame – where the hunchback lived."

Émile smiles grimly and the left-hand side of his face almost seems handsome. Somehow that makes the broken side look worse – one half of him a mockery of the other. And to think, he'll live like that for the rest of his life. My heart aches for him.

"Will we see the Eiffel Tower?" I ask, forcing

myself to sound happy again.

"Stay on board an' you will." Something in his voice makes me look at him more closely. His one good eye meets my gaze. "Stay on board as long as you like," he adds quietly.

"But ... I–I can't. My brother. I told you."

He shrugs. "So earn the money to save 'is farm. There's plenty o' work on the river. Good wages. I need a deck hand, someone to go ashore. I'm sick of people starin'."

"Oh, Émile."

I want so much to help him, to repay my debt to him. But this? It's impossible.

He slows the barge, then we come to a stop and wait for another boat to manoeuvre through the highest central arch of the bridge. Gulls wheel above us, crying noisily.

"I've always got coal an' food aboard," Émile goes on. "You'd be free to come an' go. Them wages would be yours, mind. Not your brother's or your father's or husband's. An' if the Germans take Paris, we'll sail to Spain. England, if you like. It's all the same to me."

The hope is clear in his voice, and I realize now how lonely he must be – generous, too. Work can't be easy to come by, even in Paris.

"Won't ever be your farm," he adds quietly when I don't reply. "Always his. Forever an' ever."

"I know. And thank you for the offer. But..." I shrug.

He shakes his head. "Worth the sacrifice, is he? Your brother?"

"He is! Really, he is!"

"An' what if he don't come home? Many won't."

"But he will. I know it. He *must*."

"Must?" Émile lets out a short, bitter laugh. "This war won't end till the last soldier's dead."

I look away, refusing to believe him, knowing my certainty might be foolish, but despair would be far, far worse.

"I'm very sorry," I say, "but my uncle is waiting. He'll be worried. Mother too. Will you let me off, please? I have to find the Gare d'Orléans."

Émile grunts. "Go for'ard, then. Grab a rope. That's the station over there."

From the river, the Gare d'Orléans looks like a long, low factory. It's an ugly, dirty building, lined along the nearest side with multiple arches.

The stink of the city hits me as soon as we've moored by the quay and the pungent smoke from the barge's engine has drifted away. It's replaced by fish odours and dog mess, exhaust fumes and rotting cabbages.

The geese blink at the daylight when Émile opens the hatch. They ruffle their feathers and honk at him, refusing to leave the comfortable warmth of the hold.

Or perhaps they like its quiet and safety.

I don't blame them. I feel anxious about leaving the barge too, but promise myself everything will be all right once I've found Uncle Gustav.

"Where you meetin' this uncle of yours?" Émile calls

down as I round up the last reluctant birds from their dark hiding places.

"Under something, but I don't know what."

"That'll be the clock. People always meet under the clock."

I drive the geese up the ramp to find Émile at the top with his scarf wrapped round his head. "Reckoned you might need a hand with them geese."

Deeply grateful, I touch his arm and smile.

Trams rattle along the street that divides the quay from the station, their noise joining the *clip-clop* of horse-drawn cabs, the shouts of the cabbies and the hubbub of people crowded together, hurrying about their business.

Alarmed by the city's bustle, the geese become skittish and headstrong, waddling wherever they will and hissing at everything. Émile and I have to circle them like a pair of sheep dogs to keep them together and moving in a straight line.

As Émile holds up the traffic so we can cross the road, a little boy in a pretend officer's uniform points at us and squeals. Émile flinches, but it's the geese the boy is excited about.

Even so, the boy's nursemaid peers at his face, her pretty mouth falling open and her eyes growing wide. Émile adjusts his scarf to cover his missing nose, but as we press on – his shoulders hunched and his head down – people still stare or glance back over their shoulders.

It doesn't help that the geese are making a spectacle

of themselves, squawking and waggling their heads. They honk back whenever a vehicle sounds its horn. I'd give anything to be able to quieten them down or slip into a backstreet, away from prying eyes.

We turn towards the station. A man is standing by a pillar at the entrance wearing nothing but a vest and trousers, shaking uncontrollably. He must be freezing cold.

I wonder why he doesn't have a jacket or coat, but when I turn to ask Émile, he just says, "Let 'im be. Walk on by."

"Why? What's wrong with him?"

"The war. What else?"

"But he's not injured…"

Émile puts a finger to his lips. "He's seen more than a man can bear. Poor soul."

I look at the man's vacant eyes and his mouth fixed in an expression of pain. Yet his jaw is square and his shoulders broad. He must have been strong. Once.

"There's worse than 'im locked up in hospitals where none can see 'em," Émile adds with a sigh.

A few coins have been left at the man's feet, though I notice people don't stare at him as they do with Émile. It's as if they don't want to see what's obvious, yet the half-hidden, half-imagined horrors of Émile's face invite curiosity.

We herd the geese into a square outside the station building, looked down upon by statues of graces and queens, their pedestals built into the Gare d'Orléans' grand stone façade.

The square is teeming with porters, soldiers, beggars, tramps, elderly ladies and gentlemen, and women holding their children's hands. Dirty urchins dodge through the crowd, while next to the station are more cabs. More horses. A stationary omnibus.

I scan the buildings for a clock, suddenly afraid that I won't find Uncle Gustav after all, that he's given up waiting and gone, and that I'll be left alone again, hopeless and helpless…

"News from the Front! Get the latest here!" a newspaper vendor shouts in my ear, bringing me back to the present. The geese start up their shrieking again.

"We'll not get 'em through this lot," Émile says, frowning at the crowd. "We need to pen 'em in somewhere. I'll guard 'em for a bit while you take a look for your uncle."

We chivvy the flock around the edge of the square.

In a quiet spot under one of the arches I saw from the river, we build them a makeshift pen out of luggage trolleys left there by porters and passengers. Then, with butterflies in my stomach, I hurry back to the front of the building in search of the clock.

It's on the very top of the grandest part of the main façade. Beneath it soldiers kiss their sweethearts, or maybe they're husbands and wives. Other people read newspapers while they wait, or scan each face that goes by.

I stay for ten minutes, add another five, then hurry back to Émile and tell him, "I'm sure he'll be here soon. Could you wait a little longer?"

He grunts and lifts his chin, and I run back to the clock.

Couples climb into cabs. Cabbies whip up their horses. I grow sad watching them, wondering why they requisitioned our horses when Paris has plenty to spare.

Every time I run back and forth, I tell myself this time Uncle Gustav *will* be there. He has to be! Everything will be all right. He's never let me down before.

But when it's just more couples, or businessmen in suits, or some fine lady waving to her friend from a cab, my heart breaks a little more – until I tell myself, *next time. Don't worry. Be patient.*

At last Émile says he has to go or they'll fine him for mooring the barge for so long without the proper permit. I thank him with all my heart, trying to hide the quaver in my voice.

Émile considers me for a while, his broken face grave. I expect him to ask me to come back with him, or offer me another job. I'm glad when he doesn't. I don't know if I would have had the courage to refuse him twice.

"You're certain he'll come?" he asks me finally.

"I have to be."

Otherwise what's left? Blind faith is all I have to keep me going, no matter how wilful or foolish.

"Right. Well, that's me off, then."

"Goodbye," I say. "God bless."

I watch him walk away, then continue to run between the geese and the clock, over and over, not thinking or hoping or dreaming, refusing to imagine Pascal shaking uncontrollably or René with half his face spread across a battlefield, just clinging onto my reckless certainty until...

"Angélique! Ma petite!"

I stop running. "Uncle Gustav." A whimper.

A great, racking sob heaves out of me. I stand in the middle of the crowd, weeping, my arms outstretched, incapable of taking another step, as he runs towards me, tears of relief streaming down his cheeks, his arms open wide like mine.

Thirty-two

We hold each other for the longest time, spilling out our stories in no particular order.

Uncle Gustav has been in Paris for twenty-four hours, snatching a night's sleep in a cheap, flea-ridden working man's hostel and meeting every train coming from the direction of Monville.

"I knew you'd find me," I tell him. "I knew we'd find each other."

He cups my face in his hands, eyes shining with tears. Then, smiling his dear, familiar smile, he says, "Look what I made while I was waiting. It'll help us get the geese across Paris." He shows me a long piece of plaited string, with gaps woven into it.

"They're collars. See? Try one on Amandine."

Gently, I lift her up, then slip her head and neck through the first hole, but she just slips right out again.

"Oh, what a shame! I made the holes too big," he says.

"They might fit the adults. Let's see."

Amandine's mother allows me to put a collar on her, but none of the others will. They're still too agitated.

"Never mind," I say. "We'll manage."

Uncle Gustav puts his arms around me, draws me close one more time, and kisses my hair.

We set off for the Gare du Nord with Amandine and me in front and Uncle Gustav behind.

The geese bunch together, hissing and snapping at passers-by like one creature with many writhing heads, like the picture of the Gorgon I once saw in a school book.

The pavement on the bridge over the Seine is too narrow for them to walk together, so we take to the road. Motor cars honk at us; cabbies shout. An omnibus on the Boulevard Bourdon almost runs us down.

"Let's try the back streets," Uncle Gustav suggests.

We turn into a narrow road behind the Place de la Bastille, where ancient high-walled houses surround dark courtyards locked behind old iron gates.

When horses pass close by I breathe in their scents: the leathery tack and rich, warm dung. It's been such a long time.

In poorer streets we're plagued by urchins, but just around a corner a lady in a coquettish hat smiles at us. Officers point at us from cabs, and tired soldiers on leave follow us with dull gazes, then wander on aimlessly.

The geese become footsore from hours waddling on hard pavements. We rest them in a tiny garden outside a quiet church while we shelter from the cold under its pillared portico.

Uncle Gustav scatters grain for the geese and produces a stale brioche for us to share, then promptly falls asleep. The flock settles too, grey cushions in the fading afternoon light.

When Uncle Gustav wakes, it takes ages to get the geese going again and I have to carry Amandine.

At dusk, lamplighters appear with long tapers and ladders. Soon orange globes glow on every street, the light softened by the evening mists. Shop windows brighten too, into vivid pictures of plenty.

Through one window I see a sumptuous, dark-panelled world of white tablecloths and velvet plum cushions, where couples sit contentedly, reading their menus like good books.

"Maybe we could sell the geese to a fancy restaurant," I say.

"No, no. They'd drive too hard a bargain."

I glance at him, thinking back, and ask, "Uncle, is it wrong to drive too hard a bargain? You know, when people are hungry?"

He smiles. "It's the way of the world. We didn't make the rules."

"But we are tricking the officers in a way."

"Officers like them?"

He nods towards a crowded brasserie, a fairyland of glass and mirrors sparkling beneath a giant chandelier, where uniformed officers stand laughing by a white marble counter.

"Those fellows are going to pay more for their supper tonight than we'll ever get for a goose."

Stopping, I press my nose to the window, my eyes growing hungrier than my belly.

A young woman dressed in creamy chiffon is telling the officers a story, her head dipping and bobbing, her hands waving prettily. A beautiful blonde lady in blue silk listens too, smiling coolly. A waitress brings her oysters on a silver platter.

"Will we eat oysters one day?" I ask.

"And *pot au feu* and *fois gras*. Come on. I know a little place near the Place de Valenciennes."

The place is a brazier in a doorway, where a one-legged vendor sells us baked potatoes and bags of roasted chestnuts. We warm ourselves on his coals as we eat, watching the geese splashing in a fountain across the way.

Their antics draw a crowd of soldiers and women in feathered hats, and ragged boys who point and laugh. After a while we walk over to see what's happening.

Poor Amandine is trapped by the fountain's slippery sides. She's flapping and squeaking, but the boys won't let her out.

Uncle Gustav chases them off, shaking his fists, while I lift her out and dry her.

She shivers in my arms, and when I try to set her down she's too tired to stand, so I tuck her inside my jacket as we set off again.

The Gare du Nord is a sombre palace topped by imposing statues. The grand square in front of it is filled with soldiers wearing every kind of uniform imaginable.

"Where do they all come from?" I ask.

"The four corners of the earth, ma petite."

There's urgency in the air, a sort of ordered chaos in their marching feet. Their horses whinny above the din of traffic. Alarmed, the geese refuse to go up the steps until prodded and cajoled.

Inside, the smoke-filled hall is immense, the roaring of voices like the wind in trees. The geese hiss and stretch their necks, and panic at the screech of a whistle. We have to ask soldiers and elderly porters to help us herd them to a quieter platform at the end of the concourse, where they hunker down behind crates and won't come out.

"I'll stay with them," I tell Uncle Gustav.

He hesitates. "You won't go without me, will you?"

I smile and then kiss him. "Horses couldn't drag me away. I promise."

As he hurries off to find the ticket office I give the geese a handful of grain, then sit with my back against a pillar, watching the comings and goings.

The sense of an ending settles on me. This time tomorrow we'll be in Frévent. I might even have met

General Foch and asked him about Pascal. And sold him Napoleon...

I shake the picture from my head — the guilt of that betrayal is too much to face just yet — and stroke Amandine on my lap.

She's floppy and weak, exhausted by the long days, the cold and teasing. If René could see us now, what kind of a mother to our gosling would he think me?

Wagons shunt along the next-door track and disgorge their cargo of soldiers. Some are dark-skinned, with turbans, black beards and fierce dark eyes. Others are well-built and tanned, in wide-brimmed hats, and sing lustily in a foreign tongue.

When they're gone, a column of puny, pasty-faced men marches up the platform in ill-fitting uniforms and out-sized boots. They fall out into groups and light cigarettes while they wait, or sit on the wagon steps and write letters on their knees.

Their voices aren't those of Frenchmen either.

I wonder who they are. Who loves and misses them?

At last Uncle Gustav comes back, followed by a railway official in gold-rimmed spectacles, carrying a heavy ledger. He counts the geese twice — even though I tell him we have twenty-eight — then writes something down and snaps the ledger shut.

"This is most irregular," he says, handing our Requisition chit back to Uncle Gustav.

"What's irregular?" I ask when he's gone.

"He'd never seen a chit like ours before. Now, which one is our platform?"

The geese are tired and truculent, and filthy with soot. Even when we put down a trail of grain, they refuse to stand up.

"We could carry them," I suggest, but Uncle Gustav gives Napoleon a doubtful look and hurries off to find a handcart. We put Amandine's mother on it first, then wait for Napoleon to lumber to his feet.

Our platform is crowded with French soldiers weighed down by bedrolls and backpacks, and boxes strapped to their belts. Their rifles are stacked like wigwams all along the platform. We manoeuvre the cart between them until we find an empty space to wait.

Glancing back, I notice the railway official talking with a tall, slim officer who leans heavily on a highly polished wooden cane. The official seems to be pointing us out. I tug on Uncle Gustav's sleeve.

"Oh, dear. What now?" He sighs as the officer limps towards us. "Let me handle this, would you, ma petite?"

"Monsieur," the officer calls. "You have supplies for General Foch?"

"We have. Is there a problem?"

"There is if you expect to find him at Frévent."

Uncle Gustav stiffens. "But I saw his camp from the train myself when I came south."

"If you did, monsieur, you should keep it to yourself.

Military locations are not a matter for public discussion. That goes for you too, lad," the officer adds to me. "Paris is a nest of spies." He turns to Uncle Gustav again. "You have a Requisition chit?"

Uncle Gustav hands over our piece of paper. Frowning, the officer reads it.

"And who is Mademoiselle Lacroix?"

I step forward. The officer raises an eyebrow, but only says, "And these geese belong to you?"

"To my brother, monsieur, Pascal Lacroix, but he's serving at the Front. I'm hoping General Foch will tell me where he is."

"And why would he do that, mademoiselle?"

"My brother is one of his men. I think he's on the Somme."

The officer's laugh is brief and bitter. "Have you *any* idea how many men are serving on the Somme?"

"No, monsieur, I don't."

He sighs and shakes his head. "And if His Excellency had directed you to your brother's regiment, what then, mademoiselle?"

I feel my cheeks redden. What right has he to question me? I know it was a forlorn hope that Pascal would actually be in the general's camp, but was it so foolish to believe I might find out where he is and get to see him that way?

This war is so much bigger than I'd ever dreamed.

Mustering what dignity I can, I say, "I was going to give him a goose for his Christmas dinner, monsieur.

I don't see why he should go hungry when he owns the finest geese in France."

The officer looks at the bedraggled geese, then at me, then he shuts his eyes as if in pain. He rubs them and I see how tired he is, and how young. He can't be much older than Pascal.

I look at Uncle Gustav, who shrugs. We wait for the officer to speak. At last he draws a long, slow breath and opens his eyes again.

"By rights I shouldn't tell you this," he says, "so don't spread it about. There's no point looking for your brother at Frévent, mademoiselle. The Battle of the Somme is over. We won – apparently. Although how anyone could win that bloody fiasco is beyond me. And now the *Grand Quartier Général* has sent His Excellency General Foch south. It seems he's to be blamed for the entire damn mess. Ridiculous, if you ask my opinion. But there it is. No more comprehensible than the rest of this abominable war."

"So where's my brother now?" I ask.

"God alone knows, mademoiselle. And I doubt very much if even the Almighty knows for sure."

Thirty-three

I stare at him, bewildered. If neither General Foch nor Pascal is at Frévent, where do we go next?

A small voice inside me whispers, *Turn around. Go home.*

I could be with Mother when the bailiffs come. Monsieur Lamy might take us in. He'd let us hide the geese in his allotment...

But I drive the thought away. We've come too far to give up. There must be other camps, other rich officers.

Smoke billows along the platform as a belching locomotive shunts a chain of wagons up the track. The moment they stop, soldiers throw their kit aboard and climb in after it.

The officer hands our chit back to Uncle Gustav.

"Monsieur. Mademoiselle. Good luck."

With a touch of his cap, he limps off, waving the railway official away.

Uncle Gustav runs a hand over his weary face. His skin is drained of colour. His eyes look dazed.

I touch his arm. "Where will we go now?"

He rubs his face again, leaving a smear of soot across his cheek. Then he puffs out his cheeks and blows out slowly.

"We could try the Gard de l'Est. That's nearer to our sector."

"Would the geese have to walk?"

He glances at them, squashed together, heads drooping, eyes dull.

"Well… There's Amiens or the Paris markets," he says.

"Don't we have to be nearer the Front?"

He blinks at me, seeming older than his years, as if the news about General Foch has snuffed out a spark in him. "We can't just blunder about, ma petite. I'm sorry. I don't know what to do."

But I do.

I have to get him home – his home, not mine. He needs rest and food. A proper bed. I've dragged him across France long enough.

Taking his hand, I say, "There's a camp at Étaples. A British camp, you said. Couldn't we get there from here?"

His bloodshot eyes widen at the thought of home. "We'd have to change trains, but other than that…" His face falls again. "But we can't go into the camp. You need special permits."

"There'll be a Christmas market. The officers will come to that."

"It's not a very big market."

"All the same.

"They're British, ma petite, and we don't speak English."

"Once the geese are rested, they'll speak for themselves."

Still he shakes his head. "The chit isn't valid anymore. And even if we had the money to pay for our tickets, they won't let us on a military train."

Glancing around, I lean forward. "Who's to say General Foch didn't go to Étaples if his location is secret? If anyone asks, we'll say we heard he went there to talk to the British. They were on the Somme as well, weren't they?"

Uncle Gustav blinks at me again. Then a sad smile spreads across his face. "Yes, they were, ma petite. Yes, they were."

The cattle stall in our wagon is slippery with frozen muck. There's no straw to keep the geese warm, and they huddle together wretchedly.

Uncle Gustav empties the last of the grain from his pockets while I break the ice in their water trough and make sure they're feeding. Then we sit side by side against a slatted wall and I cradle Amandine's limp little body close to me.

Her feathers feel cold and damp.

More soldiers climb aboard: young men, grey-beards and everything between. Fat men and thin, some with broad shoulders, others have sunken chests. But what I notice most in the flare of their matches, as they light pipes and cigarettes, is their eyes. They all look strangely blind, as if they can't see the dirty wagon we're in, just things far away.

With a shudder, I realize why. These men are going to war. Right now. Today. This train will take them to the Front and to the horrors I will only ever read about.

My heart bleeds for them.

Is this how Pascal looks before a battle? Is René on a train somewhere, facing the unknown?

More soldiers clamber in until we're jammed together like meat on a butcher's cart. I can't help staring at them, these ordinary, silent men who will soon see the unimaginable and do such terrible things.

I hold Amandine closer, but her head flops off my shoulder and her bones feel fragile beneath her feathers. A sickness forms in the pit of my stomach, a fear I refuse to name.

"Would you like me to hold her for you?" Uncle Gustav asks quietly.

"No. Thank you. I'll keep her."

He puts his arm around my shoulder, and I rest my head against him, my eyes closing of their own accord. At last the door rolls shut. The locomotive whistles and the wagons rock slowly out of the Gare du Nord.

"Abbeville! Abbeville! All change at Abbeville!"

The voice of the guard seems to come from the depths of a well. Or perhaps I've sunk into the blackest of places, where the air is so cold that my lungs have turned to ice.

"Ma petite?" Uncle Gustav shakes my arm.

I don't want to wake up. I don't want to remember where we are or where we're going, or endure the pain of forcing my frozen limbs to work again.

"We have to change trains, ma petite."

The door is open, the night crowded with men and mules, carts and boxes, stacked rifles and crates of barbed wire. Another locomotive grumbles past, pulling a seemingly endless chain of wagons.

Suddenly panic grips me. I sit up and look around wildly.

"Uncle Gustav! Where's Amandine?"

At once, his arms are around me and he's holding me tight.

"Hush, ma petite. It was for the best."

"What was?"

"She was suffering."

For a second I stare at him, unable to comprehend. Then, *"Nooo!"*

I bury my face against him, tears streaming down my face, wracked by guilt. I brought her into this world just to let her die out here in the dark and cold. She had so little time.

"I didn't help her," I sob. "I didn't save her."

"There was nothing you could have done. She was too young. She didn't have the strength to fight. Come, dry your eyes. Quickly, now. We have to change trains."

He holds me another moment, then kisses my forehead and pushes me gently away.

Trembling, weeping, I stroke each goose as I pass them down to him. Napoleon pecks my hand so hard it bleeds, but I don't care. I just want to feel their warm, living bodies.

I ache to hold Amandine one last time and take her home with me.

As we shiver on the platform, keeping watch over the flock, I try telling myself it's wrong to mourn one little gosling when so many men are going to war. But I can't help it. Truly I can't. She was my darling, my responsibility, and I didn't even know she was dying.

Wiping my eyes at last, I count the geese. Then count them again.

Twenty-six.

I don't want to know where the missing goose has gone. Without Amandine, the world already seems too cruel.

"Not long now," Uncle Gustav says when he comes back from the ticket office. He hugs and kisses me and I lean against him briefly, still wondering why, *why* my gosling had to die.

Was she sick? Didn't I feed her properly? Didn't I love her enough? As I fret, other trains come and go, offloading soldiers or taking them aboard, a constant ebb and flow.

Sometimes a song breaks out, a choir in the bitter night, but as soon as it's over the men become sullen again or sad – or afflicted by that same blindness I saw at the Gare du Nord.

Just once a ragged cheer rises as an enormous locomotive grinds through the station, shaking the platform with the weight of its load. One of its wagons is a solid black shape – a colossal cannon with a gigantic barrel aimed at the sky.

"They call those the Devil's Guns," Uncle Gustav says.

"I see it," I reply, but nothing tonight could possibly make me cheer.

At last our train arrives. I try to bury my grief for Amandine and the other goose, and concentrate on the needs of the living.

We wait as horses are led aboard our wagon, and three squealing pigs. The geese have to share a stall with them. A squad of soldiers climbs in after us – British, Uncle Gustav says, on their way to the infantry camp in Étaples.

As the train crawls through flat countryside, a young man slides the door open, and I stand beside him, looking out. The air is tainted with soot, but I'm used to that now. We watch silver pools sliding by and wild marsh grasses rippling.

All of a sudden an impulse seizes me. Why not set the geese free? Let them live? If only they could fly… But I force myself to imagine Pascal and Mother together by the kitchen fire, and step back from the door.

We clank into a siding and stop. Everyone falls quiet as the vast, icy stillness of the night enters the wagon.

The geese lift their heads. Can they sense the water and the wilderness?

I'm surprised when Uncle Gustav takes my hand and says, "Don't be afraid, ma petite. Sound carries a long way at night."

I'm about to ask what he means when lightning flickers in the east, flashing distantly again and again. Minutes later I hear the first thud of thunder.

Except that it isn't thunder. Or lightning. I can tell from the pain in Uncle Gustav's eyes.

"Is that the Front?" I whisper.

He nods. "Heavy artillery. You can feel the vibrations when they fire the really big guns."

Shocked, I watch and listen. Are those our shells raining down or theirs? Does it matter? The suffering either way must be just as great.

Soldiers climb out of wagons all along the track. They stand and stare. I join them despite the biting wind that freezes my tears to my face.

Quietly, Uncle Gustav gets down too, and lays another limp goose on the ground.

I don't know how long we stay there, how many hours the sky glimmers and the dreadful rumbling rolls across the land.

Outside, I'm numb. Inside, I burn with pity – for Pascal and René, for the men who stand beside me, for the living and the dead.

For Father, too.

At last a bugle sounds and the soldiers move as if waking from a trance. Uncle Gustav and I climb aboard, and the train heaves forward.

We enter Étaples at dawn. In silence.

Thirty-four

In the station, as I pass the geese down to Uncle Gustav, I keep thinking I've forgotten something and turn to search the wagon. But then I remember: I've lost Amandine.

The shame of it is I do the same thing over and over, glancing behind me or stopping to think, as if part of me can't believe I'll never see her again.

The other geese peck listlessly at the gritty snow piled against a fence, or preen half-heartedly as we wait for the horses and pigs to be unloaded and the men to march away.

On a hill above the station, giant white tents heave and strain in the wind. Long wooden huts stand shoulder to shoulder with them, and rank upon rank of smaller tents.

"The British infantry camp," Uncle Gustav says. It dwarfs the station, a canvas and wood city rising to the skyline. "And that's where they bring the injured."

He points under the arches of a tall, soot-blackened

bridge, but all I can see is a cat's-cradle of crossing tracks.

"Can't they send the injured home to be near their families?" I ask.

"Britain's Empire reaches halfway round the world, ma petite."

"And they come all that way to fight for France?"

The thought makes me proud and grateful, but also homesick and sad. As the last soldiers disappear, I stand for a moment, looking at the camp.

"Could we go, perhaps, ma petite?"

He rubs his arms and stamps his feet. He looks dog-tired as well as filthy and freezing cold.

"I'm sorry, yes. Are you all right?"

He glances at me with red eyes and manages a weary smile.

We have to poke and prod the geese to their feet. They look dreadful too, their eyes glazed with tiredness and their feathers matted with muck and soot.

"We'll all feel better once we're rested," I say, as the geese hobble out of the station.

The street outside is slippery with slushy snow. It's filled with British soldiers, their horses and trucks. Baker's boys on bicycles weave among them.

"That's the officers' canteen," Uncle Gustav says, pointing to the ground floor café of the railway hotel on the other side of the road. I crane to see the men I've put my trust in, but they just look like ordinary soldiers to me.

"Are they *very* rich?" I ask.

Uncle Gustav shakes his head. "The rich rent villas by the sea. You'll see them later in town." He rubs his arms again and blows into hands.

The geese have found a patch of ground where blades of grass stick up through the snow. They're tearing them out by the roots, all except one elderly gander who is lying down, too tired even to tuck away his beak.

"How long till the Christmas market?" I ask sadly.

"What day is it today?"

"Thursday, I think."

He stares at me with troubled eyes. "Are you sure?"

"I think so. Why?"

"We've only got until tomorrow, then."

"Tomorrow?"

We look down at the famished, filthy, exhausted geese, and without another word shoo them off the grass into the teeth of the icy east wind.

Grit from the railway peppers our faces. The geese put their heads down, slipping and sliding on every patch of ice. The elderly gander tumbles over and I have to help him up. At least we're going downhill, following the road as it sweeps in a wide arc inside the curve of the railway tracks.

"Is your farm far?" I ask Uncle Gustav.

He shakes his head. "A kilometre. No more."

Soon both road and rail bend right, and the terraced houses give way to turnip fields and allotments, thatched cottages and chicken sheds. An embankment rises on the left, hiding the railway tracks and sheltering us from the wind.

"That's better," I say.

Uncle Gustav nods.

There are more local people here, and fewer soldiers. We could be in a country town – until another train thunders along the embankment, its whistle shrieking.

We turn right again, into a rutted track between snow-capped, mossy walls. The lane ends by a large church, which stands alone on a mound. In front of the church is a duck pond, frozen solid, but Napoleon still honks in excitement, scenting the water underneath.

He stumbles forwards, then launches himself onto the ice, sending a flock of gulls skyward. They rise, crying, on pure white wings.

The other geese totter after him, skating clumsily until their weight cracks the ice. They splash in the shallows, dipping their heads and flapping their wings.

My eyes sting. If only Amandine were here...

I turn to Uncle Gustav, but he's watching the elderly gander standing alone on the bank.

"He's ill, isn't he?" I say. "Like the other geese were, the ones who died."

"I don't think so, ma petite. They were just tired. I know I am!"

I take his hand as we watch Napoleon waddling across the ice into the middle of the pond, honking loudly, lord of his new domain.

When he flaps his wings, pieces of ice skim away across the surface, making eerie echoing sounds, and the gulls rise again screaming.

Twenty-five. Just twenty-five of my beautiful birds have reached journey's end. I love them now more than ever, and hate the idea of our parting. It had seemed such a simple decision to sell them to save the farm. But now...

I think about Amandine and the other birds we left beside the tracks, and the wild geese on the heath by the windmill. Had those dead birds been sick? Did our geese catch some infection from them? But then I remember Amandine hadn't mixed with the wild geese, so she couldn't have caught anything. Uncle Gustav must be right: it's just been too long a journey.

He coughs, then stoops stiffly to pick up the elderly gander. "Let's get this fellow indoors," he says, "and then find your aunt. She'll be so pleased to see you."

Aunt Mathilde. I'd forgotten about her. I shake my head.

"You go. I'll stay with the geese."

I don't want to miss their last precious moments of freedom.

Uncle Gustav returns a few minutes later with a sack of grain to tempt the geese out of the pond – although we have to throw chunks of ice at Napoleon before he'll oblige – and also the news that Aunt Mathilde isn't at home.

I smother a sigh of relief.

I can't remember why I never liked her. It began when I was little, I think. But it's been such a long time since I've seen her, I can't recall her face — apart from her stubbly chin, which scratched whenever she kissed us.

Putting that memory out of my mind, I lead the geese around one final corner to Uncle Gustav's farm.

The house is squat and white-washed, separated from his snow-covered yard by a muddy lane. We coax the geese into a long, stone barn that sits at the back of the yard.

At one end are three small wooden stalls, kept warm by a deep thatch of sweet-smelling hay stored in the loft above. We divide the geese into three groups of eight and lure them into the stalls with grain.

They settle at once, preening and murmuring to one another through the partition walls.

"Where's the old gander?" I ask. "Shouldn't he be here with them?"

Uncle Gustav puts a hand on my shoulder and says nothing.

I look at him for a moment. Then, "No! Not him as well?"

"It was the kindest thing. He was suffering."

I nod. He's right. But I still can't bear it. I turn away, a lump swelling in my throat. That gander was the gentlest of creatures. I'd known him all my life.

"Go to the house, ma petite. Your aunt will be there soon. She'll make you something to eat."

I shake my head. "The geese need water."

He sighs. "The pump's outside."

It's frozen solid. We push the handle and jerk it. We hit it with a lump of wood. Still it refuses to budge. "Ice in the cylinder," Uncle Gustav says gloomily. "We'll have to melt it."

We return to the barn.

At the farthest end from the hayloft are a small forge, a large coal bunker, an anvil, a row of hammers hung on nails and a little pot-bellied stove.

Uncle Gustav lights the stove, puts on a cast iron kettle, then draws up two rickety chairs. The stove's heat soon chases the pallor from his cheeks, but I notice he's shivering.

"Why don't you go to the house?" I say. "I'm sure I can manage the pump."

"Let me show you, just this once," he replies, but then a puff of smoke from the stove sets him coughing and he can't seem to stop.

Back in the yard, I'm trickling hot water from the kettle over the spout of the pump while Uncle Gustav jiggles the handle free, when I hear the click of a latch.

Uncle Gustav looks up – and a smile breaks out on his face. "Mathilde! *Ma chère!* You're home!" He hurries across the yard to embrace her.

I take a moment to prepare, then stand and turn to face her.

Only her outline is visible behind Uncle Gustav. Wide hips. Big arms. A thick woollen shawl over a dark brown dress. Her raw, red hands are around his waist – hands that used to scrub Pascal and me behind the ears with a stiff horse brush.

I remember that much about her now. How she hated dirt…

I look down at my muck-stained trousers and filthy boots, at the grime ingrained under my fingernails. I smell the stink of our journey rising off Pascal's jacket.

Ah, well. I paste a smile on my face.

Uncle Gustav turns around, beaming. "And look who's come to visit, *ma chère*." As he steps aside, I put out my hand.

Then stop dead, my heart thudding. My hand drops. My jaw too. It's like I've seen a ghost. Aunt Mathilde is the spitting image of Father.

Thirty-five

How could I have forgotten that Aunt Mathilde is our blood relative, not Uncle Gustav? She's Father's older sister. Stouter than him, and shorter, but otherwise horribly alike.

"Pascal? Is that you?" She squints at me short-sightedly. "Where's your uniform?"

"It's me, Aunt Mathilde. Angélique."

I take off my cap to show her my face, and her eyes grow round with astonishment.

"But you're wearing boys' clothes?"

"Yes." I shrug. "I'm so glad to see you, Auntie."

"Likewise." She frowns, then turns to Uncle Gustav. "What's going on? Why's she here?"

Quickly he explains about the Requisition and the geese, but makes no mention of Father's drunken gambling or his debts.

Aunt Mathilde looks me up and down while he's talking, and when he's done she grunts as if she suspects there's more to the tale than he's telling.

"You'd best come in," she says. "You'll be hungry, no doubt, as well as in want of a bath." Then she strides out of the yard without a backward glance.

Uncle Gustav puts a comforting arm around my shoulders.

"Off you go, ma petite. You and Mathilde have such a lot to talk about. Really, you do."

"But the pump…"

I appeal to him with my eyes. I've got nothing to say to her. Less than nothing. The thought of being alone with her fills me with dread.

He kisses my forehead, then squeezes my shoulder.

"Don't worry if she seems a bit fierce. She's just surprised to see us. That's my fault. I should have written to warn her."

And with that, he gently pushes me away.

Aunt Mathilde is waiting for me in the hall, arms folded, her broad shoulders filling the narrow passage. It's cluttered with boot racks, coat pegs, a hat stand and a receptacle for umbrellas. There's a small table too, with a vase of china flowers on it.

Nailed to a beam above her head is an embroidered sign on a framed piece of silk. The words are sewn in rose and lilac thread: *Cleanliness is next to godliness.*

"I–I'm sorry," I say, glancing down at my clothes.

"Can't be helped."

She watches me peel off Pascal's jacket and hang it on a peg. I unlace his boots and make room for them on the boot rack. With a sniff of satisfaction, she steps out of her clogs and fidgets her swollen feet into fluffy sheepskin slippers. My sweaty socks leave footprints on her polished tiled floor as I follow her into the kitchen.

A cold, white light pours through a high window, bouncing off pots and pans, sharp knives and copper ladles. In an alcove, a black cast iron range radiates heat; it draws out the ripeness of my clothes.

Aunt Mathilde sniffs again.

"You can fetch the bathtub in here," she says, "then wash your clothes through there." She nods to a low, arched doorway. "Now let's see about a dress."

She leads me across the hallway and up dark, creaking stairs.

Two small doors lead off a landing, one to Aunt Mathilde and Uncle Gustav's bedroom, the other to a tiny box room, where frost sparkles on a narrow iron bed. Ice coats each pane of glass in the window of a crooked dormer roof. Outside, icicles hang from the eaves.

Apart from the bed, the only furniture is a big, old-fashioned wardrobe which takes up most of the space. There's barely room to stand under the steeply sloping ceiling.

"It's lovely," I say, shivering. "Thank you."

Aunt Mathilde looks at me. "Oh, you're very welcome, child."

Something in her tone makes me shudder, though I tell myself to stop being silly. Whatever battles we had when I was little can't matter now.

The windowpanes rattle at the approach of a train. I walk over and look out across a hotchpotch of outhouses and small backyards. Beyond them, on the rise of the embankment, a locomotive is being overtaken by another, which hammers and shrieks up the line.

Its thunder breaks off an icicle. Ice slithers down the glass.

"A hospital train for the injured," Aunt Mathilde says.

"How can you tell?"

"They're always the fastest."

Again, there's something in her voice that disturbs me deeply. Turning, I find her watching me, her expression colder than the room.

"Poor men," I say. "It must be horrible for them."

"Grievous, some of them are. Faces shot away. No legs. Bits of them hanging out. Fritz is a slapdash slaughterman at times."

I stare at her, appalled.

"We don't see the worst of it," she goes on, "not even here, where there are hospitals everywhere."

She speaks slowly and clearly, as if she'd prepared for this moment, thought long and hard about it, and wants me to hear every word.

Suddenly I realize we're not talking about the hospital train at all. This is about Father. I'm sure of it.

With a flutter of fear in my belly, I ask, "Why not?"

Her eyes drill into me. Her face twitches. Then she controls it again and says, "Because the worst get left behind."

My hand covers my mouth, a picture of Father's face more broken than Émile's flashing into my head. Is this what she thinks happened to Father? He was left behind because he was too badly injured to be saved?

"But ... he didn't suffer. It was a direct hit. Pascal said. He called it a mercy."

"I know."

"You do?"

"Oh, yes. You told Gustav all about it in your letter."

My letter? *Mon Dieu!* She read it? In my panic, I can't remember a single word I wrote. I stare at her, failing – I'm sure – to hide my shock. She turns her back and opens the wardrobe door.

"The funny thing about this war," she says, "is that no one who dies in battle dies cruelly. Everyone gets a clean bullet in the chest, or a direct hit from a shell they never saw coming. No one ... *suffers.*"

She says the word precisely, pausing for another long moment. Then she stoops and picks up a parcel, wrapped in tissue paper, and lays it carefully on the bed.

"Every letter says so," she adds, running her fingertips over the parcel. "It's always there in black and white. Did you know that, Angélique?"

"No, I didn't, Aunt Mathilde."

"Not many do. And fewer still bother to find out."

I hang my head, wishing she'd leave me alone. I don't want to think about what she's saying. I don't want to imagine my father's destroyed face or bits of him hanging off...

Aunt Mathilde pats the parcel, then walks to the door. "Bring your dirty clothes down when you're ready. I'll heat some water for that bath."

Alone, I stare at the parcel, pulse racing, the cold seeping into me. The smell of moth balls rises through the tissue paper.

As I unfold the first, flimsy layer, it crumbles to dust in my hands. The next layer is greyish white, almost transparent, with a whorled pattern within it. Cautiously, I part the folded sheets, thinking back to the last time I'd seen Aunt Mathilde.

It was summertime. She'd wanted to help me search for eggs in the hedgerows, but I insisted on doing it by myself, and ran away, and got beaten for it.

I peel back another filmy piece of paper, trying not to tear it. It's so delicate and beautiful.

I can't remember if Aunt Mathilde was there the time Uncle Gustav took Pascal and me swimming in the river, but she was definitely at the fair in Monville. We went on a swingboat together and I was sick on her skirt.

Lifting another fragile piece of tissue, I think about my birthday when I was four or five. Father made me a swing in the orchard, in the big old walnut tree. I remember it so clearly – Uncle Gustav pushing me up, up into the dappled leaves, and Pascal shouting beside us. "My turn! My turn! Me next!"

Parting another sheet of paper, I remember how I screamed and screamed when Pascal pushed me off the swing, and then broke it by going too high, and how Aunt Mathilde tried to quieten me. I shut my eyes, not wanting to remember Pascal's cries after Father found out.

And now the letter.

What had I said?

I think I'd just been honest. I told Uncle Gustav how much I hated wearing black, how glad I was it wasn't Pascal who'd been killed, how wonderful it would be when he came home again.

My palms are damp as I open the last piece of tissue and see what's inside. Aunt Mathilde's revenge. A long, black, old-fashioned mourning dress.

Thirty-six

I lay the dress on the bed. It's mended and patched, the lace preserved from a bygone age. The buttons on the bodice reach up to a high, starched collar.

It fits me well. The hem is a bit short and so are the sleeves, but the waist is perfect. Aunt Mathilde can't have worn it for years.

Part of me wishes it didn't fit. When you're in black nobody notices you. They only see the dead person behind you, their ghost.

But that's the point, isn't it? Aunt Mathilde wants people to see Father's ghost. She wants me to see it.

I look at my reflection in the mirror on the back of the wardrobe door: a thin girl in black with dirt on her face, in mourning like so many others, and a whole long day to wait before she can sell her geese.

Reluctantly, I go downstairs, trying to work out

how on earth I'm going to make my peace with Aunt Mathilde.

The kitchen door is shut. From behind it come splashing sounds. Uncle Gustav must be having the first bath.

I wait my turn in the parlour – a room made for two, with matching armchairs either side of an empty grate, two upright seats at a card table and a china shepherd and shepherdess on the mantelpiece either side of a loudly ticking clock.

Behind the door is a small mahogany bureau with two framed photographs on it. One is of Aunt Mathilde and Uncle Gustav arm-in-arm, their faces young and serious. It must be their wedding day. A little boy with a mighty grin on his cheeky face is holding Uncle Gustav's hand.

In the background is my home, La Mordue. Aunt Mathilde's home back then. A long-dead vine creeps over a porch that no longer exists, and a flowering rose rambles up the wall where honeysuckle now grows.

For a moment I picture René and me in their places – though we'd be smiling on our wedding day. Then, with a sigh, I look at the second photograph.

Father stares at me sternly out of the frame. He's wearing his uniform. It's the same picture Mother keeps beside their bed. This one is tied with black ribbon rather than draped in a veil.

My father, Aunt Mathilde's brother.

She must have missed him terribly all the years they were apart. Of course she's grieving for him now. She loved him, like Mother did. It's only me who hated him from the depths of my soul.

And now?

There's a sound in the hallway, then creaking from the stairs, followed by a deep chesty coughing from the bedroom overhead. Through the floorboards I can hear Aunt Mathilde gently urging Uncle Gustav into bed.

I want so much to go up and see him, to ask how I can help him, but I know I wouldn't be welcome so I go to the kitchen instead and bathe quickly in the tepid tub.

"Is he all right?" I ask when Aunt Mathilde brings down his dirty clothes and takes them to the washhouse out the back.

"We need mattresses at our age, child, not floorboards and sacking."

"I'm sorry. Truly I am."

She glances at me, her jaw set hard. "Snap your fingers and he comes running. Then you expect me not to mind when you bring him home like this?"

"I never meant to hurt him. I love him. You know that."

"Love him or need him? They're not the same thing."

In silence we prepare a mutton stew. I eat mine alone. When she carries Uncle Gustav's bowl downstairs untouched, I beg her to let me help her look after him, but she just snaps, "You let him be! You've done enough damage already! I know how to nurse him."

In floods of tears, I rush out of the house and across the lane to the barn.

Uncle Gustav has made the geese wonderfully comfy. The stove is lit, clean straw lines each stall, their feed and water troughs are full. There's nothing for me to do except sit and watch them.

I tell myself this is all Uncle Gustav needs too — warmth and rest, and food when he's ready. I pull up one of his rickety chairs, wishing I could stay here all day — all night as well: it's warmer in here than the box room. But that would be ungrateful. I have to talk to Aunt Mathilde somehow, and apologize for that letter.

She's in the kitchen, heating pans of water on the range.

Without being asked, I take the coal scuttle out to the barn and fill it from the bunker, then I lay a fire in the parlour and scrub my clothes clean in the washhouse.

She's already washed Uncle Gustav's things. I wring them out with mine, and when I hear her going upstairs, I bring them into the warmth of the kitchen and hang them on the rack above the range to dry. Then I sit at her scrubbed and polished table, preparing what I'm going to say.

It's hard when I haven't thought about her in years. It was always Uncle Gustav I loved, never her. Maybe I was jealous of her. Of his love for her.

Then I think, was I jealous of Mother as well? Because Pascal loved her despite everything? Somehow everything seems tangled together, all my feelings — the love and hate and regret, as if the past were an ugly ball of string trailing behind us forever.

"Aunt Mathilde," I say when she comes in. "I'm sorry my letter upset you. I didn't mean it to."

"You mean you didn't expect me to read it. What did you think? That Gustav would hide it from me?"

I shake my head. It hadn't occurred to me for one second what he might do with it. It must have come as a terrible shock, out of the blue like that. Did they even know Father was dead? Had Mother written to them?

Lowering my eyes I say, "I'll leave straight after the market if you want me to."

"You'd run out on Gustav when he's sick?"

"That's not fair! I'd do anything for him! Anything!"

"Then boil this." She thrusts a heavy pan of water at me. "The steam helps his chest."

Long, slow hours tick by. I heat water, she takes it up. Uncle Gustav's wheezing grows louder and his bouts of coughing seem endless.

Once I creep upstairs and listen at their door. But the creaking boards betray me, and Aunt Mathilde opens it at once, her face strained, her mouth turned down.

"What?"

"Isn't there anything more I can do? I could fetch a doctor, or something from the pharmacy."

She opens her mouth as if to scold me, but shuts it again, then hustles me downstairs into the parlour, where she scribbles a note and gives it to me.

"The pharmacy is in the Place de la République, on

the corner by the town hall. Don't take any nonsense about returning later. Gustav needs this today."

She gives me money and directions, then adds, "Come straight back. No window shopping."

"Of course not, Aunt Mathilde."

The afternoon light is pearly and bright. Piles of swept snow line both sides of the lane and the ruts are hard with ice.

At a corner, the barns and allotments give way to terraced houses, then a long, straight thoroughfare of shops crowded with hawkers and shoppers, and soldiers milling about.

There's a market of handcarts selling greeting cards, shoe polish, needles, thread and squares of white silk printed with Sacred Hearts in red.

No one takes any notice of me, a stranger in black in a cold, grey town, until a veiled widow nods at me slightly. I smile in return.

At the end of the rue du Marché, British soldiers block my way. They're laughing and joking, waving money in the air. I crane to see what it is they're so keen on buying.

Fish cakes. Hot fish cakes.

But I don't suppose they'd care if they were buying bottled air. It's the girl behind the handcart they've come to see.

She's enchanting, with sparkling eyes and dark skin. Her hands are quick, her gestures pretty. Her hair is tied back in a reddish-brown turban that shows off her lovely round face.

She's laughing with the soldiers, teasing them, including each one in her bewitching smiles. And they grin back, happy as boys, and put their hands in their pockets again and again, handing over more hard cash than I've ever seen in my life.

Enthralled, I watch. Either she's a brilliant actress or selling fish cakes really is her greatest delight in the world.

The soldiers guzzle them down, then wipe their moustaches and come back for more, and she pretends to be shocked that they ate them so quickly, and makes them wait their turn.

Soon I want to try one, though I know they'll just taste of fish and potato, and her charms aren't meant for me.

I shake myself. I haven't time for this. But I can't help thinking about the market tomorrow, and the rich British officers I hope to tempt into buying my geese.

The Place de la République swarms with workmen preparing for the market.

A butcher's lorry is already parked beside a timber-framed hall, while other stalls are being hammered together or decorated with bright awnings.

The square itself is longer than wide, overlooked at the far end by a tall, handsome, red-brick building. Chandeliers glitter behind its leaded windows. A white-faced clock in a fancy tower shows a quarter to three.

A very fine town hall indeed.

I take the pavement to avoid the bustle inside the square, passing an ironmonger's, a crowded café, then a fancy patisserie and the Hotel Albert.

Across the tramlines is a brasserie called the Lion d'Or. Accordion music floods out of its open door, along with gusts of beery, smoky warmth.

Four French officers play cards at a table in the big plate-glass window, each with a jug of wine at his elbow. One has a small dog on his lap, a wiry brown terrier.

At once my mind leaps to Pascal and little Poilu. For a foolish moment I scan the faces inside, hoping against hope…

But there aren't any ordinary soldiers inside, just officers – the French in pale blue and the British in their dreary khaki.

A spasm of resentment grips me. Why should men like these have Pascal's geese? He's fighting for his country just like them. His future shouldn't be decided on the whim of strangers. Deep down, I feel anger stirring again against Father and his drunken gambling.

Head down, I walk on.

On the corner opposite the town hall is a shuttered *boulangerie* and a busy butcher's shop, but no chemist's.

I hurry across the town hall steps and find myself in a wide, empty street where the breeze tastes of salt and tar and fish, and the weeping cries of gulls compete with the noise from the square. There's blown sand under my feet. The sea must be near.

The sea.

All of a sudden I want to see it very much – something bigger than me and my troubles, something bigger than the war. But Aunt Mathilde is waiting and Uncle Gustav is sick. I turn around and hunt down the sign for the pharmacy.

Thirty-seven

That evening Aunt Mathilde decides the medicine I fetched isn't working quickly enough, so she sends a neighbour's grandson for the doctor.

He arrives with fresh snow on his boots and stamps it off in the hall, then disappears upstairs with his black leather bag, leaving instructions with Aunt Mathilde that he's not to be disturbed. Her expression as her eyes follow him is darker than the night.

I light the parlour fire and sit with her in silence, each in an armchair either side of the grate, listening to the mutters from the bedroom overhead and the ticking clock on the mantelpiece.

At last she gets up and takes the wedding photograph from the desk, then sits again, stroking the frame with her thumbs as she holds it in her lap.

"Uncle Gustav looked very handsome back then,"

I say in the hope of offering her some small comfort.

"He still does to me, child."

But then her frown fades as she sinks into memories and the hard corners of her mouth soften. I want to reach out to her, to find some way of talking to her, like Uncle Gustav wanted me to. In the deep lines of her face I see how Father would have looked if he'd lived to grow old. But she's not the same person as him; she's someone who might have been close if I hadn't wronged her. Finally I ask, "Who's the little boy in the picture?"

She glances up.

"Don't you know?"

I shake my head.

"That's your father."

She says it levelly, watching me. I stare back, then down at the photograph. He looks innocent, gleeful. Sweet. How could a boy like that have become the brute I knew?

"He wasn't always angry," she says, as if reading my thoughts.

"But I didn't know him any other way," I reply, studying my hands.

She grunts, then looks at the photograph again – and sighs.

The ticking grows louder.

There are creaks and indecipherable words from the room overhead. When Aunt Mathilde glances up, her eyes are wet.

"The doctor will give him something to make him

comfortable," I say, and she nods. I take another moment to pluck up courage, then add, "Aunt Mathilde, I'm very sorry about that letter, and for being horrid to you when you visited La Mordue."

"There are worse things to forgive than childish bad temper," she says.

Her eyes meet mine.

"I-I don't understand," I say, a fluttering in my stomach.

"I don't expect you do."

She levers herself up from the armchair and puts the photograph back on the mantelpiece, then sits down again heavily and stares into the coals.

When at last she speaks, her voice is different – distant and sad.

"We left him behind, Gustav and me. We shouldn't have done. But we were too young to think, and I was in such a hurry to get away."

"From the farm?"

"From him, the old devil." Her voice is bitter. I wait for her to go on.

"Three long years my brother had to wait until the drink took him."

"Took who?" I ask quietly.

"Our lout of a father, your disgraceful grandfather."

She looks at me, her mouth hard again.

"Wasn't your mother alive?" I ask, my chest tightening with sympathy.

"He'd sent her to her grave years before. A release, it was, in the end. No more belts and fists."

"You mean…?"

"Like father, like son?" She nods. "He'd thump the living daylights out of my darling baby brother."

Her darling baby brother.

I shut my eyes, knowing now why Uncle Gustav said Aunt Mathilde and I had a lot to talk about. There's so much I didn't know, that I hadn't guessed at – that I hadn't bothered to ask about.

"I'm very sorry for both of you," I say and I mean it, deeply and truly at last.

She nods slowly, then stares into the coals.

"And now it's going to start over again. Another war, another soldier, more drink…" She glances up. "Did Gustav tell you about Metz?"

I straighten up. "He began to, but…" I look at her closely, then lean forward. "There was this other man, an old couple, the Chevaliers, they live in the woods. He told me good men didn't get out of Metz."

"He would."

"You knew him?"

She nods. "His father and ours joined up together for the last war. His didn't come back. Ours did."

She shrugs.

"But the Chevaliers can't blame our family for that."

She laughs without humour. "Half the country said Marshal Bazaine lost us the war when he surrendered

Metz. His men became prisoners of war and drank their shame away."

She gives me a penetrating look. "But then I think you know our glorious army never runs out of wine – even at Verdun."

Verdun. My heart quickens. She can't be talking about Pascal, can she?

"What do you mean?" I ask, shrinking back a little.

"You said in your letter your brother's been drinking."

"But he was celebrating being alive. That's not the same."

"They've all got their reasons."

"But it's the army that gives them the wine."

She leans back. "It's how they keep them fighting. It helps them forget. But afterwards they can't stop, and then…"

She shrugs again, then sighs more deeply than ever.

"That won't happen to Pascal," I say in a small voice.

"I hope not. But we can't pretend it doesn't run in the family."

We can't pretend it doesn't run in the family.

I wrestle with that dreadful idea as silence falls between us. It's like a monster just walked into the room, an anguished, tormented thing. Or maybe a ghost. Yes, that's it. A ghost that's been haunting me for months, ever since Mother's warning:

Soldiers see terrible things, they do terrible things.

She must have known about Metz, and Father's child-hood, and how soldiers drink. No wonder she thought my blind faith in Pascal no more than a childish dream.

The doctor comes downstairs and we hurry into the hall to meet him. He says Uncle Gustav has bronchitis and prescribes a good night's rest.

"I've given him a draught to help him sleep," he says, already reaching for his hat and coat. "I'll call again tomorrow. Scrub your hands with carbolic soap before and after touching him. Good night."

Snow flurries into the hall as he hurries out.

"As if I need telling to wash my hands," Aunt Mathilde mutters as she bangs the door behind him.

"Should I heat more water?"

She shakes her head. "I'll do it. But you could get some coal for me. Then go to bed. You've been travelling too."

Taking the scuttle, I step into a maelstrom.

The wind is wild, the air thick with swirling snow. The cracks of light from the house vanish before I'm across the road.

Blindly, I fumble for the gate. The metal latch is burning cold, the deep drifts in the yard treacherous.

The barn timbers creak in the wind and the embers in the stove cast an eerie glow. Weird shadows leap as I light a lantern. With a sense of trepidation, I walk slowly towards the geese.

They're grey shapes, asleep, indistinct. Only Napoleon

raises his head. But the others' beaks are tucked under their wings. I breathe a sigh of relief until…

My knees go weak.

A goose is lying with her head on the ground, blinking. Quickly, I open the gate and take her away from the rest, then find a crate and lay her in it, near the stove, warm and safe.

"It's only till morning," I whisper, refusing even to think what the morning might bring.

Thirty-eight

That night I sleep fully dressed. The air is too cold and blankets too thin to lie down in anything less. Uncle Gustav's sleeping draught wears off at some frozen hour. Shivering, I listen to his gurgling coughs and Aunt Mathilde's voice, and the snow-muffled whistle of a train.

In the blackness, her words haunt me again.

We can't pretend it doesn't run in the family.

What's the point of saving the farm if Pascal is going to come home a violent drunk? Béatrice couldn't marry a man like that. I can't marry René if that means leaving Mother alone with another brute.

I scold myself. How can I think that of him? I knew he'd need the farm to heal. This is just more proof that I have to save it.

But what if the Place de la République isn't packed with rich officers desperate to part with their money?

What if that's another childish dream? I can't abandon Uncle Gustav for some forlorn hope. Aunt Mathilde would never forgive me, no more than I'd forgive myself.

As the night creeps towards an uncertain dawn I sleep fitfully.

The sky is leaden when the doctor wakes me with his insistent knocking on the front door.

Through the walls I hear Aunt Mathilde soothing Uncle Gustav's horrible, hacking spasm of coughing. I run downstairs to let the doctor in.

He shakes snow off his coat and hands it to me, complaining loudly about the weather. Thick snowflakes swirl and skitter on the wind and clouds sag just above the rooftops.

"Have you lit the fires yet?" he asks curtly as I shut the door behind him.

When I say I haven't, he orders me to get on with it.

As soon as he's upstairs, Aunt Mathilde hurries down, looking exhausted. We start boiling water at once, this time to wash Uncle Gustav's sweat-soaked sheets.

On his way out, the doctor asks why I haven't made Aunt Mathilde breakfast.

"She must keep up her strength to nurse him," he snaps.

But when he's gone, she says she's too tired to eat.

She rests in the parlour instead while Uncle Gustav falls into another laudanum sleep, and I offer up a prayer that Mother can hold off the bailiffs for a few more days.

* * *

I'm taking the scuttle outside again when I almost run into an old lady in black, standing on the doorstep as if about to knock. Two more women in black are wading through the drifts towards the house. They stop behind the first woman and look at me expectantly, as though I should have known they were coming too.

"Is Mathilde in?" one asks.

"She's resting."

They nod. "Don't let us stop you. We know what to do."

And with that, they brush past me into the hall.

Perplexed, I'm crossing the lane when the elderly neighbours from last night hurry towards me. Their grandson, Bertrand, the one who fetched the doctor, is with them.

"We wondered how Gustav's doing," the man says.

I remember Aunt Mathilde had called him Monsieur Martinez.

"Resting," I reply. "So is Aunt Mathilde. If you'll excuse me..."

"She'll need something hot when she wakes," Madame Martinez says, then she, too, bustles past me into the house.

Monsieur Martinez shrugs an apology, then his face brightens. "Ah! You're getting coal. We'll do that, won't we, Bertrand?"

The boy nods, but I draw back, telling Monsieur Martinez I'd rather get it myself. He just smiles at me cheerfully.

"We won't get in the way, will we, Bertrand? We've all got to do our bit at times like these."

They follow me into the yard.

The drifts are high, the snow banked deeply against the barn door. We have to force it open. The warmth from the stove rushes out.

While Bertrand and his grandfather busy themselves with coal and shovels, I take a deep breath and kneel by the ailing goose in her crate.

She's so still that at first I'm convinced she's dead. I cover my mouth, fighting tears, but then she blinks and I'm almost sadder than before.

I ought to end her suffering. That's what Uncle Gustav would do. But I can't bear it. She might get better. We never gave the old gander a chance. I open the crate and lift her head and help her drink some water.

"Better wash your hands or Mathilde will have something to say," Monsieur Martinez says quietly behind me.

"That's only when we touch Uncle Gustav."

"All the same."

I look at him.

He shrugs. "Can't be too careful. That's what my wife always says."

With a nod, I rest her head back down and scatter some grain in her crate. Then I search by the forge for soap and a pumice stone, and scrub my hands at the pump.

Monsieur Martinez and Bertrand insist on carrying the scuttle into the kitchen for me. His wife is making coffee for the old woman, who's settled herself in a chair by the range.

The old woman smiles at me in a familiar way though I've no idea who she is. The other two women in black take their coffee standing up. It's as if Uncle Gustav's sickness is now a public matter.

Briefly, I wonder if these women are nurses, but somehow I don't think so. They're too stern and silent. I escape to the barn as soon as I can.

The goose blinks at me sadly from her crate. She hasn't touched her grain. I inspect the others carefully, looking for dullness in their eyes, or staggering, but all I see is the graceful curve of their necks and the beautiful ripples of grey in their feathers.

"Lovely birds, aren't they?"

Monsieur Martinez makes me jump.

"Sorry," he says. "We saw you coming across, and, well, there's nothing for us to do in the house. That's women's work, isn't it, Bertrand?"

Behind him, the boy nods seriously.

Monsieur Martinez puts his hands in his pockets and rocks on his feet, staring fixedly into the stalls until at last he says, "Selling them, are you? That's what we guessed, unless Gustav's decided to breed them, of course."

"We were going to take them to market today."

"Ah. Yes, I see. What a shame, what a terrible, terrible shame."

With an anxious smile, he turns to me. "You, um, do know you're not allowed to sell sick birds in the Place de la République? The town hall's very strict about that sort of thing."

"I wouldn't sell sick birds anyway," I reply.

"No, no, I'm sure not. And, um, you've got a permit?"

"Permit?"

"Don't worry! Mathilde will lend you hers," he adds quickly. "Well, that just leaves the pen, doesn't it, Bertrand? We can certainly help you there."

The boy nods again, blinking at me with eyes as big as a baby owl's caught in the daylight.

I say, "But I'm not going to market. I can't leave my aunt and uncle."

"Not today, no! My word, certainly not." He pauses for breath, his face crumpling with concern, then he attempts another smile. "But there's always the Tuesday market, you know. Gustav might be up and about by then."

"You really think so?"

I look into his moist, miserable eyes.

He gives me another nervous smile.

"We believe it, don't we, Bertrand? Gustav's a good man, a good friend of ours. Just because the crows are gathering…" He jerks his head towards the house. "That doesn't mean anything, does it?"

"Who are they, those women?"

"They, um… Well, they come to help. At times like these. Try not to worry – and keep busy! That's the thing. It's what we do, isn't it, Bertrand? Now, where does Gustav keep his timber and nails?"

I leave them to it and run back to the house, anxious to speak to Aunt Mathilde and hear exactly what the doctor told her this morning, but the women in black won't let me see her. They say she's resting in the parlour.

"We're keeping a vigil at Saint Michel's. You should attend. Tonight. You'll find it a comfort," one of the women tells me.

Resentment bubbles inside me. They've no right to keep me from my aunt – or tell me what to do. I certainly don't want to go to church and light candles. What good is that?

I turn to the parlour, but another woman in black lays her hand on my arm and says, "She's been up all night."

"I know!"

"Then you know she mustn't be disturbed."

I vent my frustration on hammers and nails, working in silence alongside Bertrand and his grandfather in the barn.

Despite all the hints and unspoken words, I refuse to believe Uncle Gustav might be dying. It's just an awful cough. God wouldn't punish the best of us for the foolish hopes of his niece and the sins of his brother-in-law.

But that afternoon I can't refuse Aunt Mathilde's request to join her at Mass. A silent procession of women in black leads us through the falling snow and up the mound to the church of Saint Michel.

Aunt Mathilde weeps in silence throughout.

Thirty-nine

That night the rattle of wagons and shrieks of inbound trains are loud enough to wake the dead. I peer through the patterns of frost on the window and see a few faint stars.

Even standing, I feel a strange sense of weightlessness, a floating state beyond tiredness, as if I don't belong in my body any more and might drift out of the window or haunt the house.

Later, when Uncle Gustav's coughing seems to shake the walls, I get down on my knees and offer God a pact. I'll work my fingers to the bone. I'll light candles and listen to bells and breathe incense as much as He likes. I'll do everything I'm asked by the doctor and those women in black if only He'll help Aunt Mathilde to make Uncle Gustav well.

I rise before dawn and riddle the spent coal from the

range, filling the kitchen with the bitter perfume of hot slag. The old woman stirs in her chair. She seems to have taken up residence.

In the barn I discover my bargain with the Almighty didn't extend to the poor goose in her crate. Her beautiful body is stiff, her eyes glittering slits, half-closed, as if she's looking at me and asking why she had to suffer needlessly.

I sink to the ground and let the tears flow. Her lonely death was my fault, her hours of misery down to me. I knew this was coming; I knew how it would end. Yet I did nothing.

Never again.

As the lantern flickers over her corpse, I swear by all that I hold dear that I will ease their passing if any more of the geese fall sick. In this, at least, I won't fail them.

I say a prayer for her, knowing that it's wicked, knowing that animals aren't meant to have souls. But if there is any peace to be had, I wish it for her with all my heart.

The other geese sleep or preen, bright-eyed and contented, except one gander who sits apart, awake and yet unmoving. I open the gate and kneel beside him. He lifts his head without a struggle, but I put him in a crate just in case.

Then I hammer and saw, lay fires, fill the scuttle, boil endless pans of water. I even cook lunch for the women in black, then rush back to barn to check on the gander.

Monsieur Martinez and Bertrand are there again, working on the pen. They tell me Bertrand noticed one young goose seemed rather tired, but they're sure it's nothing, really.

I make her a pen out of straw and keep watch over her too.

Snow is falling again when I return to the house to make supper – large feathery flakes, drifting and gliding, whirling and spinning, kissing my upturned face, a kaleidoscope of white. A final shaft of winter sun touches the belly of the sky, and in its light I follow one snowflake's long journey down.

And suddenly I wish René was here to share this moment. We could hold hands and watch it together, and I could tell him I love him and want to marry him, and we could kiss for the longest time, and laugh and be happy, while the sky fell softly around us…

By morning, it's clear that both the goose and gander are ill.

I take the goose outside first.

A light snow bounces on the wind, skipping around the pristine lane, then alights gently on the deep drifts.

The goose appears to be blind. The light doesn't cause her to blink. She just lies heavily in my arms, warm and soft. She'd managed to preen overnight, and her white belly feathers seem to shine.

In the end, though, she struggles for life, fighting me as I tighten my grip on her neck. Her eyes see again. She squawks and wriggles free, and to my shame I drop her, and she gets to her feet, staggering in the snow.

I fall on her and clumsily break her neck. She dies in an instant. Limp. Unmoving. A light gone out. I kneel beside her, sobbing my heart out and crying "Good night" over and over again.

Behind me, feet crunch on the snow. "There, there. Come along! Hush now." Monsieur Martinez, with Bertrand gaping at me from the gateway.

"She was sick," I sob. "She was in pain."

"I know. I know."

He offers to kill the gander for me, but I say, no, I have to do it. We send Bertrand away, then Monsieur Martinez holds the poor bird still while I snap his neck.

A sense of the inevitable settles on me, a patient hopelessness. By Monday I'm almost too numb with sorrow to notice the urgent comings and goings in the house.

The doctor, more neighbours, a priest.

Monsieur Martinez insists on taking the pen to the Place de la République. A way to escape, I expect.

At some point in the afternoon, a woman in black I've not seen before comes to the barn and tells me Uncle Gustav is asking to see me.

The meaning of the summons overwhelms me. I'd thought I'd be more prepared.

In a daze, I follow her across the yard and into the lane, aware that it's snowing again but no longer feeling its touch.

Aunt Mathilde sits at the kitchen table, surrounded by silent women. Her eyes meet mine as I pass. Hers are bloodshot and despairing.

I walk on, up the stairs, knowing the woman is talking, but not hearing her words.

She opens the door to Uncle Gustav's bedroom, then stands stiffly aside, still holding the handle: a guardian of the sickroom.

"Don't tire him," she says sternly.

"I won't."

Gently, I push her hand away and close the door behind me.

Just one steaming bowl now sits on Uncle Gustav's bedside table. The lamp is shrouded by a cloth, and in the dim light his skin looks the colour of lavender.

His eyes are shut, his breathing loud, a kind of panting rasp. I hurry over, but he lifts one hand off the quilt, then lets it fall again.

"Not too near, ma petite. You don't want to catch this cold."

"I don't think it's a cold, Uncle Gustav."

"Nor me. But let's pretend, shall we?"

His eyes crinkle without opening, and I know this farewell will haunt me forever.

I pull up a stool and sit in the middle of the room, my hands in my lap, my eyes fixed on his face, gathering each tiny detail of him, storing each familiar line in my mind's eye. I ache to take his hand and be close to him.

He coughs again – an awful, thick, bone-jarring sound – and turns his face aside to spit blood-flecked phlegm into a handkerchief.

We can't pretend he's not dying. Not here, not now. This is a place for the truth, all lies and make-believe stripped away.

"This is my fault," I say. "If only I hadn't..."

But he raises his hand again. "Don't blame yourself. Not ever. These things happen."

"But, Uncle..."

He opens his eyes at last and looks at me calmly, his face quiet, as if he's not sick at all. Then another convulsion seizes him, a paroxysm of coughing, and my vision swims as I lose the battle with tears.

"I'm sorry to scare you," he says when the fit is finally over. "Please don't worry. Everything will be all right soon."

"How can you say that?" I sob.

"Because I want you to be happy. I want you to carry on. Save the farm. Live your life. Marry that young fellow of yours. What's his name?"

"René."

"Then marry René if you love him. Will you do that for me? Will you carry on?"

"How can I without you?"

"Promise me you'll try."

"I will. I promise."

"Good girl."

For a while, he's silent again, fighting for breath, his

face shining with sweat. I think maybe he's fallen asleep until, very softly, he speaks again.

"Will you do something else for me?"

"Anything."

"Be kind to your aunt. She's going to be lonely now."

I nod. "I will."

"Thank you."

He drowses after that and a sort of torpor settles on me. Sounds steal through the shutters – snow slithering off the roof, children shouting in the lane. From time to time I hear whispering on the landing too, and the swish of skirts. But I don't move. I keep my watch until Uncle Gustav opens his eyes and looks up at the ceiling.

"We couldn't have children, you know," he says quietly. "We wanted them very much, but they never came."

I shift in my seat, unsure what to say. Aunt Mathilde didn't seem to like Pascal and me when we were little.

He says, "We thought when we came down to see you that it might, you know, help things along, being around other children." He rolls his head towards me, and for the first time I see tears in his eyes. "And then there was that terrible day you ran away from Mathilde and your father beat you for it.

"She was furious with him. They had such a row. I don't suppose you remember it. You were very young."

He looks up at the ceiling again and sighs. "She'd never come down with me after that in case she got you in trouble again."

So there it is — the truth. I did drive her away. All that time she might have made our lives better, and my temper had stopped her coming. How many beatings might Pascal have been spared if I hadn't been selfish?

"And now look at you," he goes on, smiling bravely, "all grown up."

"I don't feel grown up."

"I don't think we ever do."

We don't speak again for a long while. His breathing becomes easier at first, but then he coughs and clutches his chest.

"Should I fetch Aunt Mathilde?" I ask, my heart crushed by a sense of utter helplessness. He nods and, blinded by tears, I put the stool away.

At the door, I turn to him one last time. He smiles at me weakly, and I force myself to wipe my eyes and blow him a kiss.

"Angélique?"

"Yes, Uncle?"

"There's a letter in the desk in the parlour. Read it when I'm gone."

"Don't say that!"

"It's all right. Don't be frightened."

Trembling all over, I swallow and ask, "Who's it from?"

"You'll see." His eyes crinkle briefly. "Believe in people, Angélique. Believe they're good deep down."

"Are they, Uncle Gustav?"

"I think so, ma petite."

On the landing, Aunt Mathilde is waiting to come in, her face a picture of misery. The rest of the house is empty, apart from the elderly woman asleep in the kitchen.

I wait in the parlour throughout the long night, listening to my aunt's voice through the floorboards, and the gurgling, oozing sounds of Uncle Gustav's lungs. The clock on the mantelpiece says it's half past four when Aunt Mathilde comes downstairs to tell me he's died.

Forty

I run up to see him, wanting to be near him, to stay close to him. He's lying on his back with his eyes shut and his hands clasped on his chest.

Aunt Mathilde must have washed him, too. His face is no longer shiny and the room smells of rosewater and soap.

I pull up the stool and sit next to him, taking his hand. It's still warm and comforting. Like always. His face is calm now that the lines of pain are gone.

Quietly I call his name, unable to believe he'll never answer again.

Aunt Mathilde sits down on the other side of his bed and takes his other hand in hers.

Sometimes as we watch over him she cries out his name and breaks down sobbing, but mostly she just presses his hand to her face, kissing it and telling him how much she loves him.

I tell him I love him too, that he'll always be with me in my heart, that I know his love won't ever leave me.

Then the women in black from yesterday appear in the doorway and Aunt Mathilde asks me if I want to help with the laying out. I shake my head. I don't want to share him with anyone but her.

Leaving them to their work, I go down to the parlour to look in the bureau for the letter Uncle Gustav told me to read. At first I'm not sure how I'll recognize it, but then I see Pascal's spidery writing on an envelope and know at once this is it.

But I can't read it here. Not with the women's heavy tread just above my head.

Taking the letter into the hall, I put it in the pocket of Pascal's jacket, then change into his boots and pull the jacket over my dress.

Aunt Mathilde's dress.

I feel I belong in it now.

Outside, the cold takes my breath away. Everything is white — the buildings, the lane, the sky. Looking back at the house, I don't see how I can possibly keep my promise to save the farm, today of all days. I can't haggle with strangers over the price of a goose when Aunt Mathilde needs me, and I have to show Uncle Gustav respect.

Napoleon honks the moment I open the door of the barn. He stretches his wings and beats the tips against the sides of his stall. I let him out. If I can't take him to market today, at least he'll have the run of the barn.

I open the middle gate too, but stop at the right-hand stall. Just four geese remain inside, not the six I left in there yesterday.

Maybe they escaped. But there's no sign of them anywhere.

Then, like a stab in the heart, I think perhaps they fell sick and Monsieur Martinez broke their necks. Surely he wouldn't have killed them without asking me first?

I ought to go and find him and ask him what happened, but he'll want to talk about Uncle Gustav, and that's too difficult right now. I top up their troughs with water and grain instead, and shut the door behind me.

The duck pond is an immaculate field of snow, the church roof pristine white. My feet take me past them, on and on, though I don't know where I'm going.

A quiet place, perhaps, to be alone with Pascal's letter.

Or maybe I'm running away from a decision I can't face.

In the salt marshes at the end of the lane, stiff sedges quiver in the first watery shafts of sunlight and ducks quack in meandering gullies of a sluggish river. I follow it downstream, past gloomy villas and a bridge jammed with noisy market-day traffic.

I put my head down and hurry on.

What if I can't get enough for the geese to save the farm? Failing would be a betrayal of all Uncle Gustav sacrificed. I can't go home empty-handed.

On and on I walk, past fishing boats moored by a quay. The wind is loud in their rigging and the slap of water against their hulls reminds me of Émile and his barge. But the leathery faces of the fishermen are intact, and fishwives work alongside them, sleeves rolled up, hauling baskets and lobster pots. Normal, everyday lives.

I walk on by.

When the road and river part company, I find myself on sand, climbing up to rolling dunes beneath a clear blue sky. Gulls hang on the wind. Distant figures look like matchstick men. And beyond, a bright horizon: the shimmering line of the sea.

At last I take the letter from my pocket. The stamp on the envelope is marked October. He wrote it months ago.

As I walk a short way downhill to get out of the wind, I find wooden crosses in the sand, stretching away in orderly rows. A military cemetery. The bodies of soldiers lie under my feet.

A sad place to read Pascal's letter, but a fitting one.

I sit down on the sand, huddled in his jacket.

Monday, October 16th

Mon cher oncle,

Forgive me for being blunt but there is no time to waste words.

We moved position last night. It took the whole filthy night to move two kilometres in the rain, the horses sinking into this sucking mud, the most treacherous mud any man alive has ever seen.

There's no escape from it. Even the shell craters are sucked into their neighbours, the embankments crawling and crumbling into lakes of glutinous mud. The weight of our *canon de 75* and the cart of ammunition were too much for the horses. But we didn't leave them behind. We got them out. We got every last horse out of that mud.

Then dawn came. *Mon Dieu!* I wish it hadn't. There was nothing to see but a wasteland of ditches and water. We couldn't understand where we were at first. Where were the enemy trenches? Where were ours? I can't describe the cold horror we felt when we worked out that the battlefield had drowned in the night, and that these foul canals were all that was left of the German lines and ours.

We crawled on top of the ammunition cart to look out, weighed down by the mud on our coats. We seemed to be made of mud. Our gas masks and pouches were no more than muddy protrusions. There was an extraordinary quiet. The ground didn't shake. No shells screamed towards us. No one spoke, not even to cry out for help. Only the mud moved, slithering into the water from time to time, making a splash and a ripple. Men were hardly visible, just man-shaped mud clinging to some small rise, half-drowned. Or fully drowned, like hump-backed fish, face down, their legs kept afloat by mushrooming trousers.

It looked like the end of the world. But we knew it couldn't be. Because this war has no end. It will go on forever. We know it. Every night we will fire our cannons at the Boche, and he will send his endless, endless storms of steel raining down on us, and every day we will rest in some God-forsaken hole until the night falls again.

I am sorry to burden you with this. But I needed to explain that nowhere here is safe. Please keep the enclosed letters for me and send them if necessary.

Amités,

Pascal

In the same envelope are two smaller ones, both dog-eared, mud-stained and unopened. One is neatly addressed to Mother, the other – less neatly – to me. On each he's written in pencil: *In the event of my death, please forward this to my family. Pascal Lacroix.* 33e bie/35e RAC.

I look again at the date on his letter. Mid–October. Since Uncle Gustav never sent these two letters, Pascal must have survived the Battle of the Somme as well as Verdun which, in itself, is a miracle.

I read his letter again, searching for the goodness that Uncle Gustav found inside it. Perhaps I see it too, in his care for the horses and his pity.

But, oh, his desolation. His conviction the war won't end. My heart cries out to him – it will end, Pascal. Hold on! But who will he be if he lives? What manner of man? Can goodness survive such horror?

We can't pretend it doesn't run in the family...

I shake the thought from my head, then look at the envelopes addressed to Mother and me.

The temptation to read them is great, but that would betray Pascal's trust in Uncle Gustav. And deep down I'm also afraid that opening them would tempt fate.

I put them back in the envelope and re-read the letter to Uncle Gustav, taking comfort from the sight of Pascal's handwriting rather than the words he wrote.

"Can I help you, mademoiselle?"

I jump at the sound of a man's voice, and look up, still lost in thought, to find a young British officer smiling down at me.

"Are you looking for someone?" he asks, the sweep of

his hand taking in wooden crosses. I shake my head.

"But you have lost someone," he says earnestly, his eyes flicking to the black skirt of my dress, then back to my face again. "Was he a soldier?"

I hesitate, not wanting to lie. He seems so very concerned, so serious. His eyes are deep set, his nose straight and his chin clean-shaven. But to me his mouth seems too sensitive for a soldier.

"My father was a soldier," I tell him. "But he's not why I'm here. Not really."

He nods, looking at me closely with troubled eyes, as if expecting me to explain. When I don't he looks away across the dunes, towards the sea, and says, "I'm sorry, mademoiselle. I didn't mean to intrude."

I fold Pascal's letter and put it away, then struggle to my feet in the soft sand. The officer holds out his hand to help me. He's wearing fine kid gloves and doesn't seem to notice my poor man's jacket and boots.

The wind carries a faint clanking of chains and the crack of a sail.

As I stand, the sounds grow louder and around a bend in the river the fishing fleet appears, their brown sails straining, their broad bows foaming on the glittering tide.

"How beautiful!" the officer cries. "Look, mademoiselle! Do you see?"

He runs the few steps to the top of the dune. I follow him and we stand side by side, watching the fleet heading out to sea with gulls wheeling overhead. In the brilliance of the morning, in the salt-smack of the wind, it seems unimaginably cruel that Uncle Gustav will never see such a sight again, nor feel the wind on his face, nor kiss his wife – or me.

"'At the going down of the sun and in the morning, we will remember them'?" the officer asks, and I find him looking at me again, his eyes wet.

And I realize I'm crying too, hot tears that freeze to my face.

"Is that an English prayer?" I ask, wiping my cheeks.

"A poem. I find poetry more of a consolation these days."

He glances down at the graves, then up again with an embarrassed half-smile. It makes him look younger, like a shy and thoughtful boy, unsure of himself. And all of a sudden I want to comfort him.

"Not all soldiers die," I say.

"Don't they?"

I shake my head. "My brother survived Verdun and the Somme."

"*Both* battles? Dear God! The poor devil."

"My brother isn't a devil, monsieur."

"No! Of course not! It's just an expression! Oh, dear. I've offended you again."

His face creases with anxiety. Then, blushing, he looks away and says, "I've just come out, you see. This is my first tour of duty."

His eyes find mine again and this time his smile is sad.

"I'm not afraid of battle, mademoiselle, nor of death, as such. It's more *how* I'll die, whether I'll be able to set an example to my men. That's terribly important for morale, you know."

His gaze sweeps the wooden crosses again. "They give you all this training in England, and everyone tells you exactly what it's going to be like, but when you come out, it's not what you expect at all."

"What did you expect?"

"I'm not sure. Something beautiful, I suppose. A sense of brotherhood and sacrifice, a feeling that we're part of something greater."

"And it's not like that?"

He shrugs. "No one seems to know why we're here any more – only that we'll be damn lucky to get out of it alive."

I wonder at him, at his readiness to die without knowing why. Then I think of Pascal's despair that the war will never end, and Émile saying it will go on forever until the last man is dead.

And in that moment I realize why Uncle Gustav gave me Pascal's letter. It wasn't about the horses or the pity of war. It was because he remembered Mother and me and wanted to comfort us at the end.

Even in that dreadful place, that hell, Pascal had thought to send his last farewells to safety.

Beyond tears, I look across the shifting sands, across the bodies of men who will never see their homes again, and I know at last, with a deep and absolute conviction, that whatever this war might have done to my brother, and whatever it might yet do, on that day at least, on that flooded battlefield, he'd wanted to say his goodbyes. He'd wanted to send us his love, the only gift he had to give.

I take a deep breath, wondering if Father remembered us in the end as well. If he cried out to us as that shell screamed towards him. If two dog-eared envelopes lie mouldering in a crater somewhere, torn and burnt, with my name and Mother's written on them.

Near the horizon, the fishing boats seem stationary now. The air is so clean and clear that the line between the sea and the sky is straight and precise.

I take it as a sign, though in truth I don't need one now. I know what must be done.

First, though, I kneel in the sand and with my eyes wide open I say out loud, "Father in heaven, forgive me as I forgive you for the pain that you caused me."

The officer says, "Would you like me to add a few words? I did begin my training as a priest."

"No, thank you," I tell him. "I wasn't talking to God."

Forty-one

Hurrying back, I jump over patches of ice and snow, the sun in my eyes.

By the bridge I hear the noise of the market. The road must lead to the Place de la République. Somewhere a hurdy-gurdy is playing, the tune echoing off the high buildings.

I run on, past the marshes, the duck pond and church, into the long shadow of the farmhouse. As I enter the hall, the shuttered silence of a house in mourning presses on my ears.

I check the clock in the parlour. A few minutes past eleven o'clock. In less than five hours it will be dark again and the market will shut. Five hours, then, and nineteen geese to raise 300 francs to pay off Father's debts.

But first I have to explain to Aunt Mathilde that it's what Uncle Gustav wanted. I need her to know I'm respecting his wishes.

In the kitchen, the elderly lady is asleep in her customary chair. I shut the door softly, but not softly enough, it seems, because she calls out in a querulous voice, "Who's there?"

"Me. Angélique. I'm looking for my aunt."

She eyes me narrowly as I open the door again.

"She's in church. Where you ought to be," she tells me with a frown.

My heart sinks. I can't talk to Aunt Mathilde there. But I can't wait for her either, and leaving her a note seems cowardly, as if I'm ashamed of what I'm doing.

"Would you give her a message for me, please? Tell her I've taken the geese to market."

"What?"

The woman rises from her seat like some ancient fury and points a trembling finger at me, as if casting a curse. "Gustav's not yet cold and you're gadding off to market!"

"It's not like that. Aunt Mathilde will understand."

"She'll understand you're a Godless child!"

"She'll understand my brother needs me. Now excuse me. I have to go."

I run to the parlour and search the desk for her permit to trade, hunting through the paper and ink pots, the buttons and pens, but the woman follows me and shuts the door, then stands in front of it, blocking the way out.

"You'll have some explaining to do when Mathilde gets back," she says, trembling with rage. "You're dishonouring the dead!"

"I'm helping the living. Uncle Gustav knows that."

"He's gone, child!"

"Not to me, he's not."

She moves unsteadily towards me, the wedding ring on her bony finger clacking on the chair as she clutches it for support.

"Mathilde told me about you, girl. Oh, yes. You're the one who kept her from her brother. She'll never forgive you for that – or this."

I glance at her quickly. "I don't know how long you've known her, madame, but I promise you, you don't know her at all."

Suddenly, there it is. The permit. Almost as fancy as our Requisition chit. Looking at the woman, I say, "Please get out of my way."

But she turns and locks the door, and thrusts the key deep into her pocket.

"If you're not going to church, girl, you're not going anywhere."

"Give that back at once."

"Get down on your knees and pray!"

"I've made my peace. And now I'm leaving, with or without your permission."

Advancing on her, I take the key from her pocket, fending off her frail, withered hands as they feebly smack my arms and face.

"I'm sorry," I say as I unlock the door. "But this was my uncle's wish, whether you believe me or not. Tell my aunt I'll be back as soon as I can."

Racing upstairs, I take off the dress and lay it gently on the bed.

I'd willingly wear it for Uncle Gustav – Father too, if Aunt Mathilde asked me – but no soldier wants more reminders of death. They want to see a pretty face, an enchanting smile, like the fish-cake seller's.

Taking Pascal's clean clothes from the wardrobe, I notice a piece of material behind them and take it out too. It's a long scarf, midnight blue – a rich and mysterious colour.

Dressing quickly in the shirt and trousers, I wrap the scarf around my head like a turban, showing off my face. Then, quickly, I practise my smile in the mirror until I'm sure no one could mistake me for a boy.

On the landing, I stop for a moment by Uncle Gustav's bedroom and lean my forehead against the door.

I don't want to see him laid out, stiff and formal in a suit. My memories of those final hours with him are too precious to confuse.

Instead, I picture him laughing and whirling me around on the day the colonel gave us the chit. Then I press my cheek against the wood and whisper, "Wish me luck."

The elderly woman glares at me from the kitchen as I run past the open door, but she doesn't try to stop me.

At the neighbours' house, I ask Monsieur Martinez if Bertrand could help me herd the geese to the Place de la République. His wife's eyes bulge.

"You're going to market *today*?" she says. "After—"

"I'm sure she knows her business," Monsieur Martinez breaks in.

"Well, really! What will people say?"

"It doesn't matter so long as my aunt understands," I tell her.

"Does she?" Monsieur Martinez asks.

I look him in the eye. "She will. Yes."

"That's good enough for me."

As he hurries off to fetch Bertrand, I sweep the driven snow away from the barn doors, then throw them open.

The geese honk and flap in the sudden brightness, and waddle towards me, waggling their tails and shaking their heads.

All except two, who stay on the ground, glassy-eyed and drooping. I take a few moments to steady myself. Then, dry-eyed, I take each one to the back of the barn and when the deed is done, hide their bodies so Bertrand won't see them.

I wash my hands at the pump and count the geese – seventeen, and still 300 francs to raise. That's almost... *eighteen* francs each. An impossible sum! In Monville, at least. There they really would think I'm profiteering.

I search the barn for the string collars Uncle Gustav made while waiting for me at the Gare d'Orléans. When Bertrand and his grandfather arrive, I slip a collar over Amandine's mother's neck, then give Bertrand the ball of string.

"Don't tug her. Just keep walking slowly. She'll follow you," I tell him.

Mutely, he clutches the ball in his fist, staring at Napoleon, who's nearly as tall as him – just the right height to take out his eye with one peck.

"If he chases you, *run*," I whisper.

Bertrand nods seriously.

The town hall clock is striking midday as we enter the Place de la République – a loud, insistent chime above the hawkers, the hurdy-gurdy and the haggling.

Sunshine gleams off the snow on the high roofs, and in the reflected light the coloured awnings on the stalls seem to glow.

A man in a leather apron outside the ironmongery shouts, "Ten francs for the gander!" and his customers laugh.

"You're teasing, monsieur!" I shout back.

"Twelve, then!"

"And the rest!"

"Greedy peasant!"

With a shrug, I urge the geese on, telling Bertrand to turn right. We're going to make a grand entrance, parade the flock around the square. Already heads are turning.

The geese close ranks, hissing and snapping at the crowd, a glorious gorgon again. By the patisserie, the smell of bread makes my mouth water. I tighten my belt. Hunger isn't important today.

The café is already full for the lunch hour. British and French officers stroll into the Hotel Albert. But every-where people stop and stare as we pass.

"Twenty francs for the gander, mademoiselle."

Twenty! Already. I spin round, looking for the man who'd spoken.

He's a French officer, lounging at a table outside the Lion d'Or. His long, booted legs are stretched towards a brazier.

Three other officers sit with him, their table set with a white cloth, two rows of knives and forks and eight glittering glasses. They each hold a cigarette lazily in their hand.

Switching on a bewitching smile, I say, "Fifty francs."

Bertrand stares at me with saucer eyes. Two of the officers burst out laughing and one throws his hands in the air. But the fourth man, the one who offered me twenty, smiles slowly and strokes his moustache as he looks Napoleon over.

"Twenty is already a very good price," he says.

"Fifty is better, monsieur."

My heart pounds as I say it, and I feel my smile slipping. The officer chuckles.

"I admire your ambition," he replies.

But then, with a wave of his hand, he turns back to his companions as if I didn't exist.

With a grimace still stuck on my face, I nod to Bertrand, and we herd the geese on, past the butcher's shop, the *boulangerie*, the town hall steps, then turn left into a central avenue between the market stalls.

On the right are crates of speckled hens, and grey ones, and whites. On the left are ducks of all shapes and sizes, which quack and flap at the geese, who hiss and honk back.

Then come the game birds – woodcock, pheasants, quails and snipe – and finally the goose pens. For all I think that I've hardened my heart, that I've come to terms with what I'm doing, the sight of them sickens me.

This is the end. I'm *selling* the flock to people who will *eat* my beautiful birds. An overwhelming sense of responsibility falls on me like a deadweight.

This isn't worth it unless I get three hundred francs – and I've never even seen that much money in my life, let alone demanded it off strangers. Foreigners. Rich and haughty officers who barely notice I exist.

Blinking back futile tears, I shut the geese away, then tell Bertrand he can go. I can manage. The lunchtime crowd is thinning. But in truth I just want to be alone with the geese.

He hangs around for a while, looking at the ducks and pheasants, then all of a sudden he's gone, and a white-haired gentleman with a kind face is offering me seventeen francs for a plump young goose.

Seventeen. I take it. I must, though it's not quite enough. When he tucks the goose under his arm, his money feels like Judas's pieces of silver in my pocket.

A French officer with a lady friend on his arm stops by my pen next. He offers me eighteen francs for Napoleon. I shake my head, telling him I've already turned down more, but I accept sixteen for another gander because the poor creature is honking so loudly for his mate – the goose I sold first.

Two English nurses march up next in smart, starched uniforms. They speak excellent French, which they use to tell me how dirty Étaples is.

I hold out for eighteen francs each from them.

Then I scan the dwindling crowd for a rich British officer.

But none are around.

In the lunchtime lull, the red-faced farmer with the pen next to mine leans his elbows on my fencing and says, "Nice birds."

I glance at his pen where twenty scrawny Toulouse geese are crammed together. They're miserable-looking and no match for mine.

Smiling, I say, "Yours too."

"We've not seen you before," he adds. "Not from round here, are you?"

"I have family here."

"Ah."

He calls across to a stout woman over the way, "She's got family here."

The stout woman looks me up and down, her gaze resting a long while on my trousers. She's dressed like a schoolmistress, with a tight bun of iron-grey hair and a mannish, brown felt hat. In her pen are two white Pilgrim ganders and two beautiful female greys.

"Your birds are lovely," I say.

She shoots me a look, then says to the farmer. "Funny they let her out lookin' like that. Most folk around here have standards."

The farmer rolls his eyes.

Then a motor car stops by the town hall steps and all three of us turn our attention to it as a young French soldier jumps out of the driver's seat. He opens the door behind him for a fierce-looking woman with a fox-pelt collar attached to her overcoat.

The farmer rubs his hands.

"You know who that is?" he says in a low voice. "Madame Hubert. Seven hundred chickens she's got. Supplies all the hospitals with eggs. Some people do all right out of this war," he adds with a wink.

"Who's the man with her?" I ask.

He chuckles. "Caught your eye, did he? That's her youngest, Lieutenant Hubert. Home for Christmas, I expect."

"Lucky woman," I say.

The lieutenant takes his mother's arm as she surveys the market, then, slowly, they move forward together in a stately progression.

Madame Hubert ignores the chickens and ducks. She pauses by the game birds briefly, then by the stout woman's Pilgrim geese, and finally stops at my pen.

Quickly, I fix a smile on my face, but Madame Hubert takes no notice of me. Instead, she points a gloved finger at Napoleon and walks off, leaving her son behind. A grin spreads across his freckled face.

"Ten francs for the gander," he says.

"Fifty," I reply.

His eyebrows shoot up. *"Fifty?"*

"Fifty."

He scratches his chin elaborately, then, still smiling, says, "Twelve."

I shake my head.

"Thirteen? Fourteen?"

"I've named my price, monsieur."

"So you did. And my final word is fifteen."

I swallow hard. I have to keep my nerve. Standing tall, I say, "Napoleon is the finest gander in France, monsieur, and my best price is forty-five."

He laughs good-naturedly.

"In that case, mademoiselle, I wish you good day."

As he wanders off, my legs turn to jelly. The red-faced farmer goggles at me and the stout woman mutters "silly girl" loudly enough for me to hear.

Rubbing my arms against the chill, I stare after Lieutenant Hubert's retreating back.

The town hall clock is chiming one o'clock when three British soldiers wander down the central avenue from the direction of the rue du Marché. They don't look much like officers – their uniforms aren't smart enough – but I smile at them anyway just in case.

"Twenty francs for a goose," I say when they stop. "Fifty for the gander."

They look at me blankly.

I point at a goose and then hold up my fingers, twice, repeating loudly, "Twenty francs for a goose, fifty for Napoleon."

I flash my fingers at them five times.

They put their heads together, then shrug and walk across to the stout woman, who sells them a goose and a gander at fifteen francs apiece.

She smirks at me when they've gone, but her smugness disappears ten minutes later when Lieutenant Hubert comes back and folds his arms in front of me.

"Eighteen francs," he says.

"Forty-five," I reply with a smile that's almost genuine.

"You're supposed to bargain, mademoiselle."

"Am I? I'm new to this."

He laughs and saunters off again.

After that it's quiet for another fifteen minutes, but then I sell three geese in quick succession – two females for fifteen francs each, and a gander at seventeen. Then another lull before a woman in a feathered hat keeps me talking for ten long minutes before reluctantly agreeing to pay sixteen francs for a female. Finally, just after two o'clock, I see what I've been waiting for: British officers, a large group of them, stumbling out of the Lion d'Or.

They're shouting and horsing around, and most of them have bottles in their hands. Once I would have been frightened of them, but now…

Now I'm still afraid. But I have my armour on – Pascal's jacket and boots and trousers – and the visor of a smile, and very good reasons to be brave. I watch them like a cat when golden mice come out to play.

They stagger and weave between the stalls, singing lustily, their arms draped around one another's shoulders. Their faces are red, their eyes shining. They look fiercely happy.

I smile and smile and smile at them.

I'm enchanting, bewitching. Selling geese is the thing that delights me most in this world. I call out, "A hundred francs for the gander and fifty for a goose!" And they stumble towards me, shouting back in a medley of English and French.

"*Quoi?*"

"What?"

"*Comment?*"

I wish I knew a few words of English to flatter them.

"A hundred francs for the gander and fifty for a goose," I repeat as they jostle around me, a herd of young colts, shoving and grinning, peering into my pen.

One stands out from the rest. He's impeccably dressed, with a fine great coat slung across his shoulders and a badge on his cap that glitters like a jewel. His buttons are burnished, his boots polished to a high shine.

"A hundred francs for Napoleon," I say, batting my eyes at him. "A special price for *milord*."

"*Milord?* Way-hay!" Laughter breaks out, and their eyes sparkle as they nudge one another and point at me and him.

The finely dressed officer grins. "One hundred francs?" he repeats in broken French. "That is not a lot for an emperor."

"Two hundred, then," I reply.

There's more laughter, which ripples out as the joke is handed on.

"Ask him three hundred," somebody shouts. "He can afford it!"

"One hundred francs is acceptable, *milord.*"

My heart is thundering. My face aches with smiling. But I keep it up as the Englishman looks Napoleon over, rubbing his chin, nodding his appreciation.

"Go on, Jack!" another Englishman shouts. "We'll have him as a mascot!"

"We'll have him for tea!"

My stomach knots. I clench my teeth. I laugh. Ha-ha. Perhaps they'll think my eyes are shining with joy. Then, astonishingly, *milord* reaches inside his great coat and takes out his wallet! I hardly dare breathe. Blood pounds in my ears. Will he really pay one hundred francs for Napoleon? Could this be … *it?*

Hypnotized, my smile frozen, my heart swollen, I watch his fingers. I see crisp notes. A fat wedge of them! He's carrying a fortune. But as he flicks through them — counting — a new voice calls from the back.

"Excuse us, messieurs. Make way! Coming through!"

Then an English voice, "Uh-oh, miss. Here comes trouble."

There's more laughter, more shoving. I see the blue of gendarmes' uniforms between their khaki coats. Then I see *milord* returning his wallet to his pocket.

"Another time, mademoiselle. You have visitors." He lifts my hand to his lips. *"Enchanté."*

Then he's gone, lost in the crowd, and I'm left thunderstruck, gawping at a little man with a ledger guarded by two burly gendarmes.

Forty-two

"Your permit, mademoiselle," the little man says.

I stare at him, flabbergasted, unable to believe that my best chance of saving the farm has just been snatched away.

He blinks watery eyes at me. Then sneezes.

"Your permit," he repeats, taking out a handkerchief to wipe his runny, purple-veined nose.

"Couldn't you have *waited*?" I demand. "Didn't you see I had customers?"

"Now, now. Less of that," says one of the gendarmes. "He's only doing his job."

Breathing hard and shaking from head to toe, I search my pockets for the permit, then hand it over. While the little man reads it, the red-faced farmer sidles up to him.

"She's not from round here," he says, adding when I glare at him, "She's got family here, of course."

"So she says!" calls the stout woman. "Shouldn't be

allowed. Outsiders taking our business."

I glare at her, too, but she plants her feet apart and crosses her arms.

The little man glances at her, then at me.

"This is your permit?" he asks.

"My family's, yes."

"And these are your geese?"

I hesitate. Then, "My family's also, yes."

"Like the permit?"

"Yes."

The woman snorts.

"Mind your own business," I snap.

"Now, now," says the gendarme. "I've warned you before. We'll have no trouble from the likes of you."

"Wouldn't surprise me if she stole that permit," the woman says loudly. "Picked a pocket or something."

"How *dare* you!" I shout back.

"Well, you just have to look at her," the woman goes on, as if addressing a crowd. "Dressed like a gypsy. It wouldn't surprise me if those geese weren't hers, either."

"They're mine, I tell you. Mine and my brother's."

"Prove that, can you?" she asks snidely.

I look from her to the little man to the gendarmes, hoping they'll silence her, but they frown at me instead and narrow their eyes.

"Are they yours?" asks one of the gendarmes.

"Can you prove it?" says the other.

The little man peers at me and the farmer says, "They

are nice birds. Too nice, I'd say. Yes. Definitely too nice for the likes of her."

Cold claws of panic crawl into my gut. These people are united against me, determined not to believe me. I back away, stretching out my arms to shield my geese.

But then I remember…

Straightening my back, I say, "As a matter of fact I *can* prove it." And I pull out Pascal's letter and show the little man the envelope.

"See? The name and address match the permit. And here…" I show him the letter addressed to me. "That's my brother's name, Pascal Lacroix, in the same handwriting."

Last, with a flourish, I pull out the Requisition chit.

"I am Mademoiselle Angélique Lacroix, and these geese are in my possession!"

The little man's eyes nearly pop out of his head as he reads the official paper, with its fancy scrolls and lettering. The gendarmes look over his shoulders and read it too, while the farmer cranes his neck to see.

"It says the geese belong to General Foch," the farmer tells the stout woman.

"So they're not hers. I knew it," she cries.

"No," I say firmly. "They were in transit to him. I was going to sell him my geese. They were never requisitioned."

"So why didn't you sell them to him?" the little man asks.

"His Excellency had left Frévent before we got there."

"You should have followed him," the farmer says. "That's what I'd have done. I'd have followed him and sold him his geese."

Behind him there's a soft chuckling and everyone spins around.

Lieutenant Hubert is there, shaking his head, with his mother beside him, frowning.

"Madame Hubert!" The little man almost jumps to attention.

The gendarmes straighten up too, while the farmer boggles.

Lieutenant Hubert grins. Then he strolls across to my pen and leans on the fencing, looking at Napoleon.

"No wonder you think so highly of your gander," he says. "I'd want fifty francs for a bird destined for His Excellency's table as well."

"You know this girl?" the little man asks.

"Indeed. We are deep in negotiations," Lieutenant Hubert replies, winking at me.

"But these birds are meant for General Foch," a gendarme insists.

"She's meant to find him," the farmer adds, and the stout woman nods her agreement.

Lieutenant Hubert laughs. "Best of luck with that, mademoiselle. Last I heard, the army hadn't been told His Excellency's current whereabouts. But doubtless he's informed his goose girl."

The stout woman turns away with a snort and the

farmer sidles off. The gendarmes look embarrassed, and the little man returns my permit. Then he bows to Madame Hubert and to her son, and hurries away with the gendarmes.

"Thank you," I tell Madame Hubert.

"Thank you very much," I add to her son.

Lieutenant Hubert smiles.

"I couldn't buy my mother her gander if they'd arrested you. Now, where were we? Ah, yes. I'd just said twenty francs and you were about to say forty."

I wish I could say forty. Maybe even thirty. But twenty isn't enough.

I try doing the sums in my head, but lose track. Have I sold eight geese or nine? I turn to the pen to count how many I have left.

"What's going on?" Madame Hubert asks. "Are you still negotiating?"

"One moment, please, madame," I say and turn my back to them, and discreetly count my money.

I've got 132 francs for eight geese, which means I still need… Shutting my eyes, I concentrate.

"What's she doing now?" Madame Hubert says.

"She's working things out, Mama. We shan't be long."

His mother tuts, then walks over to the stout woman's pen to look at her last two Pilgrim geese.

"She won't wait all afternoon," Lieutenant Hubert tells me quietly.

"I know, monsieur, it's just…" I look down.

"Just what?"

"That Englishman was about to pay me one hundred francs for the gander."

"Are you sure? He might have been teasing. They were rather drunk."

"He had his wallet out. He was counting the money."

"And now he's gone. And I'm offering you twenty-two."

Twenty-two francs! Once I would have jumped at such an amount. But now? Closing my eyes, I calculate again.

If I've got 132 francs, I still need 168. I've got nine geese left, including Napoleon, which means... I need nearly 19 francs for each bird!

I *know* that's impossible – even here. No one has paid that much so far and the market will be winding down soon. I have to sell Napoleon for as much as I can. I look at Lieutenant Hubert. For some reason it's important he understands.

"I'm not being greedy, monsieur. I *need* this money," I tell him.

"I rather gathered that, mademoiselle."

He leans his elbows on the pen, studying Napoleon, then says, "Twenty-five. Last word. Final offer. Please think about it carefully."

I chew my lip, though I don't know why. Twenty-five still isn't enough. I'd need eighteen francs for each bird. What chance of getting that now? Napoleon is my only hope.

"Well?" calls his mother.

"Well?" says Lieutenant Hubert.

Sadly, I shake my head. Lieutenant Hubert sighs.

"You know this might be the best offer you get. What if your Englishman doesn't come back? What will you do then?"

"I don't know, monsieur."

I let my eyes drop to the ground.

"Ah, well." He swings about on his heels, calling to his mother, "I'm sorry, Mama. She's had a better offer, one I don't think we'll want to match."

"Peasants," Madame Hubert huffs. "They're only out for what they can get."

The market seems emptier with Lieutenant Hubert gone, and soon the sun dips too low to touch the snowy roof-tops. As the shadows deepen I tell myself I can't lose hope. I mustn't. I nearly got one hundred francs for Napoleon and there's still an hour of daylight left.

Fixing a smile back on my face, I study the late after-noon crowd.

There are more families than before, wives and their soldier husbands, children with sticky fingers, elderly cou-ples and women with babies. But no rich officers.

At half past two I sell a goose for seventeen francs to a young couple, then a gander for eighteen francs to a grizzled British soldier.

One of the gendarmes from before buys a pair of birds for sixteen francs apiece. I'm so astonished when he smiles kindly at me that I forget to thank him.

I count my money again. Now I only need 101 francs and I've still got five birds left – including Napoleon. I can still succeed.

Just as the town hall clock strikes three, I sell another goose for sixteen francs and, immediately afterwards, my last gander for eighteen.

Now I've only got Amandine's mother, another goose and Napoleon, and sixty-seven francs to go – just sixty-seven francs to save the farm and the future. Pascal's future, Mother's and mine. René's and Béatrice's too.

The wind picks up. It blows flurries of ice and snow off the roofs and sends pages of discarded newspapers scurrying across the cobbles. Feathers stir in empty crates.

An old, barefoot woman appears, a tiny creature with frizzled white hair wearing a sackcloth dress. She scavenges the debris of the stalls. Workmen begin taking down the meat hall, the noise of their hammering loud once the hurdy-gurdy stops.

I tell myself not to worry. It's not dark yet. I stamp my feet and blow on my numb fingers. My face hurts from smiling and the cold.

At half past three a woman in a fur hat and fur-trimmed overcoat tries to bully me into taking fifteen francs for Napoleon. I tell her no over and over, but she won't give up.

"The market's finished," she cries impatiently. "Can't you see?"

"It's not over till dark," I reply.

She points at the sky. "What do you call *that*?"

A pale moon drifts in the cloudless blue. To the west, the sky is clear as ice, but towards the east it's already a deep, rich hue.

"There aren't any stars out yet," I say.

The woman purses her lips and studies Napoleon again, then suddenly says, "Name your price."

I calculate quickly. "Forty francs."

"Forty?"

"Thirty-five."

She snorts loudly. "There are laws against profiteering, you know." And with that she finally stalks off.

"Typical," the red-faced farmer says, rolling his eyes after her. "They couldn't tell quality if they tripped over it. If I was you, I wouldn't sell that gander. I'd breed from him. That's what I'd do."

Then he, too, packs away, loading his last ten geese onto a handcart and breaking up the wattle fencing of his pen.

The stout woman is long gone. The game birds' crates are empty, the ducks sold too. There are just a few sad chickens left. And me and my geese. I blow on my fingers and rub my arms, saving my smile for later.

The market dissolves in the twilight. Drays take the stalls. People slip away. Lights twinkle in shops and cafés, but the square looks dreary and deserted.

"I still say twenty francs is a good price for that gander."

A man's voice. French. He stands a short way off, his face hidden by his military cap and the darkness, but I recognize him all the same. He's the officer who dismissed me at lunchtime with a wave of his hand outside the Lion d'Or.

Despite his miserly offer, I'm glad to have a last chance to tempt him. Tapping into some hidden reservoir of hope, I say, "I've been offered a great deal more than twenty francs for him today."

"Offers you refused, I see."

"Our discussions were interrupted. *Milord* said he'll be back."

"An Englishman. I might have known."

He lights a cigarette and blows out a plume of smoke. "The problem with the English is, they don't know how to bargain – unless they send a servant, of course."

He tosses the match on the ground, where it sizzles and dies. Then he considers Napoleon for a while.

I wait in silence, doubting anything I could say will persuade him.

Finally he says, "How much did he offer you, this English *milord*?"

"One hundred francs."

He whistles. "No wonder you're waiting for him in the dark. Make sure you only sell him a goose, mademoiselle."

I bridle at the insult, feeling my cheeks burn. Stiffly, I say, "Are you buying the gander, monsieur? I'm open to sensible offers."

"Sensible? That's an interesting word. How much does good sense cost these days?"

"Sixty-seven francs."

He looks at me quizzically. "That's very exact."

"It's exactly how much I need."

"Ah. Need. Another interesting word."

He leans on the pen, toying with his cigarette. I'm almost sure he's playing with me, stringing me along. Maybe he has time to kill and nothing else to do. I'm about to demand he makes his final offer when a growling begins, an extraordinary sound, like some great beast. A predator.

"Oh, dear," the officer says with a sigh. "Here they come again."

"Here who come?"

"Your English *milords*. Out for a night on the town."

And around the corner by the pharmacy a motor car appears. An incredible motor car. Its shimmering white bonnet is longer than a cart, with a silver winged lady on the front. The gleaming headlamps pour streams of gold across the cobblestones and the engine snarls.

Awed, I watch it prowl past the town hall steps, the shuttered butcher's shop, the Lion d'Or. It purrs to a halt outside the Hotel Albert and six or seven British officers bundle out, already shouting, already drunk. Half of them disappear into the hotel; the rest head for the Lion d'Or.

None of them seems to notice the mad, frizzle-haired woman peering at them from the dark, or the goose girl and the Frenchman staring at them from the wind-swept square.

"And there goes any talk of sensible prices," the officer says with another sigh.

I turn to him, torn. Would any of those Englishmen really pay one hundred francs for Napoleon? What would a soldier want with a goose when he's out on the town? I daren't risk it. I daren't gamble. I look the officer in the eye.

"I'll take sixty-seven for the gander *and* the two females. It's a good price, monsieur. They're fine birds."

He nods and keeps nodding as he studies them, muttering, "Not a bad price, not bad at all, considering. Unfortunately..." He turns to me with a shrug and lifts his hands palm up.

"Need drives me also, mademoiselle. Twenty is all I have." He takes out his wallet and shows me its contents. "But I'll take those two females off your hands."

"Twenty? For two birds?"

"They are poorly."

"WHAT?"

I whip round and stare in horror at the pen.

Amandine's mother is lying flat out, with Napoleon standing over her, protecting her. The other goose is staggering on her feet. I clutch at the fence, dizzy with shock. The officer puts his head close to mine.

"You do know you aren't allowed to bring sick geese into the Place de la République?" he says quietly. "But I won't tell if you don't."

"But … I-I shouldn't sell them if they're sick."

"Don't worry. They'll go straight into the oven tonight. No harm done."

I almost retch. Amandine's mother. Dead. Tonight. And the other poor goose as well. As he slips the money into my pocket I shut my eyes tightly to stop them from overflowing.

Forty-three

Shakily, forcing myself not to think, just to act — for Pascal's sake — I lift the staggering goose out of the pen, give her to the officer, then regard Napoleon. He's guarding Amandine's mother with outstretched wings, a glaze of black fury in his eyes. His sharp beak gapes.

Lightning fast, he slashes my hand before I've even reached for his mate, drawing blood. He lashes at my eyes as I bend towards her. Terrified he'll blind me, I shut my eyes and pull my face away while he attacks my arms and wrists.

When I finally manage to lift her out, he shrieks like a devil and charges the fence, pecking at it wildly, breaking a paling and attacking my boots and legs.

The officer laughs as he takes Amandine's mother from me.

"He really is spectacular! Worth every sous you can get

for him. Good night, mademoiselle, and *bon chance*."

The officer melts into the gloom with the bulge of a goose under each arm. Napoleon screeches after him, battering the fences, beating his wings. I retreat, frightened he'll break out, and stay out of sight until at last he starts honking at the sky – a terrible, lonely sound like he made on the heath that night we saw the wild geese...

The wild geese. Did they cause the deaths of my geese? Were they diseased? That would make more sense than my flock simply dying of exhaustion.

I shake my head. It doesn't really matter any more.

Gingerly, I return to the pen and wait for Napoleon to finish hissing at me. Then I take out Uncle Gustav's ball of string collars and let Napoleon see it, hoping he'll think we're going to follow Amandine's mother – hoping to save my fingers when I put a collar around his neck.

Slowly, cautiously, I open the gate and edge towards him.

With the way out clear, he quietens down and doesn't seem to notice when I slip the collar over his head. He struts out of the pen ahead of me. *Slap, slap, slap* across the cobbles. I follow at a distance. *Slap, slap, slap.* Does he really believe we're going to find his mate? I wish I could make that true. Instead I steer him towards the Lion d'Or.

The British crowd around the dark wooden counter or sit at tables on the right, while French officers occupy tables on the left and in the window. A warm light spills across the pavement. I stand outside, looking in, trying to summon the courage to put my crazy plan into action.

The accordion player strikes up a tune. A few British officers begin to dance like chained bears; red-faced Frenchmen sing. There are beer tankards everywhere, and spilt wine, and cards smacking down on wet tables. Two more French officers stagger over the tramlines.

At first I think they're drunk too, because they have their arms around each other, but then I notice one has lost a leg and the other's face is covered in bandages. They lurch and bump into crates and other rubbish left over from the market.

Hop. Crunch. Thud.

When they reach the Lion d'Or, the one-legged man elbows the door open and the bandaged man feels blindly for the handle.

Warm air floods out, and laughter and smoke. The two injured friends are greeted with a cheer. I wait until they're seated, then touch Napoleon's back, risking a peck.

"Ready?" I ask him as I slip the collar from his neck.

Very quietly, I open the door and shoo him inside. He lumbers across the floor, neck out, hissing magnificently. Officers jump out of his way, British and French alike.

Remember, I tell myself: bewitching, dazzling, enchanting. I burst through the door.

"Napoleon Bonaparte! You naughty bird! Come back here!"

For an instant I'm the centre of attention. Heads turn. Faces grin. The barkeeper throws his hands in the air.

Then Napoleon pecks a French officer's leg. Not just *any* officer: a colonel, no less. I recognize his uniform from the man who gave us the Requisition chit.

"Monsieur!" I cry. *"Oo-la-la!"*

The British cheer – until Napoleon turns on them, slapping across the floorboards, gathering speed, honking furiously. They hop on tables and chairs and climb on bar-stools, spilling beer and wine, shaking their fists and laughing uproariously as Napoleon attacks them.

The French cheer now. Even the colonel raises his glass, calling, "Bravo, *mon emperor!*" The accordion player strikes up a few notes of the "Marseillaise".

I make a feint at catching Napoleon, but luckily only succeed in riling him even more. He honks and hisses, flaps and screeches, attacking each army in turn.

"I'm so sorry, messieurs!" I shout, flashing my smile back and forth, counting the seconds before I play my last hand…

Run my last risk. Gamble.

After all, I can't pretend it doesn't run in the family.

When everyone's yelling and leaping out of Napoleon's way, I throw myself across his body and pin him down. Then I roll over and stagger to my feet, lifting him in triumph. Napoleon shrieks his outrage and pecks savagely at my hand.

"Bravo!" shout the French.

"Captured!" yells a British officer as he climbs down from a stool. "Napoleon Bonaparte is defeated again!"

"Mais non!" The French colonel slams his glove against the table. "The emperor was being a gentleman! He let the girl catch him!"

"Nonsense!" the British officer roars back, and the two armies jeer each other loudly.

I take a deep breath, offer up a prayer and then throw back my head and laugh.

"The English will never take Napoleon!" I yell. "Only a Frenchman knows his true worth."

The French stamp their feet to more cries of "Bravo!" The British jeer. More beer is spilt, more wine. Napoleon wrestles in my arms.

"Well said, mademoiselle!" cries the colonel, waving his glove in the air. He puts it down on the table and with slow, unsteady dignity, takes out his wallet and tosses some notes down after it.

"There," he says, slurring slightly. "Twenty francs for the gander – and ten for your trouble!"

Thirty francs. A good start. I flash him a brilliant smile.

"Thirty-five!" A British bid.

"Forty!" The French colonel again.

From the French tables there's low rumbling as the officers drum their fingers on the wood. Grins and rude gestures fly back and forth.

I swallow hard. Forty francs. So very nearly there.

I smile and smile, holding Napoleon tightly to my chest.

A British officer snaps his fingers at the French tables,

then swaggers into the middle of the floor.

"Forty-five francs, mademoiselle!" he shouts to British hoots and yells.

Forty-five. One more bid and I've won. Excited, scared, heart racing, I bat my eyelids at him – then toss my head in the air.

"Forty-five, monsieur?" I shout. "Ha! Put your money away! My countrymen will never let you have him!"

More French cheers, more drumming, and stamping now, too. The accordion player plays a few more notes of the "Marseillaise".

But the British officer stumbles over to me on unstable legs, rubbing the banknotes between his fingers and leering at them as if they were exotic dancers from the East.

Napoleon hisses at him, then, suddenly, wrenches his neck from my hand and lashes out at him – then at me – to hoots and roars and banging on the tables. I grab him by the throat and the whole room cheers me.

As I desperately hang onto him, the drunken British officer fans out the banknotes in front of my face. I can't help licking my lips at the sight of them. Is forty-five enough? Surely I could find two more francs somewhere.

But this battle isn't over. I feel it in my bones.

Gamble, I tell myself. Be brave. Be mad. This is for the farm.

Gripping Napoleon tighter, I turn my back on him and march to the French tables, and turn again, and stamp my foot and shout, "No, monsieur! A thousand times, non!"

Napoleon screams at him. The French cheer. The British jeer. The accordion player strikes up the national anthem and the French rise unsteadily to their feet and sing at the top of their voices.

"Allons enfants de la pa-tri-ee-ee…"

The British sway to their feet too, and raise their voices in a dirge.

"God save our gracious King…"

But the accordion music swells louder, drowning them out, and I find the words of our anthem on my lips.

"Aux armes, citoyens!"

The colonel stands to attention beside me, his eyes wet, his fist beating in time with the tune.

"Marchons! Marchons!"

The one-legged man and his bandaged friend hold on to each other as they stand and sing. Then the British link arms and sway, singing louder and louder, never stopping, never missing a beat. Among them I spot a face I know: *milord*! He smiles at me as he sings.

"Send him victorious…"

I step forward, surprised. Delighted, even. And *milord* steps forward too, both of us still singing.

"Français! Pour nous, ah! Quel outrage!"

"Long to reign over us…"

Milord walks towards me, his eyes shining. We meet in the middle of the floor, between the two deafening choirs, while Napoleon squirms and struggles in my arms until the "Marseillaise" rises to its crashing climax. On the last, lingering note, *milord* takes out his wallet and offers me *everything* inside it!

"An emperor's ransom, I think!" he shouts above the British song, and his eyes, like mine, are brimming.

"But that's too much!" I shout back as the British keep singing.

"It's only five hundred francs, mademoiselle."

Five hundred francs! I stare at it, at him, at the money again.

The British are *still* singing, still swaying, their faces alight, their voice relentless, their song unstoppable.

"Take it, mademoiselle!" *milord* shouts. "It's the rent on my villa. I'm going up the line tomorrow. I don't think I'll need it again."

"But, monsieur…?"

I look into his eyes: the eyes of a man on the eve of battle, a foreigner expecting to die far from home, a rich Englishman asking me to accept a king's ransom for the finest gander in France.

I shout, "You *might* need it, monsieur. You might come back. And I only need fifty francs."

"But we'd already settled on a hundred, mademoiselle."

He holds out the money again – all of it – as the British sing, "God Save the King" one last time, then fall silent.

"It's too much," I say. "It's all too much."

"Nonsense," bellows the colonel. "Take it, mademoiselle! Take it in the name of the *Entente Cordiale*!"

The French stamp their feet, roaring Napoleon's name.

The British join in, yelling, "Take it! Take it! Take it!" In the midst of this mad shouting, surrounded by their wild, drunken happiness, I know my job is done.

It is *my* land these men are fighting for – my farm, my mother's home, my brother's inheritance. I am a peasant, a daughter of the rich soil of France, and I, too, have a home to defend.

Slowly, cautiously, I put Napoleon down. Immediately, he attacks the colonel's boots. I grin, then lean forward and kiss *milord* on the cheek, whispering "Good luck" in his ear.

Then I close my fingers around his money. I grip it in my hand. Triumphant, elated, relieved beyond measure, I punch my fist in the air and yell, *"SOLD!"*

Forty-four

MONVILLE. Summer 1919

I'm helping Mother find a table on the crowded terrace of the Grand Café de la Gare when the rumours spread from the street: the train has been spotted, waiting on the edge of town. They'll blow the whistle as soon as they're ready to enter the station.

My heart quickens. Mother grips both my hands.

"He's here," she whispers. "Home at last."

"René too." My eyes prickle with tears.

Miraculously, they've both written home to say they're sound of body. And their minds? I chase away the memory of the shaking man outside the Gare d'Orléans.

"Shall we go and meet them?" I ask her.

Mother shakes her head. "I'm sorry. It's the sun."

"Of course."

I remember all too well the heat burning through a black mourning dress. But a seat on the terrace in the shade is almost impossible to find with so many widows in town.

A lot of men are wearing black too, children as well. Despite all the noise and the laughter, I can't help thinking about the crowded soil of France. Her silent fields.

I glance at Mother, wondering if she's thinking about Father as well, but all I see is joy in her eyes. I must make sure she sees nothing but happiness in me too.

"I'll wait with you," I tell her when at last we find an empty table inside the Grand Café.

She squeezes my hand. "Go and find your friends, my angel – and tell Béatrice she can't have Pascal all to herself. Not today. You look beautiful," she adds as I turn to go, "and so grown up. Give my love to René."

Blushing, I hurry outside.

The summer breeze is hot, the faces in the crowd pink and perspiring. Brightly coloured bunting flutters overhead, and the pavements are packed. I edge my way up the boulevard towards the road that runs past the station itself.

Over the bobbing heads, with their bonnets and caps and sober black hats, I can just make out the station's freshly painted railings and its scrubbed red-brick façade.

Musicians from a brass band push past me, heading towards the station too. Their instruments gleam in the sunshine. Standing on tiptoe, I crane my neck, trying to spot Béatrice and Claudette. Or Monsieur Lamy. Anyone I know.

My heart sinks when the first person I recognize is Madame Malpas.

"There you are," she cries. "I've been left all alone and quite lost!"

"Perhaps you'll find some of our neighbours in the Petit Café," I say, not wanting to burden Mother with her.

I try to slip past her, but she steps in front of me wringing her hands.

"Those poor souls," she says, her voice wavering and high. "Those poor, poor souls."

"Who?" I ask reluctantly, still scouring the crowd for my friends.

"Our soldiers. Who else? They'll be exhausted in this heat."

"They'll be glad to be home."

"Glad? After what they've been through?"

Shaking her head, she lowers her voice. "Their dreams will be haunted, Angélique. They'll never forget. Believe me. Those men are marked for life."

Stiffening, I reply to her curtly. "In which case, madame, we have a duty to be cheerful and help them forget. Now, if you'll excuse me…"

I start to push past her, cross that she's made me angry.

Why does she always try to spoil things, even this wonderful day? Why did she come at all? It's not like she's meeting anyone.

But even as I think it, I know in my heart that's the problem: Madame Malpas has no one to love. With a last forlorn look for Béatrice or Claudette, I gently rest a hand on her arm.

"The war is over, madame. The fighting has ended. Everyone can be happy about that."

"Wars never end, child. Peace is just a lull. When you're my age you'll know that."

"But this was the war to end all wars. Everyone says it."

She snorts. "You think our enemies won't want revenge? The defeated always want revenge. Just like we did!"

Heads turn towards us. She's spoken too loudly. I notice one man frowning.

"That's no way to talk," he tells her sharply. "Our armies defended our nation with courage and élan." More heads start nodding. "Remember Verdun?" he goes on, booming over the general hubbub. "The order was: They shall not pass! And they did not pass – nor will they. *Vive la France!*"

His speech wins him a round of applause – and dark looks for Madame Malpas.

Swiftly, I guide her away.

"Perhaps you could wait quietly in a café," I suggest.

She clamps her knobbly hand over mine.

"Find me a seat? No one will give theirs up for a poor old lady today."

I roll my eyes – but also tell myself off. I should have seen that coming. With a sigh, I turn around and take her back the way I just came.

Despite my silence – and attempts to hustle her along –
Madame Malpas walks slowly, talking constantly. Her
words are full of complaints about her age and her health,
her fear of the crowd...

"Any one of them could be sick. This influenza is horribly contagious."

"The influenza is over, madame. Monsieur Lamy said.
It was in one of his journals."

She sniffs. "That's not what I read in the papers. The
Spanish newspapers, mind. You can't trust ours. The cen-
sors make *them* write nonsense."

Stopping, I peer into the window of the Petit Café.

René's parents have a table near the counter. Monsieur
Faubert catches my eye and smiles. I wave back, then steer
Madame Malpas away, knowing René's mother still hasn't
forgiven Madame Malpas for calling her an interfering old
nag the day René left for war.

Madame Malpas is still listing calamities befalling the
world. Strikes. Mutinies. Those Bolsheviks in Russia...

"And it's not just influenza. There was that other awful
disease, the one the British had. What was it? I told your
mother all about it. Putrid something-or-other, or was it
prurient...?"

I try to block her out.

All of a sudden the air is split by three loud blasts of a
train whistle.

"They're here!" I shout.

At long, long last!

On the terraces and inside the cafés, people stand and cheer. Women burst into tears. Men on the street kiss on both cheeks. Laughing, I turn to embrace Madame Malpas.

"Purulent," she says with satisfaction. "That was the word. They had purulent bronchitis."

I turn away in disgust. *She's* the disease. Spreading her misery.

"I have to go," I say, shaking off her hand.

"But my seat? You promised! Oh, dear me. Oh, no! I'm going to faint. Here I go…"

She sways dramatically, flailing her arms.

I'm almost tempted to let her drop to the ground. Ridiculous woman. Instead, I grasp the top of her arm and propel her into the Grand Café de la Gare.

Mother's eyes widen when she sees us.

I say, "I'm very sorry, Maman. She says she's feeling faint."

"Does she now? Leave her to me. You go."

"Are you sure?"

Mother nods. "Find Pascal for me and bring him back. That's all I ask, Angélique."

Running outside, I'm met by a tide of people surging towards the station. They chatter and smile, their faces eager. In the station square, the brass band strikes up a bold marching tune.

But somehow it all seems less real than the pictures

inside my head of Pascal and René jumping down onto the tracks, smart in their uniforms.

Are they together, I wonder, and talking about home, or still with their regiments, bidding sad farewells to their brothers-in-arms?

"Angie! *Come on!* Bee's wetting herself!"

Claudette grabs my sleeve.

"Where is she?"

"By the gate. They won't let us any closer."

Hand in hand, we dodge through the crowd, then weave our way along the railing fence. Béatrice is jumping up and down, waving frantically and shouting, "Over here!"

"I thought you'd left me," she scolds when we reach her. "I thought you'd gone to find Pascal without me." There are tears in her eyes.

I hug her. "We'll find him together, I promise."

"We better had – or else!"

The police have erected a rope barricade to stop people from spilling into the gateway. We push against it, straining our necks to see into the station square. Claudette laughs at our desperation.

"They won't come out any quicker for you two flapping like hens."

In the brilliant sunlight it's impossible to believe that Monville station is the same place where Uncle Gustav and I brought the geese on that dark winter's night. Now the building is festooned with bunting and flags, and dignitaries line the steps where last time ragged children begged.

As I look up at the clock the past seems to tumble on top of me.

"Angie, don't cry," Béatrice whispers in my ear. "He'll be here soon. René, too. Everything will be all right."

"I know. It's just…"

I feel dizzy as well as weepy. How on earth can I pretend Pascal and René won't be haunted by the past when I can't even look at a clock without welling up?

"We all love him," Béatrice is saying. "You and me and your mother. We'll all take care of him."

"I know. Aunt Mathilde too. She said she'll come down as soon as I let her know he's home."

"Write to her tonight, then."

"I will."

I'll ask after her health, as well, just in case Madame Malpas is right and this horrible influenza isn't over.

Claudette shrieks. "Look! Over there! Here they come!"

The first line of soldiers is marching out from the goods yard. A roar erupts from the crowd. The dignitaries wave their hats. The soldiers wheel around to pass the station steps, then stamp across the square, out through the gate and onto the main boulevard.

We cheer them wildly, scanning each and every face.

But these men are older than Pascal or René, and soon word goes round that the battalions have been reformed so that the longest-serving soldiers can be demobilized first.

"Pascal should be first," Béatrice cries. "He served in the hardest battles!"

But it's men like Father who went to war on that very first day – and survived till the end – who take precedence.

We cheer them on. Every column. Every man. Each time the band plays a new tune Béatrice snatches my hand, crying, "This *must* be him!" But it never is.

At midday, a squad of Algerian riflemen marches up the hill from the military hospital for colonial *mutilés* in town. Those with missing legs lean on crutches; others have empty sleeves pinned across their chests.

"Ew!" Claudette screws up her nose. "Look at that one's *face*!"

"Shut up, Claudie," I growl.

"But it's ... *gone*!"

I frown her into silence. "If you don't cheer them I'll tell André Cousin you've been pining for him the whole war."

"You wouldn't dare!"

I narrow my eyes. "I'll tell him you kept his picture under your pillow."

Béatrice giggles. "You'd make such a sweet couple. You and little André. Tiny little André..."

Claudette glares at us, then she pushes forward and blows the riflemen elaborate kisses. We tease her about it long after they've gone.

More soldiers march out of the yard. The band plays

on. Then it stops, and suddenly the air seems unnaturally quiet.

"What's happening now?" Béatrice asks, her voice edged with panic. "Is it over?"

Alarm grips me too. What if they weren't on this train after all? I couldn't bear another day of waiting.

"Let's go to the station and find out," I say.

"I told you. We can't," Claudette replies. "We're not allowed inside."

I give her a look, then hoist up my skirt, seize Béatrice by the hand and clamber over the rope barricade.

We move quickly and quietly, staying just inside the railings, keeping a sharp eye out for anyone who might try to stop us – a railway official or some busybody officer.

The dignitaries are wiping their shiny faces and sweating necks. Some disappear inside the cool station hall. The bandsmen sit down on the steps. We dash across the square and plunge into the shade of the covered goods yard.

Scores of soldiers are milling about in that half-ordered chaos I'd seen at the Gare du Nord. More men stand by the tracks. The train seems endlessly long.

As we pass between them, searching each face, some grin at us and a few look us up and down, but most just watch us impassively, their expressions indifferent – hopeless, even – as if they're used to waiting for orders that never come.

"They don't look very happy," Claudette whispers.

"They've been through so much," Béatrice says,

glancing at me. "But they'll be fine, won't they, Angie? They'll be happy as soon as they're home."

"I hope so, Bee."

"Only hope?"

I manage a smile. "I believe so. Truly, I do."

Claudette tugs at my arm. "Angie. Look."

"Where?"

"There!"

"Is it Pascal?" Béatrice's voice trembles.

"No," I breathe. "It's René."

He's standing alone, a book in one hand, leaning on a polished wooden cane with the other. He looks more handsome than I remember. More assured. Taller, somehow. I can't think of a single thing to say to him. I'm not even certain my legs will carry me to him.

"For pity's sake, Angie." Claudette shoves me in the back. "Get over there!"

"But, Pascal..."

I look at Béatrice, suddenly afraid I'm abandoning her, that I'm being selfish...

"We'll wait. I promise," she says. "We'll find him together, like we said."

Claudette pushes me harder.

"Go on," she hisses. "He won't wait for you for ever."

Then she links arms with Béatrice and bites her lip. They both look so anxious for me.

I turn towards René. And find his eyes on me.

I take a step forward, my pulse racing, my throat tight.

He puts his book in his pocket and slowly walks towards me, flourishing his cane. Somehow I keep walking too, until we're close enough to touch. Then I stand stock still, my mind whirling.

I blurt out, "Since when have you needed a walking stick?" Instantly I wish I hadn't.

"Good, isn't it?" he says. "I made corporal. That's nearly an officer."

"Is it?"

"Not really."

He laughs – the same easy laugh as always – and I laugh with him, tears of relief pouring down my face. He doesn't sound crazed or haunted. He's not shaking uncontrollably. There's hope for Pascal, hope for them all.

"Hey!" He brushes my wet cheek with his hand. "None of that."

A shiver runs through me at his touch.

"Sorry." I dry my face with both sleeves, trying to be calm and sensible, and not make a fool of myself. "How are you?"

"I'll be better when they let us out of this place."

"Your parents are here. They'll be so pleased to see you."

He nods. "Have you seen Pascal?"

"Not yet."

"We can go find him if you want."

I hesitate – but only for a moment. Then, "In a minute. Can we talk first?"

"If you like."

My head fills with all the things I've got to say to him, all the explanations I owe him. I glance back at Béatrice and Claudette. They're hugging each other and grinning at us like idiots.

René says, "They seem excited."

"We all are. Shall we find somewhere quiet?"

We walk side by side along the platform, so close that I feel the heat of his body and smell the soot on his uniform. Up ahead, an enormous locomotive steams quietly. Two officers smoke in silence on the step of an empty wagon. A soldier and his sweetheart sit on a bench in a soot-blackened alcove, their foreheads pressed together, their arms entwined.

René smiles at them, then – tentatively – at me.

Our hands touch.

Our fingers mesh.

I don't notice if there's anyone else on the platform after that. If there's noise, I don't hear it. All I know is that René and I are holding hands. That he still wants me. That I love him. For now, nothing else matters.

He stops and I stop beside him, feeling his breath on my skin.

"Here we are," he says softly.

"Here we are." I pause, then, "René, I'm sorry—"

He puts a finger to my lips. "You're with me now. That's enough."

Shutting my eyes, I lean against him. He folds his arms around me and draws me close. I feel the beat of his heart beneath the coarse material of his jacket. Somehow it seems familiar.

Then I realize his jacket reminds me of Uncle Gustav's great coat, and how I buried my face in it. And never will again.

I tighten my arms around René's waist, wondering if any of us will ever be able to forget the past. Forgive it, yes, but forget?

"What are you thinking about?" he asks quietly.

"I'll tell you later."

He nods.

The faint strains of yet another marching tune filter in from the brass band outside. The two officers throw away their cigarettes and stand. They button up their collars and straighten their caps, then stroll towards the goods yard.

René sighs. "I should go."

"Yes, you must."

We don't move.

Doors bang in the hall. Voices are raised in the yard. At last the other couple rises from their bench, their heads still together. All of a sudden the young man gets down on one knee.

Shyly, I glance at René. Is now the right time to tell him? His lips are so close to mine. Gently, he traces the outline of my cheek with his fingertips; his eyes are warm and serious.

"I love you, René."

The words seem to come of their own volition.

"I love you too, Angelique."

We kiss. Tenderly, slowly, breathing as one. Rene's mouth is soft, and in the circle of his arms, I fill with a sense of the rightness of things and a sweet ache of desire.

Afterwards Rene's eyes shine and his smile is the most beautiful I've ever seen. I don't want to let him go. We linger for a moment. Then, taking my hand, he says, "Come on. Let's go and find Pascal."

Author's note

This story began with a photograph I saw many years ago on a TV documentary about the origins of the great "Spanish" influenza pandemic, which swept around the world in waves during 1918 and 1919, transported by soldiers returning from World War I.

The black-and-white photograph showed a huge flock of farmyard geese crowded together in a French marshalling yard near a railway station. It was being used to illustrate the theory of British scientists, led by Professor John Oxford, that a domestic goose, duck or chicken sold at a local market had introduced bird flu to the British infantry and hospital camp in Étaples, northern France, during the winter of 1916.

Doctors at the camp reported an outbreak of "purulent bronchitis" that winter, a deadly disease which Professor Oxford says later became known as "Spanish" influenza – the name probably derived from uncensored Spanish newspaper reports about its terrible impacts at a time when both the British and French press were heavily censored because of the war.

I remember that photograph whenever I see news reports about another outbreak of bird flu today, or hear scientists warning yet again that it could mutate into a human disease. Thus, when I had a chance to write about World War I, that same picture immediately sprang to mind.

I knew from the start that I wanted to write about a goose girl from the countryside around Brive-la-Gaillard, my model for Monville, where I'd first seen free-range Toulouse geese. But I didn't know why this girl would herd her flock all the way north, nor what powerful reason would keep her going, nor what dark forces might make her falter and turn back.

As I imagined, then reimagined her story, my research expanded from scientific papers and medical reports to wartime diaries of women and girl farmers and the hardships they'd suffered while working the land. I also read textbooks, novels, poems, military websites and collections of letters from the Front. I watched newsreels and films, studied battlefield maps, listened to sound archives and visited museums, art exhibitions and memorials.

At the Royal Artillery Museum, London, the archivist allowed me to copy from the notebook of a British major who, in October 1916, had been fighting just a few miles from where Pascal's regiment (the real one, a copy of whose official *Journal des Marches et Operations* I downloaded from the website of the French Ministry of Defense) had also been in action. The notebook was small, with a moleskin cover. You can buy ones just like it today. I was thrilled just to touch it. Then I opened it up, and to my shock and amazement found its pages still spattered and stained with the notorious mud of that dreadful campaign.

Another time, while touring the battlefields of Verdun and the Somme, my husband and son found a dud World War I shell, mossy and rusted in the undergrowth of Trone's Wood, near the site where my great-uncle fell on 30 July 1916.

We stood together in the green summer shade, reaching out across time, immersed in our thoughts about him, trying to conceive the industrial-scale slaughter that had taken place a century earlier beneath unimaginable storms of artillery shells.

In honour of the fallen of both sides, I have tried to be as accurate as possible about the history of the time, but some facts I did change to make them fit my story.

The incident of the farmer hanged for shooting a Requisition officer actually took place in 1917 in Ariège. Also, I can't be sure if the Requisition would have taken King George and the chickens as well as Angélique's cow, but I needed to force her into the tightest possible corner. I also needed the geese to show signs of illness, whereas chickens infected with the H7N9 strain of bird flu that emerged in 2013 reportedly displayed no visible symptoms at all.

For Angélique's railway journeys, I borrowed from my grandfather's account of being sent by cattle truck to Devonport on his way to the Dardanelles. I also delved into my own memories of days-long trips across India when I was a student, and the filth of those enormous steam locomotives.

In the passage about the harvest, I wanted to pay tribute to the courage and endurance of subsistence farmers who work the land by hand – then and now – including the AIDS-orphaned child farmers I met in Uganda, breaking their hard-baked fields with nothing more than handmade tools, and the women and girls I've seen across Africa and in India and south America, carting great stacks of firewood and fodder on their backs.

But I didn't want Angélique's story only to be about serious subjects, so I wrote about things that make me happy as well – like love, animals, friendship, the beauty of nature, and France itself, where I used to live and work as a Reuter's foreign correspondent.

Having poured so much I care about into one book, perhaps it's not surprising that in the end I didn't want Angélique's geese to be the ones to bring bird flu to Étaples. In my own mind I've decided that Napoleon lived out his days in the garden of a chateau in Montreuil, happily terrorizing all and sundry for years!

And why not?

For in truth we'll never know what type of bird did carry the original virus into the British camp, nor exactly how it mutated into a highly contagious human pathogen. Pigs and horses might well have acted as "staging post" species; lung damage from weaponized toxic gases could have played a pivotal role in the severity of infections, while cramped conditions in the soldiers' huts and the camp's twenty-six military hospitals most likely increased the numbers infected.

What we do know is that early estimates of the death toll from Spanish flu were almost certainly too low. At the time of writing, scientists calculate the global pandemics of 1918 and 1919 killed between twenty million and fifty million people, making it one of the deadliest infectious diseases ever to have struck humankind.

ROWENA HOUSE is a journalist as well as a writer. She graduated from LSE and spent several years on Fleet Street, reporting for various news agencies. She has lived and worked in France, Africa and Belgium as a Reuter's foreign correspondent and covered the fall of Addis Ababa at the end of Ethiopia's thirty-year civil war. More recently she has settled in Devon with her husband and son but continues to work as a freelance journalist. In 2013, Rowena won a competition run by Andersen Press, which published her winning entry, "The Marshalling of Angélique's Geese", in *War Girls*, a collection of short stories about WWI as seen through the eyes of young women. *The Goose Road* is her novelization of that story.